Sherlyn Stahr

The Trail of Revenge

*Never give up—
on your dreams!*

Sherlyn

For information: smslive120@gmail.com

ISBN: 978-0692411506

Cover design by Cathy Kriznik
Author Photograph by Jay at JH Photographers

Published in Partnership with
Purple Distinctions Self Publishing
www.purpledistinctions.com
Venture, CA 93004

Printed in the United States of America

To Bev
I feel blessed you're in my life, Sis! I couldn't have
written this book without you!

To Kent and Aida, Ryan and Amanda, Kegan and Kathy
You're amazing and I love you! Never give up on your
dreams!

To all my friends and beta readers
Thank you for your support and words of wisdom
and grace. You're the best!

To S.A.R.T. staff members, police officers,
and Special Agents
Thank you for your tireless work and dedicated service that
you perform each day to help the survivors of sexual
assault and our communities!

To survivors
You have remarkable courage and wisdom! Shine your
light for the world to see!

A percentage of the proceeds from the sale of this book will
be donated to a S.A.R.T. program and/or to the National
Center for Lesbian Rights (NCLR)

PROLOGUE

Tuesday 2:11 a.m., 23 September 14

The car radio was turned on full blast pelting out the final bars of Christina Aguilera's *Fighter* as she turned into the parking lot and began to search for an empty parking space. After her car gently touched the concrete block at the head of the space, she methodically pulled on the brake, turned off the car, picked up her Coach purse, and took out her Calvin Klein wallet. Slowly, she slid her driver's license and health insurance cards out of their leather holders, and carefully placed them on the dash. She pulled out her cell phone with the electric blue case and checked her messages and email before she returned it to the pocket in her purse.

Taking the cards off the dash, she clenched them in her fist as she opened her car door. A blast of hot night air hit her as a hint of a breeze jostled her baggy white running shorts. A few steps later, she clicked the key fob and waited to hear the "beep" that let her know her car was locked.

She allowed herself to shiver slightly as she looked up at one of the parking lot lamp fixtures, whose light cast a dirty, yellow glow spreading like an infection toward the multistory building spanning several city blocks. On a mission now, she forced herself to stand up straight as she marched toward the sliding double doors, pausing only long enough to read the blindingly red lit "EMERGENCY" sign that was displayed prominently overhead.

Walking through the automatic doors, the left side of her body brushed against the hall wall to put as much distance as possible between her and a man on a stretcher.

5

She noted a doctor in blue scrubs who was deep in conversation with an anxious couple in a small side room. Avoiding a large nurse's station where a sniffling child sat on a parent's lap, a man was holding his bloodied hand, and another man was bent over in pain, she continued down the blindingly white and sterile corridor.

With unrelenting resolve, she searched for the vending machine where she had plunked in a couple of quarters for a power bar only five months earlier while on a tour of the facility. With each step she took toward her destination, the emotional tornado that she managed to contain on the two-hour drive threatened to demolish and destroy what little reserve she had left.

She paused at the vending machine, lightly caressing the buttons as if they were old friends, and then turned down the side corridor that elbowed left off the main hallway. The corridor was empty now, except for a nurse sitting at the far end behind a nurse's station. As she neared the station, she focused on the bold blue letters, "S.A.R.T.," that were printed on a white background. Carefully, she placed her cards on the counter so the nurse could easily read her name.

"May I help you?" the nurse asked with a friendly smile.

"Yes. I've been raped."

And as the tornado hit and the room spun, she soundlessly slid to the floor.

CHAPTER 1

Friday, 26 September 14
New Case Assignment

Special Agent Mary Hatchert looked down at her regulation heels and stifled the urge to toss them off. Heels weren't her style. Nor was the A-line, army-regulation, blue skirt that was creeping up her thigh as she sat there in the sagging visitor's chair in the Colonel's outer office. The white tailored, long-sleeve shirt was more to her liking, although nothing felt better at the end of a long day than to pull on her blue jeans, racer back t-shirt, and dark chocolate sandals. She imagined she were home right now, relaxing in her outdoor lounge chair with a cold beer.

Hatchert liked things that were simple, just like her house. She pictured her small, two-bedroom, two-bath Spanish style adobe with its red tile roof welcoming her home. She could almost taste the dark beer and the fresh green mixed salad with ranch dressing and grilled chicken as she drank in the view of the sea greens and blues of the Pacific Ocean from a little table at the corner of the inner courtyard off the pool. If she imagined hard enough, she could almost smell the scent of jasmine and sweet-smelling roses that tumbled down the sides of the large clay pots that were carefully placed around the pool and courtyard.

She basked in the thought of how it would feel to take a plunge into the pool where the blues of the Spanish tiles around its edge blended seamlessly into the sky and sea making it feel as though she were a part of them. And how she would lie on the chaise lounge looking at the city lights and the stars overhead as the hot night air caressed her body.

Hatchert thought about bringing some of the women she dated home with her, but it never felt right. She came close with Danika, the owner of a rock climbing gym where Hatchert trained. Danika's muscles were so toned she bragged she could bounce a penny off of them—and she did it one time to prove it. But, it didn't work out with Danika. She wanted commitment and Hatchert wasn't ready yet. One day, she hoped to be ready for that special someone in her life, but right now she had a job to do.

Damn it! She almost had him, she thought disgustedly as she fumed silently inside; Jason Perkins, the man she'd been chasing for the past three months was still out there in that stifling supply warehouse in a South Carolina town where two military women had been raped. It was her job to find the rapist and get him off the street. She hated it when she failed, which wasn't often.

The South Carolina town was ripe with places to rape. It had over fifty city parks, a huge 40,000-acre national park, as well as 60,000 undeveloped acres the army base used for training purposes. One of the city parks was filled with weeping cherry trees whose thick, arched branches touched the ground like a parasol providing a great place to play hide and seek for children by day, but served as a site for one of Perkins' rapes at night. He chose a historical structure that was down an old dirt road in the national park to rape his second victim.

The small upstairs studio Hatchert called home while on assignment had no air conditioning—a big mistake when the previous record of 112 degrees was broken the first three days she lived there. When the humidity hit 93%, her long auburn hair looked like soggy spaghetti noodles dipped in dark, brown barbecue sauce—not a great way to entice a rapist, she chuckled to herself.

Except Perkins was one sorry excuse for a man. He was 5'8" tall, overweight, and a thirty-six year old civilian contractor who was hired four months ago to handle the purchase orders for an army supply warehouse. Hatchert wondered if he owned anything other than the tacky, loose-fitting double-pleated cotton khakis pants, moth-eaten tennis shoes, and those two ridiculous Hawaiian shirts with a hodge-podge of food stains he alternately wore to work each day. His black plastic round glasses that encircled his near-sighted eyes were oversized for his nose, and the deep pockmarks along with the thin, red spider veins painted a haphazard, grotesque landscape across his face. As Perkin's administrative assistant, she'd spent hours answering phones, taking messages, and listening to his endless raunchy jokes as she quietly gathered evidence.

Hatchert thought distastefully about all those times she let him stare at her cleavage and acted like she enjoyed the attention. She even let his pathetic barrel-belly slide against her breast in his sickening seductive play. She drew the line at French kissing him the day he had too much beer and tried to force his tongue down her throat. She nearly decked him, but managed to keep her cool.

Hatchert probably knew Perkins' habits better than he did: that he always ordered a tall, caramel macchiato with extra whipped cream every Thursday at lunch, that he wore cheap aftershave lotion bought at a local grocery store, that he replenished his stash of dark beer in the supply cupboard every Monday morning, and that his left eye twitched when he made an appointment with his local prostitute. And, she almost had the concrete piece of evidence she needed to put him behind bars when it all blew up on her.

It was a stroke of rotten luck the new forklift driver was someone Hatchert met on her last assignment. He recognized her immediately and burst out with a "Hi, Selena. I didn't expect to find you here. How are you?" while Perkins was chomping down a burger close by. It would have been fine if she'd used Selena for this job, but she'd chosen Victoria instead. She managed to deflect the newbie's attention away from her, but Perkins got nervous real fast.

She updated the Colonel at 8:00 a.m. yesterday. Her cover was blown. They both knew the case would have to be turned over to another agent.

It never failed to amaze her how often rapists walked away free. She winced as she remembered hearing the "not guilty" verdict at Crocker's trial. He raped six women and got away with it because his lawyer used Crocker's babyish, innocent look to convince the jurors that someone like him couldn't possibly be a rapist. She hated losing. *Let it go!* she chastised herself. *It doesn't help.* But, she never forgot the cases she lost and why. She spent hours drinking coffee and studying the behavior patterns of the rapists after those cases, to see what she missed that could have sent them away to jail where they belonged.

So, here she was, sitting in the Colonel's beige, carpeted outer office wedged between the American flag and the Army flag. It was good to be back in Southern California where the sea breeze cooled things off at night. From her courtyard lounge at home, she could watch the Navy ships come and go. Hatchert thought about going Navy, but she liked the Colonel and he was Army, so she went Army.

Her headache, that began as she was approaching headquarters, was now producing a deep thud at each temple. Hatchert had been plagued with them since she turned eight.

The Army got her away from home. She had no idea when she signed up that she would end up in intelligence tracking down rapists. The work served her risk-taking side and challenged her intellect; and she loved the way her body felt when she pushed her muscles, heart, and lungs to the max. There was nothing better than to chase down a rapist, or to force him to his knees as she cuffed him. Or, better yet, she almost smiled, to see the shocked expression on the rapist's face when they realized a woman was the one who brought them down.

Hatchert's headache was now spreading slowly from her temples, behind her eyes, and across her forehead as she forced herself to focus on the picture of the Colonel that hung behind the administrative assistant's desk.

She knew Perkins kept the scarab amulet and chain that he hung around each girl's neck before he raped her. The more Hatchert stroked his ego and sex drive, the more he talked. And finally, after all these weeks, he told her about the amulet and its powers—how it had the power to cleanse the soul. They were supposed to go to his place where he could show her how it worked that night. Hatchert felt repulsed that he religiously believed he was cleansing their souls by raping them. All she needed was to find the amulet and chain and he was going behind bars.

"*Damn skirt*," she swore silently as it continued to creep up her thigh.

"Special Agent Hatchert?"

"Yes, ma'am" Hatchert replied as she noted the new administrative assistant's name was Carol Lionel.

"Can I get you anything while you wait?" Carol asked as she smiled provocatively.

11

"No, thank you, ma'am."

As Carol moved away from her and bent down to pick up a paper that had fallen to the floor, Hatchert noticed how Carol's short, green dress barely covered her thighs and clung to every curve. Wonder what happened to Lucy, Hatchert thought as she studied Carol. Matronly Lucy sure didn't look anything like Carol. It was obvious that Carol worked out and liked to show off her figure. The green dress complimented Carol's dark brown hair and green eyes, so Hatchert had to give her points for knowing what color to wear to enhance her look. A little too much makeup perhaps, but you never know, Hatchert thought, as she debated the possibilities.

"Colonel Highland will see you now," Carol said with a sexy smile.

As Hatchert unfolded her long crossed legs and pushed off the chair, Carol unabashedly stared. Any female worth her salt would be hard pressed to ignore the 5'9 1/2" sultry woman who sat straight as a rifle barrel and hadn't so much as twitched since she arrived. Her fingers itched to undo the pillow-soft, auburn hair that was pulled back into a regulation bun and let the reddish-hued mass of waves cascade down her shoulders so she could get lost in it.

You could fall into her dark cognac eyes, she mused, if it weren't for the flashing warning sign that emanated from them. The only thing that stopped her from being drop-dead gorgeous was her nose that was slightly large for her square facial structure. But, those lips more than made up for her nose. They were lush and full, curving slightly upward and painted with a hint of rose-colored lipstick—a mouth that someone could nip, tease, and sink into. Oh well, sighed Carol as she watched Hatchert disappear into the Colonel's office.

12

As Hatchert walked into the Colonel's office, she relaxed. She looked at the picture of the president hung on the wall behind the large, 8-foot long, dark oak desk. The papers were neatly stacked in obvious order and his engraved nameplate, "Colonel Steven Highland," sat front dead center. The Colonel's imposing 6'4"-tall, well-built frame and posture demanded respect from everyone who was under his command.

Commendations, certificates of recognition, and degrees were strategically placed around the room. She looked at the pictures of the Colonel shaking hands with General Wesley Clark, General Ann Dunwoody, and President Obama mounted in frames and placed in a quiet, logical pattern in the bookcase. There were pictures of Elisabeth, his wife; his two daughters, Lily and Chelsea; and his three granddaughters, Joni, Sara, and Connie.

Age had been good to him, Hatchert thought. The Colonel was still ruggedly handsome at sixty, perhaps even more so than when he was in his youth. The various shades of gray hair looked like they had been hand-painted by Apollo. His light olive-brown skin, chiseled jaw, and prominent chin added to his distinguishing features, along with his Greek-shaped nose that sat perfectly on his face. His large, chocolate-brown eyes held her gaze for a moment.

"Hi Agent Hatchert. Welcome home. Sit down," the Colonel said as he motioned her to a dark, brown leather chair while he sat in an identical chair opposite her.

"Thank you, Colonel," she replied as she settled into the cool leather chair.

"Special Agent Debbie Lawson is on her way to South Carolina," he continued as he watched her expression. Hatchert had been in his command since she finished boot camp. She was intelligent and had a sixth sense when it came to catching rapists. And she was gutsy—maybe too gutsy. A couple of times, she ended up a little too close to the action when the timing went wrong. She never complained. She knew the risks. But, still, he had to admire her courage for the things they required her to do.

After three years of working with Hatchert, he knew she would be hard on herself. She was probably mad the case had to be turned over to Agent Lawson to finish, but he also knew she would be a professional and suck it up.

He learned early on that when Hatchert thought she failed, the best thing he could do was to give her another case. And he needed her. The number of cases was growing and so was his headache.

"Is there any new information we can pass on to Lawson?" the Colonel asked.

"I emailed her the list of locations where I searched for the scarab amulet. The victims told me they were dizzy, nauseous, and sleepy. I figure he used Ecstasy. I looked for it, but I couldn't find it. He wanted to show me the amulet, so my guess is that he keeps it somewhere at home."

"It took you a while before Perkins trusted you. Do you think Lawson will be able to bring him down soon?"

"Yes, sir," she said as she nodded her head. "He was all hot to go to bed with me and then didn't get his chance, so my guess is he's ready to jump into the sack with the first female that looks at him. It's important that Lawson moves fast, or I'm afraid he might rape again. I've been keeping him pretty distracted, but I've seen Lawson and I know Perkins. We came up with a plan that we believe will put him behind bars soon."

"Good. I want him off the street and this case off my desk."

14

As he looked at Hatchert, the Colonel reflected on all that she'd been through in her life. Damn shame, he thought.

He'd gone to boot camp with her father. Lieutenant Colonel Hatchert was a flamboyant type and full of himself. But, they all were at that age. No one suspected what went on behind closed doors. That came out when she signed up and they did a security check. Each day Lieutenant Colonel Hatchert forced his daughter to kneel before him and bow while saying "oss." And each day she sat in silence when he said "mokusa." The silence and sitting must have been hard for a three-year old, the Colonel thought, but apparently her dad's rage was worse.

At the age of six, the Colonel remembered when her dad deemed her ready to fight others and enrolled her in classes at a local karate school. And fight she did; she went against kids twice her age and won. Her dad gloated every time he pinned another blue ribbon to the bulletin board that took up one wall of their living room, or when he placed another trophy in the huge, corner display cabinet. None of that seemed to matter to Hatchert, but everyone knew that it mattered to her father. In looking back, the Colonel recalled that winning was the only thing that Lieutenant Colonel Hatchert seemed to care about, even in boot camp. Her father trained her to be tough, but it was a rotten way to go about doing it, the Colonel thought as he stared into Hatchert's dark amber eyes.

Hatchert had gotten her father's hair color and eyes, but she had her mother's body frame and chin. That's all she seemed to have in common with her mother, he reflected. Where Jeanette was submissive, Hatchert was defiant. Where Jeanette depended on her man to take care of her, Hatchert was independent.

Hatchert's cousin forced her into her grandmother's garage while her parents were away. He pulled a hunting knife out of his pocket and flashed it around for good measure, then hung her up on the wall by her wrists and raped her. And, after he took her down from the wall he raped her again on the cold, concrete garage floor. Eight years old was too damn young to experience what she went through, he thought, but that's what drove her and made her one of the best in the field.

"How is your family?" the Colonel asked in a fatherly tone.

"They're fine, sir. Mom's volunteering at the women's shelter; Dad's being dad. How are Elizabeth and all your girls?"

"They're visiting her mom. I can't believe Edna will be ninety next Saturday. She still plays golf and takes dance classes two times a week. How are you doing after spending the last few months chasing this guy?" he asked as he looked at her to see if there were any signs of fatigue.

"Mad, sir. I almost had him. But, Agent Lawson is good. She'll bring him down if there aren't any more surprises. She has my number in case she needs more information."

"We never had a chance to talk personally since you went to Cabo last February on vacation. Elisabeth and I went two years ago and we had a nice time. How did you enjoy Cabo?" he asked Hatchert observing her more keenly.

Hatchert's lightning-quick mind flashed to Cabo and Josefina. When Josefina stepped onto the stage the temperature in the room went up with each step she took. Her dress was flaming red mounds of ruffles and skirt and her plump, full lips were painted with the same red. An

16

intricately carved silver comb held her thick mass of onyx-black hair in a tight bun on the back of her head. As the music began, each of her hands grasped the bottom of her skirt. When Josefina held the skirt up, it formed a cape that she used to seduce, challenge, and swirl around her dance partner, much like a matador waves his *capote,* or cape, to bring down a bull.

At first her dance was slow. She enticed, teased, but as the music beat climbed, she became a swirling, dodging, temptress until her skin glistened under the bright stage lights. When the emotions of her audience were driven to its peak, she ended the seduction in a blinding whirl of red.

As she was taking her bow, Josefina's eyes locked onto Hatchert's and their own dance began. It was hot and fiery just as their night had been. Hatchert could still see the unending waterfall of black hair that fell to Josefina's waist after she removed the silver comb; and how she got lost in it during the night. Josefina was like molten lava and fire, and both ended up exhausted and spent by the time the night was over.

"I enjoyed Cabo, sir" Hatchert simply replied without a change in expression.

"Do you think it's time to take some leave? You've handled two tough cases since you came back."

"No, sir, I'm not ready yet. Maybe after this assignment, I'll take some leave."

The Colonel relaxed a little. He needed her. The Secretary of Defense made it clear that one of his top priorities was to solve any and all sexual assault cases and that directive trickled down to him. Now, it was his priority.

Only a few more years to go, he thought, and then he planned to retire where he could relax on his own boat with

Elisabeth and the entire clan. He already had the boat picked out: a sport fishing boat with white hull sides, stainless steel deck hardware, rod holders, and grab handles. It even had a galley, head, and a V-berth. Yes, he was going to enjoy his retirement out on the water. But, there was still more work to do, he sighed, as he shifted his attention back to Hatchert and her new assignment.

"I've got another assignment for you."

"I'm ready, sir," Hatchert replied as she cocked her head and waited.

"Are you familiar with Fort Oaks, the army base near Hamilton City?" the Colonel asked.

"Yes, sir. I read about it when I thought I would be assigned there for basic," Hatchert nodded as she observed the Colonel's jaw muscles tighten for a split second and then disappear.

"Three women have been sexually assaulted in the past week in the Fort Oaks area. Two are ours and the third is a civilian. The two military women won't file an official report. I'm hoping you can change their minds. They reported what happened to them to Dr. Calloway, one of the base psychiatrists, and she reported it to Colonel Delaney, the base commander."

"What do the files look like, sir?"

"We have Dr. Calloway's reports and the civilian report. There isn't much there, but it looks as though we're dealing with the same perpetrator. The two military soldiers live in the same barracks on base. The civilian lives in a small town southwest of Fort Oaks. All three sexual assaults took place on the Vista Point trail. It's a public trail operated by the state that runs up and down a mountain near the ocean."

"Sounds like he's in good shape, sir" Hatchert noted as she watched the Colonel shift slightly in his seat.

"Yes, it appears that way. Robert Girard is the chief of the Vista Point police force. He's handling the civilian case and will be your point of contact. I've checked him out. He's got a good reputation and record. He grew up in a Los Angeles ghetto, played football, and became a police officer. He worked on the L.A. police force for a few years before he moved to Vista Point. He's solid, and I believe he'll be a good person to have on our side."

"That's good to know, sir. Some cops get pretty territorial," Hatchert said as she took the flash drive from the Colonel.

"The base commander is Colonel Delaney. Your father and I went to boot camp with him. He's tough and sharp. I've let him know you're coming. We aren't telling base security since we don't know who's involved."

Hatchert nodded her head and their eyes met and held each other in a brief moment of camaraderie and sadness that one of their own might be the perpetrator.

The Colonel continued as his knuckles turned white while he absentmindedly gripped a pen. "The press would have a field day if word got out that it was one of our own which is something we want to avoid. More importantly, we need to stop him. Your cover will be as the research assistant to Dr. Calloway. She's been informed of the security level and priority of this case."

"When do you want me to report, sir?"

"You report to Colonel Delaney on Monday. He'll brief you on any new information when you see him."

"Hatchert nodded her head as she noted how the Colonel looked unusually tense. She learned early on to observe a person's body language. Based on what she saw, she knew the Colonel had something else on his mind. He was upset, that much was obvious to her trained eye. More importantly, Colonel Highland was like a father to her, more than her own father would ever be. She knew the Colonel's moods almost as well as she her own, and right now, his jaws looked like they could crush an armored tank.

Most of her birthdays passed by unnoticed as a child. But, on the rare occasion when there was a party, the Colonel was quietly there. He was a safe lap to climb on when she was a toddler, and as she grew older she respected him—and perhaps loved him, although it was hard to tell; she had shut down her feelings a long time ago. But, his presence always calmed her and she liked being under his command.

So she sat there longer than necessary and waited. He would tell her in his own good time. Patience was a major part of the game. If you didn't have patience, you wouldn't make it in this line of work.

"Hatchert. This one's personal," the Colonel said slowly as he focused on her eyes. "The Vista Point victim is my niece, Josie Green. She's stubborn and won't accept my help. She's also a civilian, which means she's out of our jurisdiction and we have no legal basis to help her. If there's a way you can keep an eye on her without direct involvement, I would appreciate it," the Colonel said with solemn eyes that held her gaze.

She didn't blink. "I'm sorry, Colonel. I'll do my best."

"I know you will, Hatchert."

Hatchert stood on the curb in front of the building and watched the oranges and reds of the sunset sky as she waited for a cab to arrive. She looked off into the distance where she saw the hill that her house sat on. As she stood

20

there with her suitcase beside her, she started to relax. Just a half hour from now and she would be home.

The taxi pulled up and the trunk popped open. Hatchert tossed her suitcase onto the bottom of the trunk while the cab owner got out and came to the back.

"Hi," Hatchert said.

"Hi. Where are you going?" the thirty-something cabbie asked as she shuffled the suitcase around the way she liked it and slammed down the trunk lid.

"1623 Blue Haven Hill."

Hatchert climbed into the back seat. She didn't want to play twenty questions with the cab owner.

As the cabbie slid into the driver's seat, she looked in her rearview mirror at the serious young woman who was seated in the back. Guess she doesn't want to talk, the cabbie thought, and began flipping channels on the radio. Soon, the car was filled with light rock as piano, guitars, and drums blended in with the car horns, exhaust, and squealing brakes as they inched their way along the six-lane freeway.

"*God damn it, MOVE IT, YOU ASSHOLE!*," was flung through the air as Hatchert observed a petite woman, the size of a large Mickey Mouse doll, screaming out her driver's window at the car in front of her. The cab owner was humming along to Elton John's *Bennie and the Jets* and seemed oblivious to the anger and the traffic.

They crawled past the main city and started the climb up Hatchert's hill.

"How much?" Hatchert asked as they pulled in front of her house.

"Fifty," the cabbie responded with a cheery fixed smile.

"Here," Hatchert said as she handed her sixty-five. "Keep the change."

"Thanks," and hit the trunk release. She was halfway to the trunk when she noticed Hatchert was already reaching for her bag.

"Got it," Hatchert said as she grabbed her suitcase out of the open trunk.

"Have a nice afternoon," the cabbie said pleasantly as she jumped in the driver's seat and drove away.

Hatchert stared at her house and took in a deep breath as if she were inhaling a rich, dark chocolate espresso. She studied the new hot-pink flowering bush to the right of the front door that her gardener must have planted while she was gone. She unlocked the solid-mesquite, Spanish-style door and stepped inside to her living room. She looked at the plush, dark-brown leather couch and almost gave into the urge of running and jumping into the midst of the deep blue and varying shades of orange throw pillows that were lying in soft piles against the seat back.

She stroked her finger along the rough slab of mesquite with its bark that served as a mantle on the fireplace. The fireplace surround had terra cotta tiles with a border of Spanish tiles in deep blues, greens, and oranges. In this climate, she almost never used the fireplace except when El Nino hit. She loved to light a fire and watch the flames dance as the wind whistled over the chimney flue. She looked at the dark mesquite bookcases she had custom-made that went to the ceiling on both sides of the fireplace. She picked up the silver comb that was lying on the third shelf and slid her fingers along the prongs and smiled before she carefully put it back in its place.

The first order of business was to throw her dirty clothes from her suitcase in the laundry room and then head

22

for the shower. She emptied her suitcase and tossed the dirty clothes onto the tiled floor by the washer, slipped off her clothes and added them to the pile. It felt good to let the warm, night air embrace her naked body. She walked back to her bedroom and into the master bath, stepping into the shower lined with more terra cotta and Spanish Mexican tiles. The shower spray rained down on her, as she felt cocooned in its warmth. Her muscle aches and headache were swept away as she stood there drinking in the feel of the warm water as it slipped and slid over the curves of her toned body.

Stepping out onto the ocean-blue, cotton shower mat, she towel-dried her long auburn waves and let them hang loosely about her shoulders. She pulled on her deep blue, terry-cloth robe and headed to the kitchen allowing her bare feet to soak in the warmth of the tiled floor. Grabbing a beer, she slipped outside to the courtyard and stretched out on the lounge chair. Looking at the city lights and the stars overhead, she finally began to unwind. She inhaled the sweet scent of lemon and oranges in the warm night air and basked in the feeling of being home—at least for the next two nights.

She listened to a neighbor taking out the garbage and Zookie, the little Yorkie that lived two doors down barking. Wait for it, she said to herself as she smiled. Sure enough, Ms. Kittredge yelled, "Zookie, you'll wake the neighbors. Be quiet." And Hatchert had to chuckle because Ms. Kittredge's yelling was always louder than Zookie's bark. Hatchert was content to finally have neighbors. The noises and sounds they made seemed to be the sounds of one gigantic family without all the fuss. Except for Mr. Forsythe, when he got out his weed blower at 6:00 a.m. and began blowing the leaves out of his front yard. Oh well,

Hatchert thought, he only did it once a month, which wasn't too bad all things considered.

She took her empty beer bottle back to the kitchen where she dropped it into the recycling bin. She swapped out one load of clothes in the washer for another and tossed the wet ones into the dryer. The hum of the machines was like music to her ears because it meant she could do laundry anytime she wanted, unlike the last three months when she had to haul them to a laundry mat. No coins to worry about and no one taking her silk blouse either, she grimaced. That was a great silk blouse, Hatchert lamented as she headed for her bedroom.

She let her bathrobe slide to the floor and dove into bed. She loved the feel of the crisp, cotton sheets against her skin and enjoyed the luxurious feeling of being spread-eagle in her own bed. She was glad she decided to go with a king instead of a queen bed, even though it meant giving up a small bookcase she'd planned for one wall of the bedroom. She rolled over and pulled out a brochure on Machu Picchu and Africa. Partway through reading about the cheetahs in the Serengeti, she drifted off into a deep sleep.

CHAPTER 2

Saturday, 27 September 14
Relaxing between assignments

The morning light streamed in through her bedroom window dancing across her eyelids. She rolled over in bed and stretched her arms and legs out wide, relishing the fact that she had nowhere to go this morning. Almost heaven, she thought as she opened the Spanish style mesquite door with the wrought iron that curled lazily against the full-length, clear-glass door panels. She stepped into the courtyard, walked to the edge of the pool, and dove in. As she floated to the surface she turned over and simply drifted, allowing the water to cradle her body. Her long, auburn hair moved gently on the water currents that spread out like a halo around her. She looked up and watched the clouds slip by across the morning sky. Now THIS was heaven, Hatchert grinned as she drifted about letting the pool's current provide the direction.

Soon, she was swimming laps creating her own pattern of current and bubbles. Pushing her lungs and muscles until they screamed, she finally rolled over and drifted once again. Stepping out of the pool, she almost giggled as the water droplets tickled her skin as they scurried downward. She plopped onto the deep-blue cushion on the lounge and let her body absorb the sun's rays. It would be interesting to meet the Colonel's family after all these years. Her heart did a flip as she wished she were his daughter, but she quickly extinguished any sentimental spark that might have been struck.

Restless, she headed to the kitchen and grabbed a chocolate-brown coffee cup from among the precisely aligned cups and bowls that occupied the top shelf of the dark oak cabinet shelf. After she poured rich Kona coffee into her cup, she drew in a deep breath inhaling its nutty scent and then, ceremoniously took the first sip letting it slip and slide over her tongue. She stood at the kitchen window and spooned in a mouthful of yogurt and granola while she watched a ruby-throated hummingbird feed on coral-colored honeysuckle that grew along the trellis by the fence.

She thought about her two best friends she was going to meet for a late lunch. Hatchert met Lea and Kate at a local lesbian event when she made her first foray into the gay world five years ago. For most of her teens, Hatchert remained a loner. Moving each year to match her father's assignments made it difficult to establish friendships. It was hard to explore who she was when there was no one to explore it with. But, Lea and Kate changed all that. They took Hatchert under their wing and helped her establish contacts and find places where she could explore her sexuality. She wasn't "out" at work. Hatchert felt her personal life was private and her sexual orientation was none of their business. She was looking forward to seeing Lea and Kate after being gone for so long.

Grabbing her laptop off her desk, she took it outside and sat at the little wrought iron table in the courtyard. She clicked on Laura Brock's file. Laura Brock was the first victim and had been sexually assaulted on the previous Tuesday around 5:40 p.m. She was nineteen years old, blond, 5'4 1/2" tall, and weighed approximately 145 pounds. She grew up in Prescott, Arizona and was an only child. Her mother, Karen, was a drug addict and rarely saw

26

Laura, except when she needed more money. Hatchert studied the mug shot of Laura's mom taken when she was arrested for selling drugs. She had the classic smaller-than-normal pupils, bloodshot eyes, and drawn thin face of a drug addict.

"Must have been tough for Laura," Hatchert thought as she clicked on a photo of her father and Laura as they stood in front of a souped-up, tropical turquoise 1957 Chevy Belair. Laura loved anything to do with engines, a joy she shared with her dad. She joined the army to be a mechanic and according to her file, was one of the best students the teachers had run across in a long time.

Ben, Laura's dad, was an electrical engineer for a local power company. He seemed to be drug-free, and was educated at Arizona State University where he met his wife who was bussing tables in the college cafeteria at the time.

Hatchert smiled when she saw Laura dressed in the uniform of Scotty, the chief engineer of the starship Enterprise, taken when she attended the Trekkie convention last August. She would be deployed to a base in Germany in four months.

She clicked on Cindy Cunningham's file, the second victim. Cindy was sexually assaulted on Saturday around 8:00 a.m., four days after Laura's attack. According to her bio, Cindy entered the Army one year ago, was 5'8 1/2"" tall, blond, and a curvaceous 130 pounds.

She was twenty years old and grew up in Boise, Idaho. Hatchert clicked on a photo of Cindy in her cheerleader outfit as she waved her pompoms for the Mountain High Cougars at a football game. Clicking on the next photo, Hatchert studied the beaming 16-year old Cindy standing behind a counter on her first day of work at a coffee house.

Her dad died in Afghanistan six years earlier, the same year her younger brother Stephen was born.

Hatchert pictured a skinny girl with carrot-red hair in her sixth grade class whose father died in action. It was Hatchert's first realization that her father might not come home one day. She learned to deal with it, as all military kids do, but it didn't mean it was easy.

Turning her attention back to Cindy's file, she noted they were a military family through and through. When Cindy decided to join the Army, her mother understood and supported her. She was getting high marks from her language teachers and was scheduled for an overseas assignment in South Korea in six months.

Josie Green was the civilian victim, and was sexually assaulted on Monday around 4:40 p.m., two days after Cindy. "Busy boy, aren't you," Hatchert said out loud as she thought about the four-day time span between attacks.

Josie's parents were Samantha and Bill Green. Samantha Green was the Colonel's 55-year-old younger sister who had graduated from Cal State Berkeley in finance and accounting at 23 years old. She worked at a local Wells Fargo Bank where she met Bill Green. She was twenty-five years old when they married and two years later they had their one and only child, Josie Marie Green.

As she looked at Samantha's picture, she observed that Samantha had the same light-olive-brown skin of the Colonel, but her sea blue eyes, dark blonde hair, petite nose, and jaw must have come from their mother. Samantha sat on the local Salvation Army board, the local historical preservation committee, and the school board.

Bill Green was the son of a local rancher, Kyle Green. His mother died when he was born. Instead of following in his father's footsteps, Bill chose to farm. He had great business sense and earned the title of being one of the wealthiest men in the valley. As Hatchert studied a picture of Bill Green in cowboy attire taken when he was president of the rodeo, she saw how his 6'2" tall, 210-pound body, honey-blond hair, high cheekbones, and striking Scandinavian blue eyes probably broke some hearts in the valley. She clicked other photos of him as a city council member, an agricultural commission board member, and a United Way board member.

Hatchert grumbled as she clicked through the file and realized that photos of Josie Green were missing. Josie lived in Vista Point, a tiny ocean community south of Hamilton City and Fort Oaks. She was 5'9" tall, 115 pounds, with the honey-blond hair and height of her father. She graduated with honors from Stanford with a doctorate of Philosophy in English at the age of twenty-two and published two short stories and one poem. She was a member of the National Writers Association and taught writing twice a week at a local church.

She was bright, you had to give her that, Hatchert mused. But, what kind of life was it to sit in coffee shops and in writing groups, she thought with a sneer. She could picture her now, wearing an oversized sweatshirt, tattered blue jeans, and thick, ebony, round glasses—all designer of course: a fancy nerd; sitting in a library somewhere with her head among piles of books. Nerds weren't her type. But, Hatchert reflected, you had to give her credit. She must be in fairly decent shape if she runs the Vista Point trail.

Josie's Wednesday night writing group has eight members composed of two males and six females. The Thursday night group has ten members and only one male. Hatchert wondered how he felt about being the only male in a mostly women's group. Guess she would find out, she thought as her stomach did a one and one half somersault just thinking about the writing class. She could rule out the females in the writer's group leaving her with three male suspects.

Looks like I'm going to get to know the Vista Point trail and have a nice workout at the same time, Hatchert thought as she closed her laptop. But now, it was time to get dressed, run some errands, and join Lea and Kate for lunch. Hatchert smiled as she grabbed her laptop and plopped it back on her desk.

She walked into her bedroom and scanned her closet. My old standby, Hatchert grinned as she pulled on her favorite pair of blue jeans with the rips that were strategically placed to highlight her strong legs and tight butt. She pulled on a deep blue t-shirt, slipped on her black tennis shoes, and headed to her car. Backing out of the driveway, she made a mental note to pick up a bottle of wine to give to Kate and Lea.

The errands didn't take long and soon she was headed to the Mexican restaurant run by Claudia and Elena who were one of the first lesbian couples to marry in California. Claudia and Elena were amazing women and between the two of them, they bought and renovated an old rundown pizza joint. Instead of flaking pea-green paint and hot pink fluorescent light fixtures, the walls were now the rich earth tones reminiscent of Santa Fe. The heavy wrought iron chairs and mesquite tables fit the southwestern theme, and the rich colors of oranges, browns, and turquoise blues were seen in exquisite artwork hanging on the wall by some well-known Santa Fe artists. It was a festive and fun place, and Hatchert's stomach grumbled as it anticipated all the wonderful Mexican food it was going to receive soon.

How lucky can she get, Hatchert thought as she pulled into a parking space right in front of the restaurant. At one of the outdoor tables she could see Lea and Kate who were busy laughing and talking with Elena. She took the time to drink in each of these women. She looked at Elena, who had sultry, black hair, rich mocha skin, and an infectious smile that lit up the world. Hatchert smiled as she remembered Elena dancing the salsa at the last potluck she attended.

Then she looked at Lea. Lea had beautiful, snow-white hair, wore dark brown glasses that framed her deep brown eyes, and was dressed in a tan plaid shirt, and Khaki pants. She was a quiet, nature lover who worshipped the ground Kate walked on.

And then there was Kate, Hatchert laughed. Kate had short blond hair, sparkling blue eyes, and wore blue jeans, a green t-shirt, and a long, gold necklace along with a pair of large, gold hoop earrings. She was a whirling spirit of happiness and energy and she loved everyone.

"Hi Hatchert! What are you doing sitting there? Come on. I can hardly wait to wrap my arms around you!" Kate belted out with a huge smile as she waved for Hatchert to get out of the car and join them.

"Be right there," Hatchert shouted back with a huge grin on her face as she grabbed the wine bag from the passenger seat floor.

"Sit over here," Kate motioned to the chair opposite them as Hatchert set the wine bag on the seat beside her.

"Hi Lea. Hi Kate. What's up with you two? You look like you just won the lottery or something," Hatchert asked as she searched their faces for a clue as to what they were all excited about.

"First things first," Kate said as she leaned over and plunked a kiss on Hatchert's cheek. It's so good to see you again," she said, as a smile as wide as Texas spread across her face. "Now we can order and then we'll share about why we're so happy," Kate said with a devilish grin.

"Hi Hatchert. It's nice to see you again," Elena said as she laughed at Kate's girlish giggle and Hatchert's amused, but curious eyes.

"I had to come out and say hi to you Hatchert. It's great to see you!" Claudia said as she came over and gave her a warm pat on the shoulder. "Are you home for a while?" she asked as Hatchert took in the beautiful blend of spice and delight of Claudia, the one who ran the business side of the restaurant.

"Only today. Tomorrow I leave on my new assignment, but it's in California so I can take my baby with me," Hatchert grinned as she looked at her shiny, black 1989 Miata sparkling in the sun.

"Well, it's good to see you. Maybe next time you'll stay for a while and we can catch up. I've got to head back to the office. Nice seeing you gals again, and congratulations again Lea and Kate," Claudia said with a smile and a wave as she headed inside to her office.

"What can I get for you gals today?" Elena asked with her electric grin.

"I'll have two of your artichoke and mushroom enchiladas with beans and rice along with a big glass of ice cold beer," Kate sat with a twinkle in her eye.

"I'll have a chicken tostada and a beer," Lea said.

"Chicken fajita for me," Hatchert chimed in, "and I'm ready for an ice cold glass of beer."

"Coming right up," Elena said and set off to turn their order in to the cook.

Hatchert turned her attention back to Kate and Lea.

"Well, are you going to tell me, or do I have to get tough with you?" Hatchert jokingly teased.

"We did it!" Kate said with a huge smile on her face.

"Did what?" Hatchert asked quizzically.

"Wait! You've got to have your beer before she tells you," Elena said enthusiastically as she set down three icy mugs of beer. "There, now you can tell her, Kate."

"We got married on Thursday!" Kate blurted out as she leaned over and gave Lea a giant kiss right on the lips. Lea beamed.

"That's awesome!" Hatchert said, although her heart skipped a bit because she wasn't with them on their special day.

"It was a spur of the moment type of thing. Don't feel bad," Kate replied as she noticed the quick wave of disappointment sweep across Hatchert's face. "We didn't know ourselves until Thursday. We flew up to San Francisco on Wednesday to visit Jennifer, Lea's college roommate, and to go to the Melissa Etheridge concert with the San Francisco Symphony. We started laughing and talking and had a great time at dinner. Jennifer teased us that we should get married while we were there because our twentieth anniversary was the next day. The concert was amazing and we walked away floating on air. Lea and I have been talking about getting married for a while now."

"I remember you mentioning it the last time I was home," Hatchert nodded.

"We had breakfast at this cute little café near Jennifer's apartment. Jennifer kept talking about how wonderful it would be to celebrate our twentieth by getting married. One thing led to another and we went to the courthouse where the first gay marriages were performed and we did it! It happened so fast I think we're both spinning."

"How are you feeling around all this, Lea," Hatchert asked knowing that Lea was the quiet one in the partnership, which is why their relationship worked so well for both of them.

"I'm happy. We both wanted to get married, but it never seemed like the right time. The weather was perfect. We were having such a great time and it finally felt right. I don't like a lot of fuss when it comes to the whole wedding ceremony business," Lea confessed.

"I'm happy for you. Cheers!" Hatchert said as they all clunked their beer mugs together and took a big sip in unison.

"Here's a bottle of wine to celebrate," Hatchert smiled happily as she handed them the bottle of red cabernet that was neatly tucked into a bright blue wine bag.

"She didn't tell you the best part," Lea said.

"Yes, I did. Getting married was the best part. But, we have more to share. We're going on an all-lesbian cruise! The ship leaves next Sunday out of Rome and we're going to see Italy, Turkey, and Greece!" Kate gushed.

"Wow! You guys will have a great time," Hatchert cheerily replied as she took another swig of beer.

"Here's your enchiladas, Kate," Elena said as she set a large, oval plate filled with enchiladas, black beans, and Spanish rice in front of her. "What do you think about their news?" Elena asked as she waited to see Hatchert's reaction.

"I think it's great! Cheers to the newlyweds!" Hatchert toasted them again.

"Those look yummy, Elena," Kate said as she inhaled the aroma of Mexican spices, bubbling cheese, and beans.

"Be careful. The plates are hot," Elena said as she set the sizzling cast iron fry pan in front of Hatchert and the tostada stacked a mile high with lettuce, cheese, and chicken in front of Lea.

Hatchert still marveled at how Lea's petite stomach was able to hold all that food and how she never seemed to gain an ounce.

Hatchert could hardly wait to dive into her fajitas that were sizzling on the cast iron plate.

"How are you?" Lea asked noting the tired lines around Hatchert's eyes.

"I'm fine. It was hot in South Carolina and I'm happy to be back home."

"Did you meet anyone while you were there?" Kate asked as she spooned in a mouthful of enchilada.

"No, I didn't have the time. I'm glad to be home though," Hatchert sighed as she rolled a pepper around in her mouth letting its hotness harass her tongue.

"Tonight we're having a party at our house to celebrate our marriage. We'd like you to come. Can you make it?" Katie asked with a grin so wide it almost touched her ears.

"I'd love to come," Hatchert replied.

"Yahoo!" Kate giggled as she stabbed the last bit of cheese-and-sauce coated artichoke onto her fork and pushed it into her mouth.

"This was so nice. I miss you guys," Hatchert said as they got up to leave.

"We miss you too," Kate said as she leaned forward and gave Hatchert a big hug.

"See you tonight!" Hatchert said as she gave Lea a quick hug.

The rest of the afternoon flew by. After running to the drugstore to pick up some suntan lotion, to the hardware store to buy a carbon monoxide detector, and to the post office to drop off her bills, there wasn't much time to do anything more. She finished her laundry and it was time to dress for the party.

She pulled on her slim-fit blue jeans, and a deep-green t-shirt where the "V" ended a little below her cleavage. She slid on her black tennis shoes and turned the lights down low. As she opened the garage door and backed out of her driveway, she thought about how nice it was to be home, even if it was only for a little while.

Jumping onto the coast highway, Hatchert aimed her car toward Lea and Kate's home that sat on a cliff-edge across from the ocean, north of the city. The drive was pretty as the warm night air blew through her hair. Traffic was fairly light and she made the drive up the coast in no time. The ocean was calm and looked like a sea of scattered blue sapphires sparkling in the sun.

As she neared Lea and Kate's house, she saw that cars had spilled out of the driveway and onto the winding road that led up to their house. When Kate and Lea threw a party, everyone came. Hatchert pulled her car off the road and parked behind a black Porsche.

She hiked up the sloping road and driveway. The modern front door was wide open welcoming their guests into the main living space. It was a huge single room with an open kitchen opposite the wall of glass that faced the ocean.

Kate was in the kitchen checking on the shrimp puffs. Lea was standing near the barbecue grill on the large outside deck that spanned the full width of the house. The smell of the barbecue chicken and steak had Hatchert's stomach growling again and her mouth watering. She hadn't tasted barbecue in months.

36

"What can I do to help?" Hatchert asked as she gave Kate a hello kiss on the cheek.

"Nothing. Lea and I have it all under control. Go have some fun. You deserve some time off. Sue and Lisa are over there, Kathy's in the garage getting more ice out of the freezer, and Melanie's over there talking with Kris and Pat," Kate said as she swept her hand in the air.

"I haven't seen Sue and Lisa in a long time, " Hatchert said as she moved toward them.

"Hi Sue. Hi Lisa," Hatchert said with a smile as she settled in for some nice conversation and fun.

Soon the party was in high gear. The food came off the grill and people were sitting everywhere, including the floor. Melissa Etheridge, k.d. lang, Taylor Swift, and Beyoncé's melodic voices drifted from the stereo system. It was wonderful chaos as old friends caught up with each other and new friendships were formed. The evening was wonderful and as Hatchert took a break on the outside deck overlooking the ocean, she was thankful Lea and Kate were part of her life. It was sometimes hard to picture, but she hoped that someday she would find a partner and have a partnership just like them.

Well past midnight, the party finally started to wind down. People slipped away into the night while Hatchert lingered to see if she could help them clean up.

"Here are the plates from the deck table," Hatchert said as she put it next to the sink where Kate was rinsing dishes and placing them in the dishwasher.

"Scat! We can take care of this," Kate said as she tried to shoo Hatchert out of the kitchen.

"I don't mind. It's so nice to be home among friends, and helping with the dishes relaxes me. I feel like I'm part of a family when I can help out with simple things like doing the dishes," Hatchert confessed as she looked at Lea and Kate.

"You *ARE* family," Lea responded looking into Hatchert's amber eyes. "You know you're welcome anytime."

"How's your job going? I always worry about you going after these men that rape women," Kate said looking at Hatchert and wondering how she could put herself into such a dangerous position. It certainly wasn't something she would do.

"It's a lot of work and it does require a lot of patience. But, I feel so good when I meet the victim and I'm able to tell them I caught the guy who assaulted them. They're relieved and, better yet, the guy goes away for a long time, so hopefully, they can feel some measure of safety as long as he's in prison."

"Well, you're brave and I'm sure those women appreciate you," Lea said. "I hope the military appreciates you," she said more as a question as she looked at Hatchert.

"Yes. Colonel Highland has my back and I've got all kinds of support when I need it."

"I hope you know we're always here if you ever need us," Lea said as her walnut-brown eyes softened as she spoke.

"Yes, I know that. I'm really grateful for both of you," Hatchert replied as she hugged them both goodbye.

When Hatchert got home, she stripped down and landed on the bed. It was a great evening. She opened the Machu Picchu brochure and read about the Inca Empire knowing that some day she would see it in person. And with that, she fell into a deep sleep.

Sunday, 28 September 14
Santa Barbara, CA

When the morning sunlight beamed its light on the bed, it was already made, complete with the deep-blue pillow shams that lived there while Hatchert was gone.

Hatchert's suitcases were already tucked neatly in her car trunk. She planned on driving two hundred miles today to Santa Barbara where she hoped to walk on the beach and prepare herself mentally for another perpetrator.

The freeways weren't as crowded on Sunday morning as she slowly weaved her way up the coast highway breathing in the smell of kelp, salt, and fish. She watched a spray of water shoot vertically into the air from a passing whale and it never failed to amaze her that such beautiful creatures were within such easy reach.

"That's what life's all about. Just swimming along in good company and eating," Hatchert thought as she cruised along the highway thinking about Lea and Kate's party as the same ache swept through her body when she thought about the possibility of finding someone to love.

The miles ticked by and soon she was in Santa Barbara. She chose a hotel on the beach. It had been a while since she did a beach run, and the thoughts of the sand smooshing between her toes gave her an extra burst of energy. She pulled up to the hotel entrance and handed her key to the valet.

The twenty-floor hotel was a five-star hotel. The lobby was grand with tan marble floors and interior potted palms expertly placed near light-brown leather seats that provided their guests with comfort wherever they turned. Hatchert walked up to the desk clerk and registered.

She found her room on the tenth floor. It was facing the ocean and had a king-size bed, small kitchenette, and a marble-tiled bathroom. A knock on the door and a few dollars later, Hatchert had her suitcase spread open on the bed. She tossed the clothes she was wearing onto the side chair and pulled on her running clothes. With her room key now safely tucked into the zippered pocket of her armband, Hatchert headed for the beach. She walked by the pool where some kids were throwing a giant beach ball around, women and men were working on their tans, and hotel service personnel were quietly serving the guests.

When she stepped onto the tan, course sand she began a slow jog down the beach. She passed by red, orange, blue, white, and multi-striped beach umbrellas. She jogged by sisters burying their brothers in the sand, sunburned teens, and watchful parents. She smiled as she saw another brother sister team building a sand castle together, and another young boy who had a long piece of kelp that he was using as a jump rope throwing sand everywhere.

There were other runners and soon she joined into the beach rhythm making her way beside the lapping foam of the ocean. She ran about five miles before she stopped and drank from her water bottle. She walked along the tide pools and peered down into them watching the hermit crabs scurrying about in the cracks of the rocks. Little fish swam around in the small pools waiting for the tide to come in so they could escape. Sea anemones had their tentacles spread out looking like a bouquet of frilly sea flowers. Pyramid-shaped limpets and 8-arm starfish were clinging to the rocks.

Hatchert removed her running shoes and ran her feet back and forth across the coarse sand grains as they massaged her tired feet. She sat on a large log that long ago had been tossed onto the shore and watched the ocean waves crashing against the rocks. She heard the cars that were traveling on the coast highway in the distance. Another runner jogged by and they exchanged a quick smile. She sat there a long time letting the calmness wrap around her.

As the sun started down, Hatchert slid into her shoes and began her jog back to the hotel. She chased a runaway beach ball into the surf and sent it flying back to its six-year old owner. She watched a dog dive into the foamy water and come up with a soaking wet tennis ball in its mouth. She jogged by jellyfish that had been swept onto the beach. And she watched sunburned parents carrying tired kids and sand pails in their arms as they made their way back to the hotel.

In her room, she took a hot shower and washed the salt off her body and out of her hair. Refreshed, she slid open the sliding door to the little private balcony that had a small table and two chairs. Hatchert put her laptop on the table and the turkey club sandwich and iced tea she ordered from room service.

She clicked through the files again. The Colonel was right, there wasn't much to go on right now. The perp was carrying the extra weight of the women and still managed to take them to the summit and down again which meant this guy was in excellent shape. She would run the trail herself to see if she could draw him out of his lair. She was used to being bait. It was part of the job.

It looked like the most sensible way to watch Josie was to join her writing groups. Only for the Colonel, Hatchert said to the air as her stomach nosedived at the prospect. She didn't have to worry about THAT right now, she reasoned. There were three whole days before the first writing group met. She was hungry as she eyeballed her turkey club sandwich and iced tea.

After she ate, she watched the sunset with its oranges and reds spreading out like a Japanese fan across the horizon. Nature never failed to amaze her as she watched the colors subtly dim as the night took over. Time to put the files away and hit the sheets, she thought as she watched the last bit of color disappear from the sky. Her days of luxury were over for now.

CHAPTER 3

Monday, 29 September 14
Fort Oaks and Vista Point, California

"This is a wake-up call," the electronic female voice echoed in the phone as Hatchert listened, then pushed down the button to silence it. She punched the front desk button.

"Good Morning. This is the front desk. May I help you?" chirped the desk clerk.

"Could you please have my car brought around?"

"We'll have it ready in a few minutes," he chirped again.

"Thanks," Hatchert said as she hung up the phone and wondered how anyone could be so exceedingly cheerful at this hour of the morning.

Checking her email, she read a message from her mom.

Hi Mary, How are you? We haven't seen you in over a year and wondered when we can expect your next visit? Love, Mom

She hesitated, and then typed.

"Hi Mom, I'm on another mission. I'll email you when it's over. Love, Mary."

Looking out the window at the ocean, she watched the waves and waited to feel something other than the headache and knot in her stomach that always arrived shortly after she read her mother's emails. Nothing.

After tossing on her clothes, she packed her suitcase and took one last look around the room. She slung her briefcase over her shoulder, grabbed the handle of her rolling suitcase, and headed for the lobby.

"We have your car out front, Ms. Hatchert," he chirped once again with a toothy wide smile. "I hope you enjoyed your stay."

"It was very nice. Thank you," Hatchert mumbled as she shook her head and walked away.

She noticed that a few early risers were in the restaurant ordering breakfast. She eyed the scrambled eggs and bacon and settled on the fresh fruit and yogurt. Sitting at a table across the room, she watched a 3-year old boy racing in circles around his older sister while Mom and Dad were working hard to eat their breakfast. A pang zipped through her abdomen. Kids? Me? She shook her head and did her own race for freedom and inhaled deeply trying to shake the funny twinge from her heart.

Glad to see the only baby she wanted right now, she looked at her Miata that was faithfully waiting for her. As she drove along the coast, she looked to the west at the sea gulls drifting around in the sky as they soared over the miles of blue water. To the east, she observed the mega-million dollar custom homes that were squeezed together along every square inch of hillside. They looked like little stucco jewel boxes with their glistening windows and metal railings. With the wind blowing through her hair, she settled in for the luxury of quiet and a beautiful strip of highway.

Two hours later, she turned onto a two-lane road that would take her over the hills and drop her into the hot valley on the other side. Large coastal oaks with their gigantic canopies looked like greenish-black umbrellas left scattered in a hotel lobby waiting to dry after a winter rainstorm. Herds of black cattle with black faces and brown

44

cattle with white faces grazed on the short tufts of brown grass that had survived the drought, but not their appetite. She passed by a barn that was propped up with giant wood beams. As she drove further, she saw another barn whose roof almost touched the ground and she wondered how it was still standing. Some of the barns were painted, but most wore patches of peeled, white paint that clung to the bare bones of the gray and light brown wood skeletons. Rusted tractors and plows from another generation sat stoically in front of some of the barns. Others housed modern tractors and laser equipment under their rafters.

As she dropped down into the valley, Hatchert's stomach grumbled. A highway sign showed there was food at the next exit. She pulled off the road and into a fast food restaurant. Today, she was going to have a hamburger with the works. As she waited for her order, Hatchert thought about the new assignment. The perpetrator already hit three times. Her gut told her this guy was going to be real trouble. He was in good shape, unlike Perkins, which means she'd have to be more careful. She was confident her karate and army training would take him down, but she wasn't a fool either. Strong meant more danger.

As she bit down into her burger, she thought about her job. She liked what she did most of the time. It felt good to put a slime bag away. But, there were times she missed the simple, quiet life. Being at home with Lea and Kate always seemed to bring out the domestic side of her. It was hard to find a partner when she was gone for months at a time. And when she did find her, she was going to have to be independent and strong—someone who understood and accepted the danger that she faced each time she was on assignment. Hatchert leaned her head back against the bench seat and sighed. For now, this was what she wanted to do. Time would tell when it came to her personal life.

As she settled into driving once again, she noticed the air was getting cooler. The hills were receding more as the valley spread wider. Soon, she saw row upon row of lettuce in varying varieties and colors. She was entering the food belt of River Valley.

The rich soil was gold to the farmers who planted and harvested vegetable crops: broccoli, cauliflower, lettuce, tomatoes, Brussel sprouts, and artichokes, among others. Hamilton City was a farming community at the north end of the valley, and boasted a mild Mediterranean climate year round. It was built on land that used to be an ancient riverbed, and each time it rained, the topsoil was swept from the hilltops, depositing more farmer's gold into the valley below.

With a population of 64,323 people, it was a small, fast-growing city because of the agriculture business. It became a magnet for young doctors, dentists, and lawyers who wanted in on the ground floor of something big, where they could build a highly profitable practice, and raise their children. Having the military base close by provided more income to the local economy, although that would be going away soon. The base would be closed in a year. A state university was planned in its place. It would take time for the city to recover from the loss, but they had no choice. The economic climate in Washington required that all aspects of the military be trimmed.

Hatchert pulled over to watch them harvest lettuce. The picking machines stood ten to fifteen feet tall and were almost as wide as they moved slowly up and down the two-foot deep rows. The front half of the machine was a hybrid--a mix between a large big-rig truck and a tractor. Large conveyor belts that were folded up for travel were extended on either side of the machines as they made their way down the rows.

The workers moved silently and gracefully along with the monsters. They bent down to neatly slice through the plant's stem with their cutting knives and with a wave of their hand would toss the head of lettuce onto the moving conveyor belt.

By day it was almost its own magical ballet. Colorful scarves that provided warmth at night and protection from the endless sun beating down on the workers by day were tied around their heads. Long-sleeve black or brown jackets, dark blue jeans, and heavy work boots that kept them from sinking to their knees in the muddy troughs seemed to be the unofficial uniform.

Hatchert could hear the faint sound of Mariachi music as it drifted through the air. She saw the gigantic spotlights mounted on top of the harvesters that created the effect of a small sun spreading its harsh light in all directions allowing the workers to pick well into the night. There was no such thing as an eight-hour workday during harvest season.

According to the bio, this was also cattle country, primarily Hereford or Angus, and home to one of the largest rodeos west of the Mississippi River. Hatchert watched some videos on the web to get a better feel for the town. Apparently, the rodeo was the one time during the year the community was able to cut loose and have some fun. One video showed all ages, from babies in their daddy's arms to seniors using their canes, square dancing in the street. She listened to a Cowboy band made up of locals and watched clips from four consecutive days of rodeo competition. Apparently, the Army's marching band led the parade each year since the base was established. It seemed like it would be a safe place to raise a family.

Hatchert could smell a blend of fertilizer, churned dirt, and cut plants in the air. Guess you got used to smelling it if you grew up here, she thought as she started her car and slowly merged back onto the two-lane highway.

Several miles later, Hatchert pulled into a small gas station to stretch her legs and get some gas. Must be a popular local's spot, Hatchert thought, as she pulled in behind a pearl white Toyota RAV4 to wait her turn at the pump. As Hatchert was climbing out of her Miata, the owner of the RAV4—a tall, blond-haired woman in her middle twenties—yelled to the man in the far gas lane, "Told you we would beat you!" she said as she flashed him a Hollywood smile.

"Could she be more obvious," Hatchert scoffed, as she watched the verbal football being tossed back and forth between the woman and the cobalt, black haired young man for the next five minutes.

"Get a room!" Hatchert murmured to herself. "Some of us have things to do; like getting some gas so we can move on with our life!" Not bad looking though, Hatchert had to admit as she studied the breasts that strained against the electric-green t-shirt of the blond. Too bad she bats for the other team, Hatchert thought. "Finally, she's done with the googly eyes," Hatchert mumbled, more irritated with herself because of the ache that spread through her body as her mind flashed a picture of what she could do with Miss Googly eyes in bed.

"God, I'm tired," she hated to admit to herself. Usually, adrenaline and caffeine were her faithful companions to keep her on her toes. But, the losses always took more out of her. Time to get to the base, she thought as she climbed back into her car. "Finally, you're done!" Hatchert thought grumpily and pulled forward to the pump.

As Josie Green pulled away from the gas pump, she glanced in her rearview mirror and smiled. She saw that hot, dark-haired woman pull in behind her. It was amazing luck, her best friend Michael was at the pump in the far, outside lane. It was fun to banter with Michael, and watch the woman sizzle and spit like water on a hot pancake griddle as she sat impatiently in her convertible. Any other day, she might have been brave enough to get a phone number. But, today she was on a mission. No one was going to rape her and get away with it, she thought angrily as she shoved her car into second, then third.

"I hope you've got some news for me today, Chief Girard," she fumed as she punched the accelerator pedal and headed to Vista Point.

As she was driving toward the police station, Josie thought about the Chief. He was the same age as her father, yet they were opposites. Where her father was fair-skinned, the Chief was mocha brown. Where her father was formal, the Chief was laid back. Where her father was tall and slender, the Chief was short and stocky. And of the two, Josie felt, at times, that the Chief was more her father than her own.

Ever since she was a child, the Chief's daughter Rachel was her best friend. She almost lived at Rachel's house back then. They shared toys, clothes, and adventures. On a sleepover, the Chief would sit in the white, rocking chair in the corner of the room and read them, "The Wild Things" or other tales. And when they got older, he pitched a tent in the backyard and told them ghost stories by flashlight.

On prom night, the Chief inspected and interrogated

her boyfriend right along with Rachel's as the boys waited for them to descend the front staircase in their gowns. And he was always there to protect her at local events, even saving her from some of the butt-numbing ceremonies that she had to endure as the daughter of two local dignitaries. With a sigh, Josie began to search for the elusive parking spot on a side street since all the marked ones in front of the police station were full.

Chief Girard leaned back in his chair and looked out the window where he could see a piece of the bay and his town. He glanced at the file spread open on his desk that held the information on Josie Green's rape. He'd been the police chief here for thirty-five years and he'd seen it all. But, this one hit too close to home.

Josie always had an adventurous spirit, he thought. She was the one who convinced Rachel to climb the huge oak tree behind the school when they were in second grade. Josie went clear to the top, but poor Rachel's nerves ran out partway up the tree. Josie tried to coax Rachel down, but she was clinging to that limb like an abalone to a rock. It took Frank from the fire department and the bucket lift on the fire truck to get her down.

He smiled at the memory of the forlorn Rachel and the exasperated Josie who had tried everything, including giving Rachel her favorite stuffed horse, to get her to climb down out of the tree. He remembered Josie's sullen face when her parents politely and calmly picked her up and took her home. The next day, both the fire and police departments had a small visitor who personally delivered a hand-drawn thank you note for saving Rachel. While Josie stood there sulkily and bravely, she apologized to both Frank and himself for causing them any trouble.

"It didn't last long," Chief Girard chuckled. Two days later, Josie convinced Rachel to play the role of the horse, while she rode around on her back with a broomstick, hitting a tennis ball around the backyard. One wild swing landed Rachel a stunning, black eye. Josie thought it looked great, but poor Rachel thought she looked hideous and wouldn't come out of her room for the next two days. Once again, Josie was standing on the doorstep with a hand-drawn apology for giving Rachel a black eye. And much to both their credit, Rachel and Josie were still close friends. The Chief smiled as he looked at the picture that sat on the corner of his desk with Rachel in her wedding dress and Josie in her pale blue maid of honor dress at Rachel's wedding a year ago.

Josie was civic minded, he reflected. Something her parents instilled in her at an early age, maybe too early. It was a big responsibility to be the poster child for the local agricultural industry. Her parents even began a scholarship program where the Josie Green Scholarship was given annually to a local woman who wanted to pursue a career in agriculture. As a poster child, Josie wasn't allowed to play with the other kids while her family attended countless fundraisers and charity events. Instead, she spent many hours sitting in a chair beside her parents, dangling her legs and playing makeup games to keep her little mind occupied.

Josie didn't scare easily. That inner courage is what got her through the assault, the Chief thought. He was glad that the city council voted to team with the Silicon Valley Sexual Assault Response Team, or S.A.R.T., so that Hamilton Hospital could have a S.A.R.T. nurse on site. The conviction rate was higher when S.A.R.T. was involved. He'd watched too many rapists walk free when it was one person's word against another. It was hard to dispute DNA evidence that proved a sexual assault occurred and by whom.

"The nurses and equipment aren't cheap, but how do you put value on a human life?" he thought as he shook his head.

He had to give Josie credit. Josie was the one who spearheaded the campaign for the S.A.R.T. project five months ago after he showed her how it would help the women in the community. The Chief was relieved when Josie jumped on board and spoke at the city council meetings in favor of bringing a S.A.R.T. nurse to Hamilton Hospital and to purchase the necessary specialized equipment. She toured the Silicon Valley facility, spoke with Sheila Evans the program director, and coordinated with Ms. Evans to give a formal presentation about S.A.R.T. to the city council.

So far, Josie was the only woman of the three victims who went to the S.A.R.T. facility that night. That took guts.

This wasn't the first sexual assault case he'd worked on and, unfortunately, he knew it wouldn't be his last.

The Chief leaned back in his old office chair that had molded to his body over time and stared out the window watching a whale excursion charter boat coming into dock with all its tired visitors. Not bad for an office view. He was glad his office wasn't in downtown Vista Point where all the boutiques and restaurants were crammed in, one against the other.

Being a police officer was in his bones. He knew he could retire in a few more years, but he liked what he did and felt good about protecting his community. As he leaned forward in his chair, he looked at the photo of Rachel and his wife Melissa. Later today, he had a meeting with

Special Agent Hatchert. He didn't have much to show her, he thought as he rubbed his eyes.

Just as he started to close Josie's file, he was surprised to see her standing in the doorway.

"Hi Chief," she said as she marched toward him.

"How are you doing, Josie?" he asked as he braced himself against the storm that walked into his office.

"I wanted to know if you've heard anything from the Department of Justice?" she calmly demanded as she searched his confident brown eyes for the answer.

"Nothing yet. They have their best working on it, Josie," he responded as he watched her fiery eyes ignite.

"I want him behind bars!" she burst out as she marched across the room and slammed her purse into one of the visitor chairs opposite the Chief's desk. "I'm sorry, Chief, I've never felt this way before," she said as she fought the anger that was building to a category 5 level hurricane.

"Josie, you've been through a lot in the past week and you've handled it well. Anger is a natural part of this process," the Chief said compassionately as he stood up and came around the corner to lean against the front of his desk.

She spun around and nodded. "It's awful. There are moments when I can't believe it happened. It feels like it was a weird dream, or that it's one of my stories. Then, I remember: it's real! There are times it's so crystal clear I feel like I'm living it all over again and I know he's still out there!" she said as she fought to stay calm against the gale force winds that threatened to unleash the storm inside of her once again.

"I know it's difficult, but don't be too hard on yourself. You've been through a lot and it will take time to recover."

53

"I know it logically, but I'm frustrated and angry at him for what he did to me, and I'm angry that the Department of Justice had a water leak the day they received my exam evidence. I want to know if the evidence for my case was damaged," she said as she took a deep breath and steeled herself for his response.

"I talked with them this morning. We're extremely lucky. The evidence room wasn't totally flooded from the broken water pipe. I confirmed the evidence linked to your case is safe. It wasn't damaged by the water."

She let out a gasp. "That's great news! How soon can we find him?" she eagerly asked as a smile broke out on her face.

"Josie, I don't want you to get your hopes up. They have to run it through a federal database and that could take days. Even then, they might not come up with a match. If he hasn't previously been convicted of sexual assault, he might not be in the database, and not all states keep DNA profiles on felons."

"He has to be there! Will you call me as soon as you get the results?"

"As soon as I hear something, I'll let you know. In the meantime, I wonder if you could start from the beginning and tell me everything that happened that day? You did a great job at S.A.R.T. and I have their report, but there might be a detail that you missed that could help us find him," the Chief asked gently as he searched her fiery eyes.

"I've replayed it over and over in my mind," she answered as she began to pace. "I was working on a new poem last Monday. My muscles were stiff and sore and I needed to run, so I left the house around 3:30 p.m. to run the trail."

"Are you sure about the time?"

"Yes. I wanted to get home by 6:00 p.m. because there was a program on television about Maya Angelou, and I remember I stopped to look at my bedroom clock to figure out if I had enough time to run the trail before the program started."

"Do you remember if the traffic was light or heavy that day?"

"There wasn't much traffic, so I was probably on the trail by 4:10 p.m. I ran the bottom half at a fairly normal pace, which probably took about 40 minutes. Near the summit the trail drops steeply for about fifteen feet and there's a huge, ten-foot tall boulder at the bottom. I came around the backside of the boulder and almost ran right into him," she said as she fought the twisting in her stomach.

"Can I get you some water?" the Chief asked as he noticed her chest begin to heave in and out and her cheeks turned the color of white paste.

"No, I'll be okay," she said fiercely as she took several deep breaths. "I wasn't expecting him to be there. At first, he just startled me. But, then he tasered me and I went down," she said as she clenched her fists driving her manicured nails into her palm.

"I've got a punching bag in my garage if that would help. You can use it anytime," he offered.

"Thanks. I might take you up on it," Josie smiled and threw a sample punch into the air.

"Anger's good right now," the Chief encouraged her, "as long as you release it safely. That's why I have the bag in the garage."

"Good, because I have plenty of anger," she said as she walked over to the window where she crossed her arms. "One minute I'm staring at him, and the next minute I'm on the ground in pain. He straddled me and then handcuffed me. I remember how much force he used to hold me down," Josie said as she fought the nausea in her stomach.

"He grabbed me hard and flipped me over. I started to scream when he shoved a plastic tube into my mouth and forced me to drink orange juice. He put a gag in my mouth. I tried to kick him, but he shoved me back down into the dirt."

"Did he talk to you?"

"No," Josie said as her nostrils flared.

"This wasn't random, Josie. He planned his attack."

"I know," Josie shook her head in disbelief as a shudder ran through her. "I don't understand why he chose ME!" she said as she spun around to face the Chief as her cheeks flushed the same red as hot coals and tears glistened in her eyes.

"We don't know the answer to that question right now, Josie, but I'll try to find the answer for you," the Chief said appearing outwardly calm, betrayed only by his knuckles that turned white from strangling the paper weight that he'd picked up from the top of his desk.

"Everything looked so distorted. I knew what he was doing, but I couldn't stop him," she scowled.

"The drug he gave you can cause that sensation, Josie."

"The next thing I remember, is that he threw me over his back and carried me. I don't know how long he carried me or where he took me. I couldn't focus, Chief! I wanted to and I couldn't!" she said as she began to pace again.

"He tasted like mouthwash," she continued, as she remembered how she couldn't stop him from French kissing her. "He raped me and then carried me again. I remember looking up at his ski mask while he was bending over me. He reeked of mint mouthwash," she spat out as she pursed her lips in disgust.

56

"Do you remember his face?" the Chief asked.

"No, but I think I saw some brown hair sticking out from under his cap."

That's new," and mentally catalogued this new piece of evidence to chew on later. "What kind of build did he have?"

"Medium build, like Mr. Peters."

The Chief nodded as he pictured the storeowner on Mission and Tenth Street downtown. "Do you remember the type of shoes he wore?"

"Not really. It happened too fast."

"You're doing fine, Josie."

"He carried me down the mountain, took the handcuffs off, and removed my gag. Then, rolled me under some bushes and left," she said as her eyebrows furrowed and her stomach tied itself into a square knot. "I remember lying there and not being able to move. I thought I was going to throw up," she said fighting back nausea once again.

"The drug he gave you can have that side effect," he reassured her. "I know this is hard for you," the Chief said as his deep brown eyes softened as he walked over to her and placed a fatherly hand on her shoulder.

"Thanks, Chief," she said as she drank in his warmth.

"I remember I slid down the bank a couple of times before I made it to the road. That must have been when I scraped my knees," she shared as she felt the remnants of the scabs on her knees rub against her pants.

"Another badge of courage," the Chief said with a hint of a smile as he remembered the first time Josie skinned her knee and he convinced her that all scabs were symbols of courage.

"You're right, Chief," she smiled fondly remembering that fateful ride on a piece of cardboard careening down a long grassy hill that ended in both Rachel and she tumbling and sliding down the rest of the hill on their bare knees.

Taking a deep breath, Josie continued. "When I got to the road, I started walking north. I didn't realize it at first, but the parking lot for the trail was just around the curve. I probably shouldn't have been driving," she confessed with sheepish eyes.

"You made it safely to S.A.R.T. and that's what counts. I'm sorry you had to drive all the way to Silicon Valley Hospital, but the work you've done for the past five months means other women won't have to drive that far ever again," he said as he shook his head wishing that the city had a S.A.R.T. here months ago. "You're very brave, Josie."

"Thank you, but I want to do something NOW instead of sitting around waiting for the lab report!" she said emphatically.

" Josie, you ARE doing something. The evidence you provided might take this perpetrator off the street. I'm really proud of you, Josie," the Chief said affectionately as he looked into her determined blue eyes.

"Thanks, Chief. I put the radio on full blast so it would take my mind off him," she shivered, remembering how she felt like a rag doll as she drove that night. "I told the nurse everything. She was great. I don't know what I would have done without her."

"I'm glad she was there for you, Josie. One more question and we'll call it quits. Do you go to the base on a regular basis?"

"No. I went to a concert on Memorial Day and again on the 4th of July. I answered the phones for the children's hospital telethon last April, but for the most part I don't go on the base."

"The Gala fund-raiser for the S.A.R.T. facility at Hamilton Hospital is tomorrow night. I know everyone would understand if you don't want to go."

"I'm going! He's not going to win!" Josie jerked back fiercely as she gritted her teeth.

He stood square in front of her and looked into her deep blue eyes. "He didn't win, Josie. You did. You lived, and you're taking the right steps to help us catch him. He only wins if you let him win. Promise me you won't go after him by yourself?"

"I won't go after him alone, but I won't stop until we find him!"

"Testifying in court along with the evidence you provided will help to convict him. It's only a matter of time. Trust me, Josie," he said as he held her blue eyes with his chocolate ones.

Returning his gaze with fond eyes, Josie explained. "I do trust you, Chief. I'm just mad," she said as a tear slowly rolled down her cheek.

"It's okay, Josie. I've got our top officers working on your case. Would you like a hug, Josie," the Chief offered and Josie melted into his bear-like arms. "I'm sorry, Josie. I'm sorry this happened to you," the Chief said as he hugged her.

As Josie stepped back she looked into his gentle eyes. "I know you're doing your best. I appreciate it. But, standing by the side isn't my style," she said with a mischievous grin as she wiped another errant tear away.

"I know. But, this time, it's safer for you to stand by the side," the Chief smiled back at her. "Josie," he hesitated for a split second, "I don't want to frighten you, but I want you to be careful because he's still out there. If you think you know this guy, or if you're suspicious about anyone, call me. He's dangerous."

"Promise you'll call me if you hear anything from the Department of Justice?" Josie volleyed right back to him.

"I'll share what I can. In the meantime, I'm here if you need me, and so are Melissa and Rachel."

"I know, Chief. I can always count on you guys. I'm headed home to write. Somehow it always helps to put things down on paper and maybe it will shake a memory loose," she said as she reached out for another big bear hug.

"I hope you can relax," the Chief said as he hugged her and then let her go.

"I'll try. Thanks, Chief," Josie said as she squared her shoulders and flashed him with a warm smile before she left.

After she was gone, the Chief went to the window and watched Josie standing on the curb looking out across the ocean. "I'm going to find him, Josie. He's going to jail for a long time," the Chief pledged. And with that, the Chief walked back to his desk and sat down. Out of habit, he put his pencil in his mouth as he stared at the ceiling and began to twist the mental Rubik's cube of Josie's case.

Hatchert got her first glimpse of the Fort Oaks base as she crossed the Hawkins River. It was situated between the El Diablo and El Muerto mountain ranges that formed the valley. Stretching from Hamilton City to Vista Point, the base included 200 square miles of ancient dunes covered in scrub brush, poison oak, and where the coastal oaks stretched out their heavy branches laden with acorns whose canopies almost touched the tall native grasses below. She read the warning in the file about how their shiny green, prickly leaves might be nasty against bare skin. Deer, squirrels, rabbits, rattlesnakes, bobcats, and mountain lions were the primary animals that called the base their home, along with a few bears.

Canyon Bay was on the coastal side of the base and was extremely unique. Beneath the bay's sparkling blue waters sat the largest underground canyon along the North American coast—approximately the same size and depth of the Grand Canyon in Arizona.

The creatures that called the bay their home were numerous and diverse. The sky could be filled with pelicans, cormorants, egrets, and seagulls, or other migrating birds. The tide pools contained fluorescent "worm-like" creatures adorned in brilliant colors, such as neon orange and cobalt blue. There were several varieties, shapes, and sizes of sea stars, abalone, crabs, and fish trapped in the tiny pools that haphazardly form amongst the rocks. After this case is solved, Hatchert thought, she might stay a little longer to check them out.

As she stopped at the gate, she automatically returned the salute of the guard, showed her military I.D. badge, and was waved onto the base.

Base housing was located near the gate entrance. Built on the sand dunes, the duplex units were lined up in rows: each one identical to the other. "I'm glad I wasn't on paint detail here. It must have taken thousands of gallons of beige paint to cover all these buildings," Hatchert whistled as she stared at row upon row of them as far as the eye could see.

The view was spectacular from here, she admitted. Conner Bay and the Pacific Ocean were to the west and because of the rolling nature of the sand dunes; many of the homes had a bird's eye view of the bay. Kids were riding their bikes in the street and moms and dads were sitting on the front porch protectively watching their offspring while chatting with each other. Hatchert remembered how military life could sometimes be lonely.

There was a camaraderie that develops among the families based on the common experience they share. She remembered how often they moved and how hard it was to meet and make friends; or more importantly, to keep them. Just as she started to develop of friendship with some of the kids who lived by her, or went to school with her, they were transferred again. And the process was repeated over and over again. As an adult, she began to understand what it must have been like for her mother to be left time and time again with a youngster to raise.

The family housing units faded and the 50-foot-long rectangular, beige-painted buildings that were classrooms and offices began to take over. The buildings were arranged in rows, just like the homes, planted among the sand dunes, oak trees, and shrubs. She passed by two deer that were feeding under the oak trees, and a flock of turkeys that were pecking the ground close by.

As she followed the signs to base headquarters, she noted that Colonel Delaney's long rectangular building matched the rows upon rows of similar buildings, except for the base flag and American flag that were mounted on tall flag poles in front of the building. After pulling into a parking space, she headed toward the entrance.

"Wow, look at that flowerbed," Hatchert whistled, as she approached the front walkway. Purple lavenders were placed in a geometric border around a bed of yellow yarrow with an old WWII Sherman tank as the plant bed's centerpiece.

The four-foot walkway led to a set of double-glass doors that opened into a highly polished beige tile floor.

Two brass flag stands, each with a 7' polished wood pole, stood against the left-hand wall. One displayed the American flag and the other displayed the Army base flag. One either side were more stands with the flag of each of the three battalions that called the base their home.

She noted the location of Colonel Delaney's office on the wall map and turned down the left hall that was dotted on either side with smaller offices. Nameplates of each office's occupants were placed in sliding holders beside each doorframe. At the end of the hall was a large dark oak wood reception desk. On the walls were portraits of the leadership beginning with the president, the secretary of defense, the secretary of the Army, and ending with the colonel of the base.

"Good afternoon. I'm Special Agent Hatchert reporting to Colonel Delaney."

"Thank you, Ma'am. I'll let him know you're here. Please have a seat," the young soldier said as he motioned toward the six straight-back visitor chairs that were lining the far wall of the waiting area.

Hatchert strode to the wall that held a large aerial view of the base. She barely had a chance to look at the various land features when the colonel's administrative assistant approached her.

"Special Agent Hatchert—Colonel Delaney will see you now."

"Thank you, Private."

Hatchert automatically scanned Colonel Delaney's office. The deep beige carpet had the Army star embroidered in its center. It was worn across one edge indicating that in the past, it must have laid across a heavy foot traffic area. The colonel's desk was a large, dark oak 7'-desk. He sat in a brown, high back executive chair with a commemorative brass paperweight on one corner and several scattered folders stacked one on top of the other. A laptop computer held center stage on his desk.

Hatchert felt Colonel Delaney's deep-set, dark gray eyes track her across the room. His eyes reminded her of a seasoned cop she once worked with on the Ferry mission. His eyes knew the vocabulary of body language and could accurately interpret how life molded the individual he was observing. They also understood the mental game each was playing with the other right now. He got up and stood as straight as a flagpole filling his uniform with about 210 pounds of muscle. She noted his square-shaped face and high cheekbones. She could picture him as King Solomon in a Hollywood movie, even though he was losing his hair on the top of his head. It made him look more distinguished, she thought as she continued to study him.

Colonel Delaney had been in the service for twenty years. He watched soldiers come and go. As he observed Hatchert walking through his office door, he recalled the bio sheet in her file. She was good, he had to give her that. And her laser-sharp, dark eyes were taking in everything, including him. Hatchert's eyes exuded self-confidence in their intensity, yet he could see past them into the deep scars that lie below. Her wounds enabled her to live on the dangerous side. He knew other soldiers who found the service a great way to quench their need for adrenaline and risk. Some made it, some didn't. His eyes followed Hatchert as she moved across the room with the fluid motion of an athlete stopping at an appropriate distance from him.

"Special Agent Hatchert," The Colonel acknowledged with a nod.

"Special Agent Hatchert, reporting for duty, Sir."

"Have a seat, Agent Hatchert," Colonel Delaney said as he motioned to one of the dark brown, leather chairs that sat on the opposite side of his desk. "Welcome to Fort Oaks base. As you know from the files you've been given, we have a serious situation here."

"Has any more evidence or information that might narrow our search been found, sir?"

"No. Dr. Calloway briefed me again yesterday and so far there isn't anything new to report. We're keeping the information strictly on an as-needed basis. I've been in contact with Chief Girard. He's expecting you."

"Thank you, sir," Hatchert said.

"We need to find this person and find them fast. This is a small community and word spreads faster than a sniper's bullet. We're under a microscope right now. This base is the first base to close in twenty years and how the turnover to the local and state governments is handled is under review by our president, congress, and commanders from all the services. We don't want any negative publicity about the army showing up in the national news. Do you have any questions?"

"Would it be possible for me to pull in other police officers or security if I need them, sir?"

"Yes. If it's during off duty hours you can contact my admin and he'll take care of it."

"Thank you, sir," Hatchert said as she got up out of her chair and looked into his gray eyes. "I'll do my best to find him."

"I'm sure you will. Keep me informed of your progress," the Colonel replied dismissing her as he returned his focus to a new memorandum from the Pentagon.

As she left his office, she saw the rows of beige buildings that were the barracks. She looked at her watch and still had some time left before she wanted to call it a day.

I might as well see where I'll be spending a lot of time she thought as she backed out of her parking space, and drove the five minutes to Hamilton Hospital. The hospital was in transition. It was still a military hospital, but because the base was closing, it would become another hospital for the city in less than two months. She eased her car into one of the few available parking spaces.

The building stood on the top of one of the tallest points on the base. She noticed the heavy concrete upright blocks fanning the entryway that served as a barrier to any vehicles within 100-feet of the building, installed after the Oklahoma City bombing. She swiped her security card through the sensor at the entry door and heard the click to allow her access.

Upon entering the lobby, she noted a large semicircular desk that sat dead smack in its center. Seated at the desk was a young, dark-haired military police officer. A large bank of security monitors showed each access door to the building and many of the hallways. Hatchert glanced at the monitors as she walked by them. She saw a delivery truck at the back door, a woman walking down a hall, two electricians placing new wiring in the hall ceiling, a nurse walking with a cup of coffee in the cafeteria, a pharmacist filling prescriptions, and a lab tech drawing blood.

The head of security stood 6'2" tall and appeared to be a solid 300 pounds. He looked like the epitome of a well-built, strong athlete, with short, curly black hair and scrutinizing dark eyes. Regardless, he's not someone you would want to fight with, Hatchert thought as his narrowed eyes locked onto hers.

"I'm Mary Hatchert. I've been assigned to the hospital as a research assistant to Dr. Calloway."

"I'm Sergeant Jones. Come this way. Colonel Delaney said to expect you. I need you to fill out some paperwork so we can issue you the keys to the office and patient floors."

She looked around the office that was filled with computer monitors showing the various halls and doors inside the building. People were moving in and out of camera range. The date and time were displayed on the screen in the lower right corner. She made a mental note of the number of cameras and their approximate location. Never know when the recordings from these cameras might come in handy, Hatchert thought.

Within twenty minutes she had everything she needed to begin her new assignment, except for some caffeine to calm the headache that began to grip her temples. After looking at the building directory, she walked into the elevator and punched the 3rd floor button to take her to the cafeteria. Her office was up on the 8th floor while the patients were down on the 2nd floor. The emergency room was on the 1st floor in the back of the building along with the lab and pharmacy. The 4th floor had the surgical units and recovery area.

As the doors opened, she stepped onto the 3rd floor and into a short hallway that led to a huge cafeteria. Two walls were filled with rows of floor-to-ceiling windows where you could see the rolling hills of oaks and scrub brush. One wall was lined with various vending machines that held snacks, sodas, coffee, and quick food items such as yogurt and pre-made sandwiches.

She headed toward the coffee machine and punched double shot espresso, black. Standard issue vending machine coffee, not her favorite, but right now her headache demanded caffeine so she wasn't picky. After four or five sips, her headache thanked her. As she glanced around the large room filled with four-seat and six-seat tables, she noticed a couple sitting in a corner. First date, she guessed, as she watched them kiss and flirt with each other.

Another recruit facing away from Hatchert had her head buried in a book with more books scattered around the table. The regulation bun had long since succumbed to her frantic activity with scattered strands of long, loose blond curls escaping down her back. Every once in a while, she would pound away on her laptop computer and then bury her head again. That's one eager recruit, Hatchert thought as she headed to her office.

As she walked back to the elevator she almost ran smack into Dr. Calloway. She knew it was Dr. Calloway by the name badge that was unevenly pinned to her white doctor's coat. Her short, black, straight hair was cut in a blunt cut 2" below her ears. Her bangs were cut in a straight line across her forehead that skimmed the top of her round, black glasses that framed her deep blue eyes.

"Major Calloway?"

"Yes?"

"I'm Special Agent Hatchert. I was on my way to your office to introduce myself."

"I need to grab a cup of coffee. If I don't get my daily fix, I turn into a monster during my evening shift. I'd offer to buy, but it looks like you beat me to it."

Hatchert instantly liked her.

"Sure. I understand the need to have a caffeine fix."

Pushing the double espresso button on the vending machine, Dr. Calloway had a chance to study Hatchert. Hatchert wasn't a slacker. You could tell by the intensity of those eyes. They also told her that Hatchert had been through some hard times in her life. They showed determination and drive that emanated from people who had been to dark places. Mostly, they showed a wall behind which her emotions were carefully stored.

She certainly was a looker, Dr. Calloway noted with a sigh. Must be nice to have those long legs and athletic body. She had inherited her paternal grandmother's short legs landing her at 5'2" tall.

As Hatchert shifted uncomfortably in her skirt, Dr. Calloway guessed that Hatchert would rather be in jeans. It would have been nice to have an athletic body like hers, Calloway thought. Oh well, her body wasn't going to change and her life wasn't so bad. At least she wasn't totally focused on her work as her older brother chided her so many times since she got her degree. Her brother was the exact opposite of her; gregarious, outgoing, and even though he wasn't exactly handsome, his personality had the girls flocking to him. Wish she could say the same herself. But, life was good for now.

Except for the sexual assaults. She couldn't command the girls to make an official report. They were scared it would ruin their career. But, the perpetrator was out there. And it wouldn't be long before he would rape again. They always did. She hoped, with time, the girls would file an official report. Until then, it was her job to help them through the pain.

There wasn't much to go on. Both were subdued with a taser. Both remembered the mint mouthwash. Each of them went back to their barrack to stand in a shower and wash him out of them. It never worked. He would be in their lives forever, no matter how many showers they took. And hopefully, she could help them process and move beyond the experience.

"Sorry, my mind wandered again. It's a terrible habit. Would you like to see where we work?"

"Yes. Thank you."

As the elevator doors opened to the 8th floor, Hatchert noticed a snack and soda vending machine shoved side by side into a small alcove. All the caffeinated soda slots were empty. The offices were arranged on either side of a long hallway that followed the outline of the rectangular shape of the building.

Her office was opposite from Dr. Calloway's office. It was a small 6' x 8' room with no windows. A standard size desk filled the width of the room with just enough space to scrunch by to get to a standard issue, gray, desk chair. A 5'-tall by 3'-wide bookcase was crammed into one corner and a standard straight-back chair served as a visitor chair. The walls were bare and painted standard Navajo white. A simple phone sat on one corner of the desk and a computer keyboard and monitor sat dead center.

"It's not much, but at least you have your own office. We're short on office space and I had to fight to get this one. Most of the personnel share an office with at least one or two other people," Dr. Calloway explained. "Budget cuts are killing us."

"Thank you. What are the duty times for the hospital?"

"Eight to five with a one-hour lunch, although we have staff 24 hours a day. I didn't have a chance to tell Colonel Delaney, but the two victims said they would like to talk to you and answer questions. I still can't get them to file an official report, but it's a good sign they're willing to meet with you.

70

Cindy Cunningham and I discussed you as her bunkmate and she's agreed to the arrangement. Special Agent Hatchert, the first sexual assault was last Tuesday, the second was Saturday, and the last one was on Monday. My guess is that he's going to get braver because he hasn't been caught, and he's using his high from one assault to carry him to the next. It's been one week without an incident. If my hunch is correct, he's already looking, or has found, his next victim."

"I agree with you. We're working with a very short time frame."

"I know. That's why I'm worried, and I'm glad that the women are ready to talk to you. They haven't remembered anything new. Sometimes it takes time to recover memories from something like this. Our brain is quite clever in protecting us until we're ready to remember."

"From what I've seen in my career, there is no set time frame for their memory to return. I've had some victims who could remember every detail right after it happened. I've had others who draw a blank and can't remember a thing. It's always easier when they remember, but sometimes we get lucky."

"Well, you've got your work cut out for you. I've got to check on two patients before I leave. If you want to go to dinner sometime, let me know. It was nice meeting you."

"Thank you, Major Calloway."

Hatchert decided to check out the underground parking garage. As she walked down the two flights of stairs, she thought about what Dr. Calloway told her. She didn't have much time to find this guy. She opened the door into the garage and looked around. It was a standard, underground parking facility. The parking spaces were against the outer walls as well as one row down the center. It was lit by overhead light fixtures, and she noted the location of the surveillance cameras near the stair entrance, at three locations throughout the garage, and one at the entrance-exit. Looking at her watch, she headed back up the stairwell to her car that was parked in the upper lot.

The wind blew on her face as she headed to Vista Point near the harbor district. She saw the crescent shape curve of the bay and the boat marina and wharves that called Vista Point their home. As she drove down the streets, she noticed how the sea air had rusted many of the flower stands that were scattered in front of the storefronts. Spotting the police station, Hatchert found a parking place and went inside.

"I'm Mary Hatchert. I have an appointment with Chief Girard," Hatchert said as she looked at the glass case filled with various sizes and shapes of trophies and smelled the aroma of strong coffee, leftover donuts, and yesterday's half-eaten meat sandwich.

"He's expecting you. Go right on in," his administrative assistant replied pointing to the door across the room. Not a bad place to work, Hatchert thought as she looked out the window overlooking the harbor.

"Welcome Agent Hatchert," the Chief said as his trained eyes took in this bright young woman before him.

"Hello, sir," she said as she shook hands with the Chief.

"Glad to meet you, Agent Hatchert. Please sit down," he said as he pointed to a well-worn, faded-brown, office chair whose seat sagged from a lifetime of visitors.

"I've read the files and I have your office number, but is there a contact number I can reach you 24/7?" Hatchert asked as she pulled out her cell phone.

"Yes, it's (900) 555-9735."

"How many police officers are on staff?"

"Twenty. Not enough, I'm afraid. We're starting to see some gang activity from the Hamilton gangs. But, my officers are good. I handpicked most of them myself. Any new information on your end?" he asked as he leaned back to study her.

"I spoke with Dr. Calloway and there's no new information. The perp finds his victims on the Vista Point trail. Dr. Calloway and I both agree that he will assault again soon, possibly within the next few days," Hatchert said objectively.

"I agree. I've got officers on rotation at the Vista Point trail parking lot, but I can't position someone along the entire ten miles, which is a problem. I don't want to close the trail because at least we know where we can find him."

Nodding her head, Hatchert said, "I'm going to run the trail and hope that he comes after me."

"If you need backup, let me know," he said solemnly understanding the risk she was taking.

"I appreciate that Chief Girard."

"You can call me Chief," he said as he felt her intelligent eyes scan him like an airport security device before she accepted his offer.

"Do you have the lab report on Josie Green yet?"

"No. Unfortunately, the day after she was assaulted there was a water leak that shut down the lab. It's up and running today so we should have a report within the next few days."

"That's a tough break," Hatchert commented as she studied the Chief's furrowed brow and clenched jaw.

"Could I get you a cup of coffee?" he said as he motioned toward the automatic coffee maker near the east office wall. "Caffeinated okay?" he queried as he held out the pot.

"Sure," she replied as he poured her a cup and handed it to her.

"It's been tough on Josie that the lab went down," he sighed as he settled back down in his chair and savored the woody aroma. "We're lucky Josie's evidence was untouched. Josie stopped by this afternoon and I asked her to go over what happened again. The report I passed on is fairly accurate. She's starting to remember more details. She remembered something that is not in the initial report: she remembers he has brown hair. She saw pieces of it sticking out from under the mask."

Hatchert immediately began to skim through her suspect list and the color of their hair. Walton has brown hair, she pondered as she continued to listen to the Chief.

"Josie confirmed that she's been on base for a telethon in April, a concert on Memorial Day, and another concert on the 4th of July," he commented as he took out a pencil and began to roll it between his fingers.

"You might be interested to know that the hospital where you're assigned is having a big fundraiser tomorrow night," the Chief continued as he watched Hatchert's reaction. "Josie and her parents will be there along with most of the community leaders. It might be a good time for you to meet them. If Josie's assailant is bold enough to be there, I want to make sure she's protected at all times."

"That sounds good. Is it formal?" Hatchert asked hoping he would say no.

"Yes. This is a black tie gala affair. I have to drag out my tuxedo," the Chief smiled as he heard the hesitation in Hatchert's voice. He guessed she wasn't too keen on formal wear. Most cops aren't, he thought and smiled again.

74

"That sounds like a plan. What time does it start?" she asked stoically as her face scrunched up at the thought of wearing a dress.

"6:30 p.m. for cocktails and 7:00 p.m. for dinner."

"I'll see you there. It's nice to meet you, sir," Hatchert said as she extended her hand.

"See you tomorrow night, Agent Hatchert," the Chief replied as he shook her hand and then chuckled to himself as he watched an unhappy agent get into her car and drive away.

Hatchert waited until she cleared the police steps before she allowed her anger to hit. "It isn't bad enough that I have to wear a skirt for my uniform, but now, they want me to wear a dress!" she fumed. "And it has to be a formal dress, not just any old dress! Now, I'm going to have to waste time buying the stupid thing," she snarled as she stomped to her car and got in. Throwing it into gear, she turned on the radio full blast to the sound of Melissa Etheridge singing, "Monster," to help her work off some steam as she headed back to the base.

After she stopped in her parking space at the barrack, she sat and took in her new home. It was a long, rectangular beige-painted structure with dark brown trim, just like the other buildings on base. A simple 6-step concrete staircase with old wood railings led to a large single door. The door had a clear, square window on the top half and was solid wood below.

She headed up the stairs. Flipping open the door, she found herself facing an extremely long hallway. There were twenty rows of doors on either side. One was marked "shower", another "restroom and laundry room." As she peered inside, she saw six communal showerheads and a room covered in standard beige tiles. Shower curtains hung on semi-circle rods that offered a hint of privacy. She closed the door and opened the next one. There were six stalls and four sinks. Above each sink was a mirror and a small shelf to put toiletries. The two washers and dryers were at the far end of the room. And of course, Hatchert smiled, everything was lined with beige tiles.

As she closed the door and moved down the hall she noted each single door had two pieces of paper that were stuck on it with the names of the women who lived there. The women came and went so fast, it was more cost effective and efficient to use paper instead of nameplates. She knew from her file this set of barracks housed forty women with two women per room.

She was sharing a room with Cindy Cunningham, so Hatchert began looking for Cunningham's name on one of the papers.

Well, it's a start, Hatchert thought, as she found her room—four doors down the hall from the restroom. The room was small, but had plenty of space for one set of bunk beds, two standard-issue clothing lockers, a small refrigerator, and two student desks.

Hatchert looked at Cindy's locker. It was partway open and showed that an attempt had been made to put each article of clothing in its place. A poster of Marilyn Monroe was stuck to the inside of the door. An overstuffed cosmetic bag was tossed onto the floor of the locker. The uniforms were crammed in between blue jeans and sweaters. Tennis shoes and a pair of 3-inch-high, red heel shoes were among the pile of stuff. Shaking her head, Hatchert wondered how she ever passed inspection. Even the bed looked like it was tossed together.

Just as Hatchert was beginning to relax, Cindy burst through the door like a whirlwind with her blond hair flying behind her. Books were tossed everywhere. Her eyes met Hatchert's as she started to flop onto her bed and then snapped to attention.

"Private Cunningham," Cindy said as she saluted and her eyes did a quick sweep as she bit her lip.

"At ease, Private," Hatchert replied. "Have a seat."

Hatchert recognized the recruit who had her head buried in her books in the cafeteria. She gazed into green eyes that were a combination of malachite green and soft dewy grass as she introduced herself.

"I'm Special Agent Mary Hatchert, but you can call me Hatchert. It's nice to meet you, Cindy."

Fiddling with her hot pink scarf that she'd left earlier this morning wrapped around her chair, Cindy continued. "It's nice to meet you too."

"Cindy, as you know I'm part of the investigation team that is working on your assault. I want to find this guy and fast. By staying in the barracks, I can protect you, Laura, and the other women in this barrack. Hopefully, it won't be necessary. Are you comfortable with this arrangement?" Hatchert asked as she cocked her head and waited.

"Yes. Dr. Calloway and I talked about it. We need to find him," Cindy replied zeroing in on Hatchert's eyes.

One thing you had to give her credit for was her guts, Hatchert thought as she watched Cindy's jaws and fists clench. She looked like she was working hard to put the memories of her assault behind her. It wasn't going to be easy. It never was.

Hatchert slipped into the desk chair across from Cindy.

"I know we just met, but I believe this guy is going to attack again. Would you be willing to tell me what happened?"

"Yes. I knew this conversation was coming when I talked with Dr. Calloway yesterday," she sighed. "I might as well get it over with," she said as she sat in the opposite chair.

"I was running the Vista Point trail. I run it every week on Saturday after we finish our physical training. Near the summit, there's a place where the trail drops suddenly and then it weaves in and out of some tall pine trees. Once you're through the trees, the trail starts to climb again. As I was coming around the last big tree, I felt this huge shock and went down to the ground. He tasered me, then he jumped on me. He put handcuffs on me, shoved a plastic tube in my mouth and squirted orange juice into my mouth. I almost choked because he practically dumped half the bottle in me," she grimaced as she remembered as she fought for air. "When he stuck the gag in my mouth, I kicked him. He started laughing and said he loved a fighter," Cindy's said disgustedly. "I kicked him again and he almost lost his balance. That's when he told me he would kill me if I didn't follow his orders," Cindy shuddered.

"Can you describe his voice?"

"He just sounded like any other guy," she said as she shrugged her shoulders and blew an errant curl from her face.

"Did he have an accent?"

"No," Cindy said as she twisted the hot pink scarf into a knot.

"Are you all right? We can finish in the morning?"

"No," Cindy said as her eyes turned dark. "He seemed to get a kick out of scaring me—the dirt bag," Cindy sputtered as she gave the scarf one more violent twist.

78

"Unfortunately, a rapist can feel more powerful if they scare their victim. You did really well, Cindy. You didn't lose your cool and you did what he asked. I know that was hard, but you lived, and that means you were very successful in protecting yourself," Hatchert reassured her.

"Thanks. But, I feel like I caved," Cindy said as she thumped the wall with her hand.

"I know it might feel that way, but you really did the right thing in your case," Hatchert said as she leaned forward and waited until Cindy moved her gaze from the floor to her face. "Each sexual assault is different. Sometimes it's safer not to fight, and at other times it's better to fight. And always, it's easier to replay the event and wish you'd done something else, but the truth is that you did the right thing at the time. You saved your life and that's worth something," Hatchert said calmly as she looked into Cindy's troubled eyes.

"I'll think about that. Thanks," Cindy said with a furrowed brow as she untwisted the scarf and twisted it back into a pretzel.

"We can stop if you need to rest?" Hatchert asked as she looked at the scarf that now appeared to be a gnarled rope like the one the Colonel used to tie the boat to the dock on their last fishing trip together.

"No, I want to get this over with. We have to catch him," she said as she took another deep breath to calm her churning stomach. "I started feeling like I was really drunk. I couldn't concentrate, everything got blurry, and freaky like I was underwater in a murky lake. He put me down on a flat piece of ground and raped me. I couldn't stop him, damn it!" she yelled as tears threatened to spill. "I couldn't stop him," she repeated as her chest heaved in and out.

"It's rough," Hatchert said quietly. "You're brave, Cindy. Remember that."

"Thanks, she nodded. "One minute I want to beat him up, and then I fall apart like I'm doing now. It's crazy how I can't control which feeling is going to come next," she murmured as she wiped her nose with a tissue and pushed her back into the chair.

"I've worked as an agent for three years. What you're experiencing is normal for what you've been through. I'm going to do the best I can to find him so he will go to prison," Hatchert repeated calmly once again and leaned back to give Cindy more space.

"Laura wants to meet you tonight," Cindy said as she unwound her scarf and took a few deep breaths.

"I'd like that," Hatchert said as she nodded her head, then waited patiently for Cindy to settle again.

"He carried me down the mountain. I could see the trail and bushes going by, but I can't do anything. It was weird to feel like that—helpless. The next thing I know, he put me under a bush. I remember him undoing the handcuffs and leaving. I couldn't move for a while. I don't know how long I was there."

"You're doing well," Hatchert assured her with a nod.

"After a while, I felt better and started to walk. I found the trail after some searching around. I didn't want to walk on the trail in case he was still there, so I walked beside it where there were more bushes and trees to hide me. When I got to my car, I drove back here and took a shower."

"Do you know how long you were gone?"

"I left about 7:00 that morning after physical training and I got home around 5:00 p.m. I guess I was gone about ten hours. I met Dr. Calloway a couple of months ago when I first came to the base. We both need a caffeine fix about the same time each day so I've gotten to know her, Cindy smiled. "She's cool. I went to her the next day and told her what happened."

"I'm glad you told someone."

Cindy sat upright. "Last night I remembered something. He was wearing blue latex gloves and I remembered thinking that his fingers were long for a man's fingers. Anyway, that's all I remember."

"Did you notice if the gloves went just above the wrist or did they go further up the arm?"

"They didn't look like those long kitchen gloves my mom wears. These gloves stopped here," Cindy said as she pointed to a place that was close to her wrist.

"How did the orange juice taste?"

"Like normal orange juice."

"How did your stomach feel after you drank it?"

Cindy shrugged. "I was sick to my stomach and I was having a little trouble breathing after it happened, but I felt better when I woke up the next morning. I thought it might be because I was still scared when I got back here."

"That was probably from the drug he gave you. When he threw you over his shoulder, did you have some sense of his height?"

"Well, I'm 5'9" tall. He was strong. He just tossed me over his shoulder like it was nothing. But, he had a hard time balancing me on his shoulder. He didn't seem to have a big build for a man."

"Did you feel anything while he was carrying you?" Hatchert asked.

"Oh my gosh. He was wearing a backpack," Cindy said lurching forward. "I remember hitting it with my face when we were going downhill!"

Hatchert smiled at her. "It's great you're getting more

memories back. It might help us find him. Do you remember anything about his eyes or hair?"

"No."

"You did well, Cindy. If you remember anything else, call me right away. Let me give you my cell phone number," Hatchert said as she waited for Cindy to enter it into her cell phone.

"Thanks," Cindy smiled as she scooted off the bed. "We can go see Laura now."

"Sounds good to me," Hatchert replied enthusiastically as she stood up and followed Cindy down the hall.

"It's me, Laura. I've got company," Cindy said loudly as she knocked on Laura's door.

Laura opened the door and waved them into a copycat room of Cindy's—same beige walls, bunk beds, student desks, and desk chairs with the exception of a poster of a 1957 tropical turquoise Chevy stuck to the inside door of a locker. Hatchert smiled as she remembered the picture of Laura and her dad in front of the one they'd restored together in Arizona.

"Special Agent Hatchert, this is Private Brock. Laura, this is Special Agent Hatchert," Cindy said as she introduced them and then stood beside Laura.

"Hi Private Brock. Please sit. I'm with CID," Hatchert said as she settled into a desk chair.

"Yes, Ma'am," Laura replied as she bit her lip and frowned.

"Thank you for meeting me," Hatchert cocked her head as she watched Laura struggle to catch her breath. "I want to catch this man, Laura. It takes guts to survive what you and Cindy went through. I know it's not going to be easy to share what happened, but with your help we'll get this assailant off the street so he can't do this to other women."

Shuffling around, Laura looked at Cindy for moral support. "I don't want anyone else to go through what we went through," she croaked out between gulps of air.

"I've got your back, girlfriend. We're going to nail this sucker! We can do this!" Cindy cheered and high-fived Laura and the first hint of a smile crept across Laura's solemn face.

Hatchert smiled as she looked at Cindy's flushed red face and Laura's soulful eyes. It never ceased to amaze her how women come together in adversity to support each another, even two women as opposite as Cindy and Laura. "Would you be open to answering some questions to-morrow morning after breakfast?"

"Yes," Laura nodded as she stared at a patch in the floor. "The sooner I get this out of the way, the sooner I can forget about it. This has taken up too much of my time," she said and with a rare display of force almost slammed her textbook shut as she fought for air and doubled over again.

"It's okay, Laura. We're going to get through this to-gether and then, we're gonna have one heck of a party!" Cindy said while she patted Laura on the back and her face glowed at the prospect of a victory dance.

Hatchert lips turned up slightly as Cindy's exuberance engulfed the room. Turning her attention back to Laura, Hatchert continued. "How are you doing, Laura?"

"I'm okay," she said as she shrugged her shoulders.

"With your help, Laura, I'm going to find him so he won't be able to harm you or anyone else for a long time. Can I do anything right now to help you?"

"No, ma'am," Laura thanked her as she fought the next shockwave that rattled through her body. "I want to forget this ever happened," she said as she gasped for air again.

"I'm sorry that you had to experience this, Laura," Hatchert consoled her as she watched Laura clench her fists in an effort to regain some measure of control.

"Thank you, ma'am," Laura replied through gritted teeth.

"See you in the morning. Here's my cell phone number. You can call me anytime, day or night," Hatchert said as she waited for Laura to enter the number in her cell phone.

After they closed the door behind them, Cindy and Hatchert walked back to their room.

"She's kind of a loner because she's really shy. Once you get to know her, she's pretty cool. And now that we're in the same situation we've become better friends. I'm tired," Cindy said as she yawned. "I'm calling it a night." and got her hot pink pajamas out of her locker.

"No problem. It's been a long day," Hatchert nodded her head in agreement.

It HAD been a long drive and a long day, Hatchert thought as she went to her car and got out her suitcase. After she unloaded the contents of her suitcase into the tiny portable closet and took a shower, she climbed into the bottom bunk. As her feet hung over the bottom and the top of her hair brushed the bunk bed rail, she realized how much she missed her king-size bed at home.

Staring at the bottom of the upper bunk, she wondered what the Greens would be like. They almost seemed like family in a weird sort of way. It felt odd that she was going to meet them tomorrow night. She'd seen their pictures on the Colonel's desk. Josie was a child in the photographs. I wonder how she's handling the assault, Hatchert thought as she pictured the different reactions of Cindy and Laura. Hatchert calmed her mind and soon fell asleep.

84

When Josie pulled into her driveway, she stopped and looked at her house. It was a fairytale house. The stucco exterior was painted in a light café latte color. The two-story house had a 10-foot tall solid medium oak door in the center with a large, hanging, wrought iron light fixture. On either side were twin, 8-foot by 10-foot windows with square mullions. Above each downstairs window was an upstairs window with a small balcony that had a whimsical wrought iron railing surrounding each of them. The pitch of the roof was steeper than most roofs, and there were twin, small chimneys for the fireplaces that were in each of the upstairs bedrooms. Bushes and flowers graced the foundation anchoring her storybook cottage to the world. Sprays of orange and pink blossoms were dotted throughout the planter beds. Tall cypress and pine trees bordered her property giving her the feeling of living in the middle of an enchanted forest. And the comical squirrels, cawing crows, squawking blue jays, and singing crickets added to the magical atmosphere.

Josie pulled into the garage that sat to the right of the main house. She loved the windows that brought light into a usually dark and damp place. Josie grabbed the bag of groceries out of the back seat and headed to the backdoor. Unlocking the door, she tapped in the code to her security system and walked into the kitchen where she plunked her groceries down on the black marble countertop. She put the yogurt and cheese away leaving out the organic salad and iced tea she picked up at McGregor's Grocery Store. It was Michael McGregor she had bandied around with at the gas station earlier. That woman in the Miata was so mad, Josie giggled, as she headed upstairs with salad and tea in hand to eat later after she changed her clothes into soft sweats.

Plopping among the pillows on her bed, she picked up her cell phone and dialed Rachel.

"Hi Josie," Rachel answered.

"Hi Rach. Did you decide between the black cocktail dress, or the long, sequined black dress?

"What are you wearing? Last I heard it was going to be a hot pink affair with a deep, scooped neck," Rachel laughed as she teased Josie.

"I've decided to wear the long gold dress that's covered in gold bugle beads. I want to stand out and I don't want that rapist to think I'm afraid of him," Josie said with determination as she rolled onto her back.

"Do you think he could be there tomorrow night?" Rachel worriedly asked.

Staring at the soft white ceiling, Josie thought about the rapist. "He could be. I'm going to show him that he didn't scare me off. As a matter of fact, I'm angry and I want him to know it," Josie replied stubbornly.

"I'm worried about you. I don't want you to get hurt. Please don't wander off by yourself tomorrow night," Rachel pleaded with her best friend.

"Don't worry, I'm mad, but I'm not stupid like some people want to believe just because I'm a woman," Josie replied heatedly.

"I'll be there if you need me."

"I know you will be, Rach," calming down as she remembered how many times Rach held her hand when things got tough. "Thanks for everything. I don't know what I would have done without you. You're my sis," Josie said softly.

"You're my sis too. We've been through a lot together and we'll get through this adventure too," Rachel said lovingly.

86

"So, what dress will it be for you tomorrow night, long or short?" Josie asked forcing some cheer into her voice.

"Since you're going long, I'll wear my long black dress," Rachel replied.

"What about wearing my hot pink, sequined shoes with it," Josie teased knowing Rachel would rather die than wear hot pink.

"No way! I'm going to wear my 3-inch black heels," Rachel teased back.

"That's sounds just like you. You'll look stunning, Rach," Josie said.

"What are you going to do tonight? Jeremy and I are staying home. He's had a long day and said he just wants to snuggle with me."

"I'm going to write. Maybe something will fall out of me onto the page that will help your dad catch this creep."

"I hope so. See you tomorrow night. If you need anything, anything at all, call me, day or night, okay?" Rachel said emphatically.

"I will Rach. I'll be okay. He's not going to win. I have a new security system that will stop an ant from coming inside. Don't worry. Have fun snuggling tonight," Josie said with a grin as she hung up the phone.

No man is going to get the best of me, she muttered. And, I'm not afraid to go to court and tell them what happened. So, don't think I'm scared of you whoever you are," Josie screamed out loud as she jumped off the bed.

She picked up her laptop computer and settled into her patio chair. She flipped it open and stared at the blank page on the screen. Stabbing a piece of lettuce, she shoved it into her mouth and was soon lost in her thoughts.

It was her chattering teeth that aroused her out of her writer's state as she shivered against the cold of the evening fog. In looking up, she had to orient herself as she took her mind from her task and focused on the world around her. The gray was marching in beat with her piece that swirled in the after-effects of rape.

INNOCENCE LOST

Innocence waited.
It waited to dance in joy and love.
It waited for heartthrob, the first sweet kiss.
It waited for the beloved, the one.
It waited for the explosion where fire met tinder.
It waited for the heart song, so loud the heavens would awaken to jubilee.
It waited an entire lifetime.
Stripped bare, desecrated, where the soul fought, the battle lost.
Stripped away by the darkness.
Fog descends, gray from despair,
Lost forevermore among the strewn ashes.
Yet wait.
Wisdom comes softly, gently in whispers.
Courage dances in partnership with dignity and grace.
Life floods the barren desert of her soul.
And in the mirror the phoenix rises,
A new dawn has begun.

It needed more work, but it was a start, she thought as she closed her laptop and shivered once again. She balanced her empty salad plate and glass along with the laptop in her hands as she walked inside and placed them on her desk.

Turning the hot water faucet on full blast in the shower, she stepped into it and allowed the hot steamy water to beat back the chill. As she stood there absorbing the warmth, a deep shudder swept through her like a flash-flood as her body remembered. Fighting the cold, Josie forced the red-hot rage that lived inside her to erupt to the surface. "Damn you!" she screamed at the top of her lungs. "You had no right!" and she hit the side of the tiled shower wall again and again until exhaustion overcame her and her hot tears joined the water drops as she wept.

With her blond hair creating rivers of droplets down her bare skin, she stepped out of the shower and looked at herself in the mirror. She studied her solemn reflection and saw a new wisdom growing inside of her. She towel-dried her hair and slipped into a green terry-cloth bathrobe. The blow dryer turned her wet mop into soft tresses that settled softly to her shoulders. She walked across the room and slid into bed where the soft flannel sheets felt warm and nurturing. She stretched her legs and arms out wide as she grabbed a well-worn copy of *Romeo and Juliet* out of the nightstand. Settling in against the soft mountain of pillows, she began to read and soon fell asleep among the Capulets and the Montagues.

CHAPTER 4

Tuesday, 30 September 14
The Gala

Morning reveille filled the still air. It was dark outside. Soon the barracks started to come alive. Moans and creaking mattresses along with bare feet hitting the floor could be heard. Shower water running, sink faucets flowing, and toilets being flushed were the normal sounds of a barrack coming to life. Locker doors opening and being slammed shut, and boot-clad running feet served as an alarm clock as Hatchert easily fell into the beat of the natural rhythm of the barracks.

"Morning, Cindy," Hatchert said as she climbed out of her bunk.

"Hi," Cindy replied as she jumped up and down to pull on her pants. Grabbing a hair band she twisted her hair and stuck in some bobby pins to make the regulation bun. "Crap! I'm going to be late again!" she said under her breath as she laced up her boots and crammed her books into her backpack.

Hatchert looked on with amusement. To keep from mussing her bed, Cindy slept on top of her regulation sheets and blankets under a blanket throw. Cindy shoved the blanket throw into her locker and gave the bed a quick once over.

"Bye," Cindy said as she grabbed her backpack and flew out the door slamming it behind her.

Hatchert smiled. She had done the same thing her first year. She looked at her bed and even though she hadn't made a regulation bed in over a year and a half, it all came back to her.

She lined her bottom sheet up with the end of her mattress near the foot of the bed, and thought about the routine the perpetrator was following.

The assaults on Monday and Tuesday took place in the late afternoon. The assault on Saturday took place in the morning. "Sounds like we're dealing with a working man," she muttered to herself as she tucked the excess sheet under the head of the bed.

He broke his pattern of assaulting military women when he attacked Josie, she thought, while she was making perfect hospital corners at the bottom of the bed.

She puzzled over his selection of women as she carefully put the blanket 12" from the head of the bed and tucked in the excess at the foot. None of the victims body styles looked alike except for the blond hair. What was he using as his criteria, she wondered as she laid the second sheet on top and lined it up to the end of the mattress at the top of the bed.

Her intuition told her that the perp was close as she took 18 inches of sheet and folded it over the blanket at the head of the bed. She had to find him and soon. She stood at the edge of the bunk bed and surveyed her work. Not bad she thought as she went through her mental checklist for the day.

The first order of business was to eat breakfast and find Laura to hear her story.

"Hi, Cathy," Hatchert said with a smile as she closed her room door behind her.

"Hi Hatchert. Want to join us in a card game tonight at Candy's Place?"

"Thanks for asking, but I've got other stuff to do. May-

91

be another time," Hatchert smiled as she headed toward the door.

As she slipped out into the morning dawn, she noted the location of the male barracks to the right. She needed some coffee and yogurt; make that two cups of coffee she noted as the usual dull thud began in her head

As Hatchert entered the cafeteria, she sniffed the blend of bacon, eggs, French toast, and syrup as she scanned the groups seated at the tables. Spotting Laura at the far end of the room, she grabbed a cup of strong coffee and wove her way over to the table. She noticed that Laura was lost deep in thought as she stared at the oaks and grasses spread out before her.

"Good morning, Laura. Mind if I sit here?" Hatchert asked softly hoping not to startle her.

Laura jumped, almost tipping over her milk glass. "No," Laura nodded in embarrassment as she moved the glass to a safer place.

"How's the granola and yogurt?" Hatchert asked as she noted Laura's dark shadows around her eyes.

"It's pretty good. They use fresh fruit and slivered almonds and it's not too sweet. I don't go for all that sugar," Laura replied shakily as she spooned in another mouthful.

"I don't like the sugar either, but I do like my caffeine," Hatchert grinned as she took a big gulp of her coffee. "Do you know if they serve scrambled eggs?"

"Yes, ma'am. They're a bit on the runny side for my taste."

"Thanks for the warning," Hatchert said as she took off for the food line.

Returning with two slices of bacon, fruit and yogurt, and a glass of orange juice, Hatchert grinned. I splurged on the bacon," she said as she settled down in a chair opposite of Laura. "You're right, this is good yogurt," she said after she took one bite and then spooned in another mouthful. "What do you do for entertainment around here?"

"I took scuba diving lessons when I first arrived, so I head to the beach on the weekends after my run. They've got great places to dive. It's amazing down there. There are sea otters and seals that swim right by you. You've got to be careful though, because you can get turned around and lost really fast in the kelp forests."

"I might have to check it out before I leave," Hatchert contemplated as she thought about the possibility of scuba diving.

"I could show you the best places to go, if you want me to," Laura volunteered as she bit her lip and her cheeks turned a raspberry red.

"I might take you up on that," Hatchert smiled. "Let's go outside and walk," she motioned to Laura as she grabbed her tray and headed toward the door. Dropping their empty dishes and silverware in the rubber tub, Hatchert opened the door so Laura could fit both her heavy backpack and herself through it.

"Where does this trail go?" Hatchert asked pointing to a trail that led into the scrub brush.

"It's not a long trail. I've walked it several times when I need to be by myself in-between classes. It goes past a set of old barracks that aren't used anymore. I think it was probably a shortcut to the cafeteria for the guys that lived there."

"It sounds just like what we need. Are you okay walking on a trail again," Hatchert asked her with raised brows.

"Sure. I'm okay," Laura shrugged as they started their walk.

"I would like you to go through that whole day. I hope you don't mind, but I'm going to jump in and ask questions along the way," Hatchert said as she watched Laura's eyes tear up and shrug.

"I got up, did all the normal stuff—made my bed, took a shower, ate breakfast in the cafeteria after physical training, and then I went to classes until I finished at 4:30."

"About what time do you think you were at the trail?" Hatchert asked.

"I'd guess around 5:30. I had to change my clothes and walk to my car. Traffic was fairly light so I made good time."

"Where did you park your car?"

"In the parking lot across the highway. It's not usually busy on Tuesdays."

"Was there anyone else in the parking lot at the time?"

"There were two cars parked there. One belongs to a guy named Patrick who runs a local rock climbing gym. The other one belongs to Jeff who works at a car repair shop in town. Both of them are nice guys. We see each other most Tuesdays because there aren't too many people that run at that time."

"Is it possible one of them could be the attacker?"

"No. Patrick and Jeff are really buff. They both work-out and their muscles are huge and tight and I wouldn't have missed that."

"How would you describe his body type?"

"He had muscles, but not the big ones from weight training like Patrick and Jeff. I think he was more a medium build."

"Did you notice anyone on the trail ahead of you?"

"Jeff and Patrick always run ahead of me, but once we cross the field they take off. Honestly, I like to run alone," she said as she flicked her eyes in Hatchert's direction to catch her response.

"I like to run alone at times myself," Hatchert said as she nodded her head in agreement and watched Laura's shoulders relax a little as she took in Hatchert's response.

"So you ran across the flat with Jeff and Patrick and then what happened?" Hatchert gently prodded.

"I ran up to the summit and then started down the back. At one point coming down the back, the cliff edge is solid rock. They had to cut into the rock face to continue the trail. It's really narrow at this point. Only one person can fit on it at a time. I typically walk this part because the drop-off is over 100 feet and it's basically straight down."

"Where did you run into the attacker?"

"Right after I finished the rock part of the trail, there's a couple of big trees that kind of grow out of the side of the cliff and I like to look at them. They're really cool. But, as I passed by the last tree, I got tasered from behind and I went down. He jumped on top of me, and the next thing I know, my hands were handcuffed behind me," Laura said angrily as her heart began to pound. "I know I should have hit him or something, but he was on top of me and I freaked," she said as she started to shake.

"Laura, once you're tasered, your muscles don't function properly. You couldn't have hit him. It's always easier to go back and determine what you should have done because it's easier to think when we're calm and not being threatened. You survived and you have to remember that."

"I know. But, I still think I should have decked the guy," she muttered.

"So what happened next?" Hatchert asked quietly as they continued to walk.

"He shoved a plastic tube in my mouth and forced me to drink orange juice and I almost choked. Then, he stuck a gag on me," she said as she bent over and gulped for air. "Damn, I hate that I'm reacting this way," she said as she fought through tears and nausea.

"I'm sorry too. Has Dr. Calloway mentioned anything about how to help you get through the panic attacks?"

"I'm going to see her today," Laura replied miserably.

"I've seen people move past them with help and time, Laura. It might not always be like this," Hatchert reassured her as she waited for Laura to continue.

"Thanks," Laura replied as she smiled weakly at Hatchert.

"After he tasered you, what happened next?"

"He had me down so fast I didn't know what hit me. I wasn't expecting it. I didn't know whether or not he had a gun or not. I felt like I was in some B-rated movie. Like it wasn't real," Laura said as she gulped in some air.

"Let's sit down for a while," Hatchert said as she motioned to a large rock that both of them could sit on.

"The ocean looks rough today," Hatchert said hoping to take Laura's attention away from the rape for a while. "Have you been on one of those whale watching tours?"

"Once. We cleared the dock and just as we hit open water, I started to throw up. It didn't matter what I tried, I was hanging over the rail the whole time. I did see a couple of whales which was cool," Laura said as she bent over while another hit of adrenaline screamed through her body.

"Do you need a break?" Hatchert asked quietly.

"No," she replied as she wiped her sweaty hands on her pants. "I want to get this over with," Laura replied as she pursed her lips and stared at the ocean.

"I'm ready when you are," Hatchert said as she kicked back hoping that her relaxed posture might calm Laura.

"I'm okay," Laura said as she glanced at Hatchert.

"Did you notice what he was wearing?"

"He was dressed in camouflage. Light tans, beige, and greens. He even had on a camouflage ski mask."

"Did he have anything on his hands?" Hatchert asked.

"Yes. He wore those latex gloves you get in a box."

"How do you know that?"

"My dad and I wear them sometimes when we're working on one of our engines."

"Do you remember what color they were?"

"Yes, they were blue."

"Do you remember anything else? Did you happen to notice his eye color or his hair color?"

"No."

"That's okay. You're doing well," Hatchert reassured her once again.

"He's strong. He threw me over his shoulder like I was a piece of kindling, and I'm not an easy person to carry. And he's crazy," Laura shuddered.

"Why do you say that?"

"He didn't talk much. When he did talk he snorted."

"What do you mean he snorted?"

"He snorted when he got angry. Then he said something about it being the rich folk's fault that he was going to have to teach them and me a lesson."

"Do you know what he meant by that?"

"No. He started stomping up the hill with me on his shoulder."

"Do you recall hearing anything else while he was carrying you?"

"No. By that time I was pretty spacey."

"That's okay. This is tough and you're doing really well," Hatchert assured her again. "This wasn't your fault. He's a sick man."

"I know. But, I keep thinking about combat. If I can't handle something like this, then how am I going to handle combat," Laura said as she turned to face Hatchert.

Hatchert sat up and looked into Laura's troubled eyes. "People don't know how they're going to respond to a situation until they're faced with it. You followed your instinct and survived. That's all they expect you to do in a combat situation."

"I guess," Laura shrugged.

Looking away again, Laura continued. "When he was done he carried me down the hill and stuck me under a bush. I must have blacked out. I don't remember him removing my handcuffs," Laura's voice broke as she looked at her wrists. "I crawled out from under the bushes and started walking."

"How did you feel as you walked?"

"Like Janie Muldoon in our barracks when she's had one too many. I felt sick to my stomach and I couldn't walk a straight line if I had too," she smiled for the first time all morning. "Don't you think it's weird that he dumped me so close to the parking lot. Shouldn't he have been worried about someone seeing him?"

"Many attackers are bold and think they will never get caught," Hatchert said as she wondered if he was watching each woman from a distance. She would have to check to see what else was close to the parking lot.

"I was relieved no one was in the lot when I got there. I didn't want to see or talk to anyone. I locked the doors and got out of there."

"What did you do then?"

"I drove back to the barracks and took a shower," she said angrily as she remembered how she couldn't wash him out of her.

"I noticed that you informed Dr. Calloway on Friday about the rape. Would you mind sharing why you chose to report the incident on Friday instead of Tuesday?"

"I wasn't going to tell anyone. But, one of my instructtors noticed I was shaking and thought I was sick, so he commanded me to report to a doctor. Our base doctor is a guy and I didn't want to tell a guy what happened," she said as she rolled her eyes. "I met Dr. Calloway while I was in the lab having some tests done two weeks ago. She seemed nice, so I told her." she said as she stared at a weed growing in the ground.

"That's understandable. Did she help you?"

"She wants me to file an official report, but I don't want to ruin my career. I want to put this behind me and keep going," Laura said angrily with one of the few flashes of fire Hatchert had seen from her since they met.

"Laura, filing an official report would not affect your career."

"I'll think about it."

"You did a great job, Laura," Hatchert said as she smiled.

"Thanks. I hope you find him."

"We'll find him. Ready to walk back to the cafeteria?" Hatchert asked as she slid off the rock.

"I'm ready," Laura answered as she leapt from the rock and began walking.

When they reached the cafeteria doors, Laura turned to Hatchert. "You've got to catch him because he's going to do this to someone else and I don't want that to happen."

"Neither do I, Laura. I'm going to do my best to find him before he can hurt anyone else."

"I've got to go to class. Bye," Laura said as she bolted from Hatchert and headed toward class.

She watched Laura scurrying away from her and then headed toward her office.

"Whoa! We've got to stop meeting this way," Dr. Calloway said as they almost collided again coming around a corner after she stepped off the elevator.

"How would you like to meet some of the other people on this floor? We're pretty informal around here. Since I can't address you as special agent, how would you like to be introduced to the staff?"

"Hatchert works for me."

After introductions to Calloway's secretary, three nurses, and two doctors and their staff, Hatchert settled down into her cramped office.

She dialed the Hamilton City Chamber of Commerce phone number.

"Hi. I'm new to Hamilton City and Vista Point. Are there any local hiking and running groups I could join?"

"What type of running?" Mark asked.

"I heard the Vista Point trail makes for a nice run."

"There's a group called the Trailmongers that runs the trail every Saturday morning and a group of hikers called the Trail Walkers that does the trail on Sunday mornings. I can give you the phone numbers to call if you'd like to check them out?"

"Shoot. I'm ready," and she wrote down the numbers as he gave them to her.

Dialing the first number she kicked back in her chair.

"Bob, speaking," a friendly male voice spoke.

"Hi, Bob. I'm new to the area and Mark at the Chamber of Commerce said you're president of a group that runs the Vista Point trail every Saturday. Are you open to new members?" Hatchert asked.

"Sure. We welcome anyone who wants to run with us. I don't know if you're familiar with the trail, but it's rated as difficult. The trail goes through flats and then up and down the mountain," Bob shared.

"I can handle it. What time do you run it?"

"Some of the guys work, so we leave at 6:30 a.m. from the parking lot," Bob said pleasantly.

"Great! I'll see you then," Hatchert responded and hung up the phone.

Dialing the next number, Hatchert waited for Jeff to answer.

"Hi," Jeff said.

"Hi. I called the Chamber of Commerce and they gave me your number. I'm interested in joining the hiking group for the Vista Point trail."

"You've come to the right place. We hike the trail every Sunday starting at 7:00 a.m. Have you done much hiking? The trail is pretty tough," Jeff asked.

"Yes, I've done a lot of hiking. Do you leave from the parking lot?"

"Yes, we do. We don't do any formal roll call or stuff. We have about fifteen people who are in the group. Most of the time we have at least seven who walk the trail. It's a nice group of people. I think you'll enjoy our bunch," Jeff said cheerily.

"I'll see you on Sunday at 7:00," Hatchert replied less cheerily.

"Bye." Jeff replied.

Hatchert hung up the phone and sat quietly. She rubbed her eyes and took a deep breath. Sexual assault wasn't about love or sex—it was about power. It was about a sick guy who uses sexual violence as an excuse to build himself up. Her anger and determination to find him was growing. For now, she needed a break and a dress, she thought grumpily as she headed to her car.

Police officer Michelle Davis looked at the deep amber-tinted eyes of the auburn-haired woman coming off the elevator. She dressed like a regular, but the cop in her told her that this woman was no ordinary recruit. The woman's self-confidence and the way she carried herself showed she was used to being listened to and respected. She'd bet her badge this woman was from intelligence, CID. It was too much of a coincidence that she shows up suddenly after there were rumors of sexual assaults on the base. She figured they would send someone. The military brass wouldn't leave something like this to the locals, she thought with a sneer. As if we aren't good enough. They were holding the details close to their chest. Hell, how were they supposed to catch them if they kept everything under wraps?

They told us to keep our eyes open for anything unusual. But, sexual perps were tricky. She ought to know. Her sister and family found out the hard way when her sister turned thirteen. He was a cheap bastard who lived in the upstairs apartment. Came across as a real nice gentleman. And we bought it, she raged quietly inside. Until we found out that he was a slime bucket. And it was too late for her sister, Angela. He got her. At least he didn't kill her and now the bastard was behind bars where he belonged. He should rot in that jail as long as she was concerned. And she hoped that he became the cellblock whore. Would serve him right.

She wasn't afraid of a perp. Lord, help him if she found out who he was. She would keep it legal. She believed that rotting in a cell for the rest of their life was an appropriate sentence. Instead most were let out and they did it again. At least they got her sister's offender in for ten to twenty years—not enough for what he did. Her sister would be changed forever. But, at least they got him.

She nodded and held the dark eyes that were taking her in as the woman walked by her desk. Yup, CID, no doubt about it. And she went back to watching the monitors. Officer Davis watched a lab courier walking down the 1st floor hallway with an ice chest filled with medical specimens, Dr. Calloway walking down the hall to her office, and a man on a stretcher being pushed by two paramedics into the triage room. Another normal day at work, Officer Davis thought as she kept her eye on the monitors and the people in the lobby.

Hatchert scanned her ID card through the sensor, waited for the door to click before she opened it, and headed to her car. As she walked across the parking lot, she allowed her body to drink in the 70-degree weather after being cooped up in a warehouse for the past three months where the temperatures, on some days, reached 120 degrees. She smiled when she read the email noting from Special Agent Lawson came close to blowing her cover when Perkins, the creep who thought a scarab amulet would cleanse souls, slapped her bottom as she walked by him. I bet he gave her that toothy grin that he thought made him look sexy, Hatchert laughed out loud knowing what Lawson was up against. Come this Thursday, you're going down Perkins and she sighed, wishing she could be there to watch his face as they arrest him.

Turning her attention back to the bay, she noticed that a light wind had risen resulting in a few white caps that skittered across the water. Some sailboats were skimming across the surface, bobbing up and down as they went over the waves. Charter whaling boats were headed for the wharf to drop off a load of tourists for the day. She loved being on the water and fortunately never experienced seasickness. When she got in the car, she flipped out her cell phone and punched in "dress shopping Hamilton City, CA" and hit search.

"Of all the ridiculous things I have to do for this assignment, she grumbled, "now I have to buy a freakin' dress and wear it to some fancy gala!" she fumed. "I don't do formal dresses! I don't do high heels!" she mumbled to her cell phone. "The person who thought up galas in the first place should be court marshaled!" Hatchert swore under her breath as she waited for the websites to appear.

Clicking on the website that popped up on her phone, Hatchert noted that Brown's Department store specialized in formalwear. Programming her GPS for 1546 Chavez Drive, she headed toward the coast highway.

Recalculating," the Australian female voice said as the GPS system was searching for the satellite.

"Come on," Hatchert grumpily said.

"Turn left at Harkins Road."

Hatchert looked at the blue dot as it moved toward the red flag. She was getting closer to somewhere she didn't want to be at the moment.

"You've reached your destination," the Australian female voice said as its final words. Hatchert turned into the parking lot of a huge shopping mall.

Parking her car, Hatchert got out and stared at the front door of the department store. If she would have been here to buy a pair of blue jeans or running gear, she could handle that. *But, a dress! And a formal!* That was off her emotional compass.

She stomped up to the door and flung it open landing in a blue-green sea of bed linens and towels.

As the young, redheaded salesperson looked at the beautiful, dark haired woman staring at the towels, she couldn't help but notice that this customer looked like she was ready to bolt out of the store. I'm just who she needs, thought Amanda. And it certainly would be a pleasure as she looked at Hatchert's long legs and athletic build.

"May I help you?" Amanda smiled sweetly.

Hatchert turned around and her face almost did a swan dive into Amanda's cleavage. She knew it was Amanda because Amanda's name badge was pinned precariously close to her cleavage.

"Hi," Hatchert said as her cheeks turned as red as the apple off her Mom's tree in their backyard back home.

"What can I help you with today?" Amanda chirped.

"I'm going to a gala event tonight and I need a formal," Hatchert said as her eyes narrowed and her lips pursed.

"I see. I take it formals aren't a part of your usual wardrobe," Amanda teased as she did an obvious sweep of Hatchert's body.

"No," Hatchert replied as she shifted uncomfortably under the scrutiny of her attire.

"Well, what is the occasion? A wedding, a bar mitz-vah?" Amanda asked as her eyes sparkled in anticipation of the hunt for the perfect dress.

"No. It's a gala fundraiser at Hamilton Hospital for S.A.R.T."

"How exciting!" Amanda squealed in delight. "I know all about it. I've helped several women who are attending with their dress purchases. It's going to be a wonderful event. I wish I were going," she said dreamily.

"I wish you were going instead of me," she mumbled as she followed Amanda's perky butt.

"Come this way. I have some gorgeous dresses that you'll look stunning in," Amanda said as she clapped her hands and signaled for Hatchert to follow her up the escalator.

Not bad, Hatchert said to herself as she took in Amanda's electric orange dress that hugged the rounded curves of Amanda's body.

"Right this way," Amanda chirped once again as she directed Hatchert to a rack of long dresses. "I would guess you're a size 4, is that correct?" she said as she studied Hatchert's body.

"I don't know," Hatchert muttered.

"That's okay. You're in good hands. I'll pull some dresses for you to try on. Do you have the appropriate lingerie to wear under the formal?" Amanda asked and based on the wide-eye catatonic expression on Hatchert's face added, "Don't worry, I would be more than happy to help you with that part of your wardrobe," as she headed for the dress racks.

Amanda fussed and stewed and began pulling dresses. She tossed them over her arm and pointed toward the dressing room as Hatchert followed like a duckling the first time it saw its momma. Stepping in ahead of Hatchert, Amanda hung the dresses on the hooks.

"Why don't you start trying them on while I run to our lingerie department? I'll be right back," she winked before she left.

Hatchert stepped into the dressing room and closed the door. She was surrounded with bolts of material. Some were sparkling blue, others green, and one was a hot pink number covered in sequins!!!

No freaking hot pink, Hatchert thought as she grabbed the dress and threw open the door. Feeling foolish, Hatchert looked around and saw there was no place to hang it. Almost snarling, she stepped back inside and shoved it behind the other dresses that were on the hook.

She was left with a sequined gold number, a deep-green dress with a flared skirt, a scarlet-red chiffon dress, and underneath them all, was a simple long, black dress. Hatchert took the black dress, held it up and sighed. At least this one doesn't make me look like a darn peacock, she grumbled as she took off her clothes and piled them on the tufted, pink stool that sat in the corner of the dressing room.

She unzipped the side zipper and shimmied the dress over her head. The soft, black material flowed over her curves and settled nicely to the floor. Hatchert turned around to look at herself in the full-length mirrors that covered three walls of the dressing room and gasped. The deep-v neckline stretched down past her cleavage and the sexy sheath shape hit every curve in the right place. The long black sleeves added a simple elegance. She stared at herself in the mirror.

"How are you doing in there?" Amanda asked good-naturedly hoping Hatchert hadn't bolted. "I've got some great 3-inch black satin heels for you to try on and a pair of 3-inch red ones too."

"Give me a second," Hatchert said as she took it all in. She hadn't been in a long dress since her junior year in high school when she went to the prom with Steve Murkowski.

Her mom insisted and she wasn't ready to tell her parents about what she figured out in junior high school when Becky Stevens sent her libido into a full spin.

One prom was enough and she downright told her mom, "No," when she hinted at it the following year. A lot had changed since her senior year, including her body. She did a slow spin as she watched her reflection in the mirror. The back had a deep-u shape cutout exposing her silky smooth back.

"Are you ready to try on some shoes? And I got you some great silk panties and a stick-on bra to hold up the girls," Amanda chuckled light-heartedly as she thought about what Hatchert's reaction might be when she saw them.

"Sure," Hatchert said as she cautiously opened the door and peeked out.

"Wow! You look hot!" Amanda exclaimed as she threw the door open and made the index finger motion to twirl around. At Hatchert's confused expression, Amanda repeated the finger motion and said adamantly, "Twirl!"

So Hatchert twirled and shuddered.

"You look great! Here's a stick on bra for the girls. You have to bend over and then stick this bra onto your skin and they'll do all the work," Amanda smiled as Hatchert's cheeks turned a blend of strawberry and tomato red.

Hatchert grasped the two round foamy shapes with sticky backs and held them up. "These are going to hold these up?" she said in disbelief as she pointed to her size D breasts.

"That's right!" Amanda said confidently. "These red heels will look great on you!"

"I think I'll stick with the black ones," Hatchert said as she took them out of Amanda's hand and then gasped. "How in the world am I going to walk on these things?" she exclaimed as she stared at the 3-inch spiked heels the size of #2 pencils.

"Take your time. You'll look awesome. I'll be right back," Amanda giggled and ran off again.

Hatchert slid off the dress and took the stick-on bra and looked at it. I didn't even know they made these things, Hatchert mumbled to herself as she held up two cups with an adhesive spread over them. She bent over and after considerable wiggling and jiggling, finally got each one in place. Straightening up, she felt as though they were going to fall off any minute. After she bounced around a little, she saw that they really worked. All right, she said confidently as she pulled on the black silk panty and once again shimmied into the dress.

She stepped into the 3-inch black skyscraper heels and as she attempted to stand, she tottered and almost fell over.

"How the hell does anyone walk in these things?!?" Hatchert uttered in disbelief that such a feat was possible as she wobbled back and forth and fought gravity.

After a few shaky steps, she decided to venture out of the dressing room. It took a little practice, but Hatchert finally stopped swaying and swinging.

"Look what I found!" Amanda said as she plunked a pair of dazzling drop earrings with pear-cut diamonds and a matching necklace into Hatchert's palm. "They're going to look beautiful on you," Amanda giggled as she watched Hatchert's expression.

"I don't think so," Hatchert hedged as she tried to hand them back.

"Try them. You're going to look fabulous!" Amanda said as she clipped the necklace around Hatchert's neck.

"I'm not sure of this," Hatchert stuttered as she put on the earrings.

"Look!" Amanda said as she led Hatchert to a short platform that was surrounded in 9-foot tall mirrors.

Hatchert managed to step up onto the 5-inch tall platform and stared.

A sexy woman in black stared back at her.

"Where are you getting your hair done?" Amanda asked.

"Hair!" Hatchert exclaimed in dismay.

"Yes, hair!" Amanda said. "You can't go to the gala without getting your hair done. Look, I'll call Rita. She's fabulous and she owes me one. We'll ring you up and then you can go to her salon that is two doors down from here in the mall."

Hatchert looked like a lost duckling as Amanda steered her toward the salon. In no time at all she was seated in Rita's chair while she watched her hair being pulled back off her face and secured with a crystal hairclip at the back of her head. Rita could have been her mother's age and fussed over Hatchert as Hatchert sat there in stunned silence. She took Hatchert's long, auburn hair and gently twisted it around her curling iron giving a softer look to the athletic Hatchert.

"What are you doing?" Hatchert gasped as Rita spun her around and began attacking her face with foundation.

"I'm going to do your makeup," Rita grinned mischievously. "This is a fancy ball and you have to wear makeup. Now, sit still," she scolded Hatchert who was fidgety as a three-year old in a church pew during services.

"I don't want a lot of makeup," Hatchert moaned as she submitted to Rita's fussing.

"There, you're all set for the ball!" Rita said as she stepped back to admire her work.

Hatchert looked in the mirror. The soft glow of light pink blush highlighted her high cheekbone. The dark gray eye shadow and eyeliner made her dark eyes pop. The light rose colored lipstick made her lips look lush and ripe.

"Thank you," was all Hatchert could muster as she continued to stare at herself in the mirror.

"It's almost 5:00 p.m. and time to go home, take a bath, and spritz some of this perfume on you, compliments of the salon," Rita said as she giggled at the Hatchert's gaping mouth and wide eyes while handing her a bottle of perfume in the shape of a swan.

Hatchert stared at the swan in her hand.

"Thank you," Hatchert muttered again as she gathered up her packages and headed to her car. No one had better see her from headquarters, Hatchert mumbled to herself as she put up the top on her convertible. Oh man, I have to show up at the barracks looking like this, she grumbled all the way back to the barracks.

She rolled past the guard at the gate and didn't look sideways as she gave a quick salute. Grabbing the bags and long plastic garment bag, she sprinted up the stairs and down the hall to her room. Thank goodness, she sighed when she found her room was empty as she threw the bags onto the bed. Now what?

She looked around the room like some felon who was about to get caught. *Get a grip, Hatchert! You've handled sexual perps! Certainly you can handle this! Can't you?* This is all part of the job, she said to herself as she paced the room trying to work up the courage to actually wear this stuff out in public.

Bath. She was supposed to take a bath. How the heck can she take a bath when there is no tub! Survival training. That's it. Think of it as a test of my survival skills. It's a way to test my emotional strength, just like they did at boot camp. Only instead of being tossed into a simulated combat situation, she was going to a gala—in a dress! She can do this, she repeated again and again, not yet believing herself.

As the panic began to rise, Hatchert headed to the bathroom to throw up. When she came out of the stall, she knew she had to figure out a way to "take a bath." She went to her room, grabbed a washcloth and towel and opened the shower room door.

A loud whistle pierced the silence.

"Look at you!" Brittany said while Connie continued to whistle.

"Going to a ball tonight?" Connie teased.

"Yeah. As a matter of fact I am. So leave me alone so I can get ready," Hatchert snapped as her cheeks turned pink.

"If you need any help, we're just two doors down from you," Connie said as she pinched Hatchert's butt on her way out.

"Anything at all, you hear?" Brittany said as she patted Hatchert's cheek before she closed the door behind her.

It was the fastest spit bath Hatchert ever took. She flew through it and literally ran to her room and slammed the door behind her.

It was one thing to try on a dress in the store, but to actually wear it in public was another thing. Hatchert put her head in her hands and rocked back and forth.

I can do this, Hatchert repeated twenty more times as her heart pounded in her chest. The gala started in thirty minutes. It was now or never and she wasn't a quitter. But, if anyone takes a picture and tries to send it to headquarters I'm going to personally put them behind bars, she swore as she removed the plastic garment bag and held the gown in her hand.

She flipped and flopped trying to get the stick on bra to stick on in the right places. Cussing to herself after three failed attempts, she finally got it right. She pulled on the silk black panty and slid the dress over her head. It got caught on her stick on bra and darn near tore everything off, including her skin.

"Damn," Hatchert swore out loud as she fought the bra and the dress.

Finally, the dress was in place and the zipper pulled up. Next, were the shoes. Hatchert plopped on the bed and picked up the shoebox. Pulling out the 3-inch black heels out of the shoebox, she slid them onto her feet.

She pushed up and teetered. It took a while, but finally Hatchert was able to stand erect. Okay, I have the swing of this, Hatchert said with full confidence believing she had it all under control. Until, she decided to walk. She looked like an out-of-control stilt walker who was about to crash. She teetered and tottered, swooped down and then up, trying to get the hang of walking on the tips of two knitting needles. It took time, but soon, she actually could walk across the room. As she looked at her watch she swore once again. The gala started in ten minutes. She was going to be late.

She shoved on the earrings and fought the box clasp on the necklace. She searched the bags and found the black clutch purse that Amanda insisted she buy to hold her driver's license, base ID, cell phone, and money. Shuffling through the empty bags and boxes to see if she missed

113

anything, she fought valiantly against the purse's seams as she stuffed her gun into its new silk home. It was time.

Catcalls and whistles ensued as she opened the door.

"Thanks a lot, Brittany and Connie," Hatchert muttered through gritted teeth.

"Anytime, Hatchert!" Connie teased as she slapped Hatchert on the butt as she walked by.

"Yah, yah," Hatchert said as she tried to look non-chalant while she walked through the gauntlet of women who were all too ready to have some fun at her expense.

I've got it all under control, Hatchert said to herself to get her courage up: until she tried to drive her stick shift car.

"How in the heck do women do this?" she screamed in total frustration as she looked at the car's clock and realized she was thirty-five minutes late. She kicked off both shoes, pulled the dress bottom up to her knees, and drove barefoot. "I'm never wearing a dress again!" she screamed at the top of her lungs as she pulled onto the highway.

When she pulled up to the valet parking area for the gala, she almost kept on driving. But, she wasn't a coward. Yanking the silver chain handle of her clutch out of the passenger seat, she slid on the heels and jumped out of the car.

"Oh for Pete's sake," she groaned as she looked up at the twenty-five stairs that she had to climb to reach the ballroom.

Josie stepped into a warm, jetted bath filled with scented bubbles and essential oils.

"Now this is heaven," she said as she sunk into the water. She'd spent most of the morning and early afternoon writing and her muscles were stiff and sore. She pushed on

114

the jet button and soon the bubbles and water current were kneading every part of her body. Mariah Carey's *Daydream* album was playing in the background and the scented candles that flickered softly around the tub gave off a soft lavender scent. She gave each muscle its own little massage as she moved this way and that around the jets. Forty minutes later, Josie stepped out of the tub and gently patted her skin dry. She lovingly rubbed a rose-scented skin cream over her body. Then, she slipped into a warm bed and drifted off into a deep sleep.

When the alarm went off two and one-half hours before the gala, Josie felt rested and pampered. She pulled on her green-terry cloth bathrobe and walked downstairs to the kitchen refrigerator.

"Wonder what we've got in here," Josie asked as she looked in the freezer. There was some leftover homemade lasagna from Rachel's dinner the other night. She slid it onto a plate, put it in the microwave, set the time, and punched, "START." She took a bag of mixed greens, baby carrots, diced jicama, and cherry tomatoes, and rinsed them off under the faucet. When the microwave bell rang, she took out the hot lasagna and sniffed the heavenly Italian cheeses and spices, then added the greens mix. Pouring on vinegar and oil on the salad, she settled into a kitchen chair facing the back garden. She watched some gray squirrels playing in the tree branches, some butterflies and hummingbirds feeding on the flowers' nectar, and listened to a blue jay chattering angrily at a large gray squirrel that was perched on a tree limb. She drank a bottle of water, put the dishes in the dishwasher, and headed to the library.

The Great Gatsby seemed like the perfect book to get her in the mood for the gala tonight. Pulling a green blanket out of a basket that was carefully tucked behind a table,

Josie headed to the comfy sofa where she propped her head up on a soft, green feather pillow, and stretched out her long limbs along its length. She was well into the part about Tom's affair with Myrtle when the grandfather clock struck four o'clock. It was time to get ready for the gala.

Josie headed upstairs to her master bathroom. She pulled out the custom-made drawer that held her makeup. With the strokes of a skilled artist, Josie began her transformation into the respected and admired "Daughter of the Valley." When she looked in the mirror, she inspected her artistry and touched up a few spots she felt needed more attention smiling at her reflection in the mirror. She spritzed on the perfume her mom brought from her annual shopping trip to Paris last year.

With one final glance in the mirror, Josie strode into her large walk-in closet that was almost the size of one of the smaller, downstairs bedrooms. Along with the black shoes and white shoes were blues, purples, oranges, pinks, reds, and even yellow ones in the custom-made, solid oak shoe rack that occupied one wall of her closet.

Her clothes were neatly hung by season, color, and style in floor-to-ceiling cabinets. Her gown for tonight hung on a special hook placed on the face of the cabinet just for occasions like the one tonight. Splashes of light reflected off various shades of gold as the sun's rays from the closet window hit the honey-gold fabric drenched in gold glass bugle beads. A pair of gold 4-inch heels sat at the foot of the gown.

On top of the center island that held Josie's sweaters was a solid, oak tray lined with black velvet. On top of the black velvet, sat a square-cut yellow diamond surrounded by smaller, round, white diamonds forming a pendant that hung on a 14k yellow gold box chain. Matching square-cut

116

yellow and white diamond earrings and bracelet were carefully placed beside the necklace. Another 1 ½-inch diamond cuff bracelet lay respectfully on its side waiting to grace Josie's slim wrist.

The final detail was her hairstyle. She knew it might have been more sensible to go to a salon, but the rebellious and free-spirited artist's soul wanted to see how she felt before she did her tresses. Did she feel like a princess tonight? A celebrity? A rebel? Josie stopped and stared at her dress. She imagined how she would feel wearing this gold masterpiece. When she finally saw a picture form in her mind, she knew how she wanted to wear her hair and headed back to the bathroom to begin the metamorphosis.

Thirty minutes later, Josie emerged from the bathroom and put on some soft, instrumental, background music. She effortlessly slid her breasts into her stick-on bra and secured it before she slipped into her flesh-colored, silk panty. Josie walked over to her gold gown and eased the 2-inch wide beaded straps off the hanger. She pulled down the side zipper and allowed the gown to pool on the floor and then, she gracefully stepped into it, gently sliding it up over her hips. With ease she placed a strap over each shoulder and pulled up the zipper. Turning around, she walked to the full-length mirror and adjusted each strap into its rightful place. The deep-V neckline caught just enough of her cleavage to be dangerous, but was not offensive.

Pivoting to see her back, she rebelliously smiled to see how the dress was cut in a large U-shape revealing her smooth, silky, cream-colored nakedness that some might judge to be a bit too daring. She looked at her hair and was pleased with what she saw. The messy bun, that sat like a crown on the back of her head, was just formal enough to

117

meet the elders' approval, and messy enough to match her defiant spirit. The thin, blond tendrils that skipped along her cheeks acted like a gold frame around her face and highlighted her sensuous, soft, rose-petal lips.

It was time to slide into her glass slippers, she thought as she stepped into her heels and picked up the gold clutch already filled with the necessities for a gala evening. With one final look, she took a quick breath as she thought about the money that would help bring S.A.R.T. to Vista Point and the victims who would benefit from their services. Tonight meant something to her. It wasn't just another fundraiser; it was helping out a fellow sister. And if he was there, she was damn well going to show him that what he did to her was less than the bee sting she got last summer, nasty at first, and then nothing.

She turned on the desk lamp that provided a soft light spreading a warm glow around the room. She went down the stairs and then down the hall to the connecting garage door. She set the alarm and slid into the driver's seat of her RAV4. Taking the flats from the passenger seat, she exchanged them for her high heels and soon was heading to the gala.

The night was crisp and clear and the stars were out. She passed through Vista Point and headed for Hamilton City listening to some rock and roll to help energize her for the long evening ahead. Soon, she was pulling into the valet parking area of the hotel where the event was taking place. She efficiently slipped out of her flats and into her heels before she stepped out of her car.

"Hi Peter. How's your wife and kids?" Josie asked as she handed him her car's valet key.

"They're fine. Sylvia's taking piano lessons and Brian's in little league this year," Peter answered.

"Gosh, they're getting big. See you later, Peter," Josie called out as she headed for the stairs.

"Hi, Mr. and Mrs. Ramirez. It's a lovely evening tonight. How are your granddaughters?" Josie politely asked as she gracefully walked up the stairs and into the lobby outside the large convention hall where the dinner was being held. People were packed elbow to elbow. Five bars were set up and the lines were already long.

"Hi, Mr. and Mrs. Mason. It was so good of you to come tonight to support our effort to bring a S.A.R.T. facility to our area. How are your sons doing?" Josie asked as she slid into her host role. For nearly an hour, Josie moved from guest to guest, personally greeting each of them and thanking them for their support.

The doors opened and guests poured into the massive room. Round tables that sat ten people were covered in black and white table linens. Silver spoons, forks, and knives glistened on top of the black linen napkins. Bottles of red and white wines donated by a local winery were waiting to be opened and enjoyed. Candles set in tall, 2-foot crystal vases flickered in the center of the table.

The room buzzed like a busy hive as people found their table and wine began to flow. Waiters in black ties, crisp white shirts, black slacks, and black aprons shuffled quietly in and out of the kitchen bringing the salad made with mixed greens donated by a local grower.

Just as the salad was served, Hatchert made it to the top of the stairs and into the drink area. She looked around and saw the bartenders cleaning up and preparing to go home. The noise from the ballroom made Hatchert grimace as she headed toward the din. When she stepped through the hall doors, she felt like she'd entered Oz. Tables and people filled the landscape. She looked around and then heard her heartbeat pounding in her ears. Steady, Hatchert she told herself. We can do this, even though at that moment she wasn't certain she could. She swept the room looking for Chief Girard.

"Oh, right! He's at the very front table, center stage," Hatchert gasped as she made her way at a snail's pace around the multitudes of people and tables.

Welcome," Chief Girard said with a huge smile as Hatchert approached the table.

"Hi," Hatchert said in utter relief as she sank into her chair.

"Everyone, this is Mary Hatchert. Mary, this is my wife, Brittany, my daughter Rachel, and her husband Jeremy. This is Samantha Green, her husband Bill Green, and their daughter Josie Green. This is Dan Reyes and his lovely wife Maria."

"Hi. It's nice to meet you all," Hatchert said as she stared at Josie. If that doesn't beat all! Miss RAV4 was Josie Green! And I'm sitting with the Colonel's family, she thought as she gawked at everyone at the table.

The Chief was finding it amusing to see Hatchert's well-trained mind go into outer space. Even the best can have their off moments, he smiled to himself.

"A toast. To Josie, who has led the effort to bring a satellite S.A.R.T. to Hamilton Hospital," the Chief said as he raised his wine glass. "And to Bill, Samantha, Dan, and Maria for their generous contributions to the program," he saluted and each raised their glasses and took a sip of wine.

"And I want to thank the Chief who spearheaded this idea and turned it into a reality! Thank you, Chief," Josie said as she raised her glass to honor him.

120

It was time for the main course. As the waiters served the entrees, Hatchert noticed that Josie took the prime rib. Interesting, she didn't think Miss RAV4 would eat meat, she thought sarcastically. She sure doesn't have a nerd body either and forced herself to look at the Chief instead of Josie.

As she shuffled around in her chair, Hatchert was offered prime rib, chicken, or a vegetarian entree. She was a meat gal all the way and pointed to the prime rib. Dessert was a strawberry tart from fresh strawberries picked that day in a nearby field. By the time the coffee arrived, everyone was full and content.

As Josie set her glass on the table, a sharp-looking woman whispered into her ear, and Josie nodded in acknowledgement.

"Please excuse me," Josie said as she rose and followed the woman.

Hatchert's eyes took one look at Miss RAV4 walking away from her and darn near lost it. Some thin strands of honey-gold hair seductively spilled from the messy bun kissing Josie's neck. Her body began to ache as she imagined herself gently stroking that creamy whiteness and removing the pins of the bun allowing the soft, blond curls to spill down so she could lose herself in them.

"Get your act together, Hatchert," she chastised herself as she forced herself to look at Josie's parents.

"Good evening, ladies and gentlemen. It's an honor to be here tonight. As you know, Chief Girard can use that blazing smile and quick wit to talk us into doing just about anything, " she laughed along with the guests.

"About five months ago, he turned on his Mississippi-wide smile and shared his vision of bringing a satellite Sexual Assault Response Team, or S.A.R.T. team, to

Hamilton Hospital. He had me under his spell after he explained how a S.A.R.T. facility would make a difference to our community and families. At the time, I didn't know anything about S.A.R.T. After hearing his brief explanation, I wanted to know more so I toured the S.A.R.T. facility at Silicon Valley Hospital. After the tour, I was hooked.

Sheila Evans, their current director, took an infant S.A.R.T. facility and built it into one of the most successful facilities in the state. We are extremely fortunate to have Sheila on our team. Ladies and gentleman, Sheila Evans," Josie said as she clapped and took two steps back so Sheila could take her place behind the podium.

"Good evening, ladies and gentlemen. Thank you for inviting me here to share about our program. We're excited about partnering with Hamilton Hospital to bring a satellite S.A.R.T. team to your area. It is unfortunate that we need S.A.R.T., but since we do, I've been privileged to run the Silicon Valley program for the last twenty-five years. Our facility has twenty-six nurses who handle approximately forty cases a month. Each S.A.R.T. nurse must undergo a specialized training program to conduct an examination. They are trained to support the victim, to conduct an interview to determine what type of evidence might be present, how to collect the evidence with specialized equipment that they have been trained to operate, and if necessary, how to testify in court as an expert witness should a case be brought to trial. A S.A.R.T. nurse is available twenty-four hours a day, seven days a week, and it is their dedication and commitment to the program that allows us to offer the quality service that we provide. I would like to share that the victims believe what we offer to them is a gift.   Unfortunately,   S.A.R.T.   programs   are   not typically government funded, so each S.A.R.T. facility must find ways to finance their own program. We would like to thank your community leaders for their time and effort in this project. And, we would like to thank each of you for your attendance tonight, and for your financial contributions so that a new S.A.R.T. satellite facility will soon be established at Hamilton Hospital."

"Thank you, Sheila. As most of you know, I unfortunately needed to use the services of the S.A.R.T. facility at Silicon Valley Hospital. I cannot say enough about the dedication, quality, and services that were offered to me that night. The distance I had to drive was an added burden that I don't want other victims in our community to experience. It is imperative that we offer this remarkable service at Hamilton Hospital. Your donations are greatly appreciated and we thank each of you for coming tonight. Now let's dance!" Josie sang out and flashed a lightning bolt smile to the audience.

The band began to play, *Moondance*, as Josie's father escorted her onto the dance floor to start off the evening dance festivities. Chief Girard and his wife followed, and before long, the dance floor was full.

Hatchert couldn't help but stare at Miss RAV4's curves and the flow of her dress as it slipped and slid while she was dancing with her father.

Just when Hatchert began to relax, she noticed that Bill Green was headed her way.

"Oh no," Hatchert panicked when she realized he was going to ask her to dance. Her heart pounded, her palms became sweaty, her stomach churned like a boat's propeller on full speed, and her mind went blank. She'd never stepped foot on a dance floor, not even at her junior prom.

Run was all she could think of as she began to bolt from her chair.

"I'm sure my dad would be happy to dance with you," Josie needled Hatchert recognizing that Miss Gas Station was ready to make her escape, "but, I told him that Mrs. Reyes would probably like to dance."

Massive relief flooded through Hatchert as she watched Josie's dad taking Mrs. Reyes' hand so he could lead her to the dance floor.

"Where were you going in such a hurry?" Josie smiled as she noted how the color began to slowly return to Hatchert's face.

"I was headed to the restroom," Hatchert spat out.

"I'm sure you won't mind if I join you," Josie challenged.

"It's a public restroom," Hatchert jabbed back and started walking as she tried to keep her eyes straight ahead of her instead of on Miss RAV4's cleavage.

"What do you do for a living?" Josie asked.

"Right now, I work with Dr. Calloway over at the hospital."

"What does your work involve?"

"I actually just started yesterday, so tomorrow I'll know more about my job responsibilities," Hatchert replied honestly.

"You mean, you took a job and you don't even know what you're doing?" Josie needled hoping to rattle her cage a little.

"What do you do besides throwing galas?" Hatchert angrily countered throwing the ball back into Miss RAV4's court.

"I'm a writer."

124

"Do you do anything else?" Hatchert asked rather pointedly.

"I have two writing groups I run Wednesday and Thursday nights," Josie silkily replied as she batted her black mascara-swept eyelashes.

Standing in front of the mirror by the paper towel dispenser, Josie watched Hatchert in the mirror as she refreshed her lipstick. Just as Hatchert reached around her to pull a paper towel out of the basket on the sink, Josie purposely turned and Miss Gas Station's hand landed right in her cleavage.

"Oh man!" Hatchert shouted as she yanked her hand back and looked at Miss RAV4 who stood there batting her aquamarine blue eyes.

With great restraint from all her years of training, Hatchert excused herself and stomped back to the table, or at least tried to stomp. Her heels made that nearly impossible.

Josie followed and laughed out loud as she watched Hatchert's awkward one-woman parade.

"How are you doing, Hatchert?" Chief Girard inquired with a twinkle in his eye.

"Fine," she tersely replied. "It's time I get back to the barracks," she almost snarled as she watched Miss RAV4's body float around the room laughing and chatting with each of the guests. "I'll keep in touch. Goodnight," Hatchert said to the Chief forcing a smile.

"Goodnight," the Chief said as he watched Hatchert make her getaway. Looks like they didn't teach Gala 101 to the intelligence team, he chuckled to himself and then turned to his wife and asked her to dance.

A rocket couldn't have made a straighter path than Hatchert as she headed to the front door. In looking down the

125

flight of stairs, she took a deep breath and started down them.

"Mary Hatchert!" Josie cried out in a sugary voice from above.

"What?" Hatchert grumpily shouted as she pivoted around to look up at Miss RAV4. And when she saw Miss RAV4 with her gold gown moving gently in the breeze she almost lost her balance.

"I believe you lost your earring!" Josie said sweetly and smiled as she held up Hatchert's earring in her hand.

"Great, just great," Hatchert growled to herself as she began the journey back up the stairs.

"Thank you," Hatchert muttered as she grabbed her earring.

"You're welcome," Josie said as she cocked her head and smiled.

Safe inside her car, Hatchert drew in a deep breath. The torture was over. Never again, she swore under her breath as she yanked off her heels and threw them onto the passenger floor. Pulling her dress up over her knees and with her bare feet on the gas, she was never so glad in all her life to be going back to the barracks.

Miss Gas Station was going to be fun, Josie thought as she watched Hatchert drive away. Real fun. And with that she returned to the gala to say goodnight to her guests.

He watched her from across the room and wanted her. The shimmering reflections of gold light that encircled Josie like a diaphanous veil proved to him that she was his golden goddess—only his. She'd shaken his hand and made small talk as if he was just another patron, but soon she would know what it felt like to truly be his goddess forever.

126

He had to be more clever this time. It wouldn't do to get caught. He wasn't going to end up in a 12-foot prison cell, not him. He was too smart. By the time he was done with her she would never want to leave him. It might take a while for her to love him, but he had no doubt that it would happen. With careful nurturing and patience she would be his, and if not, there was always his hand, he smiled. A few careful slaps and hits and she would know who was boss. He would take her to a place where it would only be just the two of them. She would learn that the ONLY one she could count on to take care of her was he. All in a matter of time, he thought as he smiled and joined in the chatter around the table.

CHAPTER 5

Wednesday, 1 October 14
The First Writing Group

"Good morning, this is the pharmacy. How can I help you?"

"This is Mary Hatchert. I'd like to pick up some migraine medication."

After she verified her insurance card number and answered a few questions, she hung up the phone and moaned again when she learned that it would take thirty minutes to fill the prescription. Turning on the computer in her office, she typed in different passcodes and watched the various screens pop up. *I hope you're there;* she grimaced as her head sent a wave of nausea to join in with the deafening beat of the jackhammer in her head.

"There you are," and clicked on one of files of the men in Josie's writing groups. "Let's see who you are, Sam Meade," Hatchert said as she opened his file.

She studied a picture of a baby-face man smiling back at her while he stood with his junior Olympic archery students for their team photo. His crisp white pleated pants and white buttoned-up polo shirt blended in with his milky-white skin giving the overall effect of a giant marshmallow that was wearing white tennis shoes. She stared at his round button blue eyes and balding hairline and wondered if he had any secrets to tell.

"Wow," she whistled as she opened another photo and found herself looking at the crushed skeleton of what used to be a minivan. According to the accident report, a semi-
128

tractor trailer rig fishtailed into his lane sending Meade's minivan rolling down an embankment. It took the jaws of life, five rescue workers, and one and one-half hours to free him from the car resulting in a broken right arm, left hip, and three crushed disks in his lower back and two in his neck. "Wonder if he can lift 145 pounds," Hatchert grimaced as another wave of nausea swept through her.

She clicked on David Lockhart's folder. David had a rakish smile that spread as wide as the Rio Grand as he stood in front of his dental practice sign along with his wife, fifteen year-old daughter, and two office workers. Clicking on the next photo, Hatchert studied his lanky body, side-swept black hair, and chic glasses as he presented a trophy to the regional bowling champion held the morning Cindy was assaulted. "That rules him out," Hatchert thought as she rubbed small circles around her left temple.

She clicked on Matthew Walton's folder. A picture of a brown-haired Ken doll leaning against a brand new BMW Z4 roadster popped up on her screen. She studied his dark weasel eyes and arrogant smile. "What you are doing here since you had a successful therapy practice in Kansas City less than eight months ago?" Hatchert wondered as she clicked on the next photo.

Walton was seated among various-aged children dressed in hospital gowns. His pasted-on smile, preppy, navy-blue sweater and laced white deck shoes seemed out of place in a pediatric oncology unit. As Hatchert studied the faces of the children she was caught off guard as a twinge of what might be love surged through her heart. She took several deep breaths. It must be the headache, she thought as she shook off the feeling.

A still shot of Walton crossing the finish line at the Big Sur Marathon in last year's race popped up on the screen. "Looks like we need to become running buddies," Hatchert moaned as another shotgun of pain blasted through her head.

She clicked on a message from headquarters. Sergeant Jones and Officer Michelle Davis passed all security clearances. Picking up her cell phone, she dialed Colonel Delaney.

"Colonel Delaney," he said with a decisive voice.

"Hi Colonel Delaney, this is Special Agent Hatchert."

"Agent Hatchert."

"I would like to pull Sergeant Jones and Officer Michelle Davis onto my team for the next three weeks. Would this be possible?"

"Consider it done. Anything new on our assailant?"

"Not yet, sir. I have some ideas."

"Keep me updated, Agent Hatchert."

"Yes, sir," she ended as she hung up the phone.

Hatchert groaned as her head felt like it was being crushed between two semi-tractor trailer trucks. Shutting down the computer, Hatchert headed to the pharmacy. As she walked past the allergy section, she was surprised to see Cindy and Laura.

"Hi Laura, hi Cindy," Hatchert said as she walked down the aisle toward them.

"Hi," Cindy replied. "Guess what? Laura remembered something. We were going to call you right after we got some allergy medication for her. She's allergic to oak trees. Bummer since we're surrounded by them," Cindy said as she looked sympathetically at Laura wiping her runny nose with a tissue.

"Would it be possible for me to meet you in the cafeteria in a few minutes," Hatchert asked as she studied Laura's puffy red eyes. "I've got to pick up some stuff here and then we can talk."

"Great, we can grab something to eat. I'm starving, how about you, Laura?" Cindy asked as she searched her friend's face.

"Sure. I have to pay for this," Laura nodded as she pulled out her wallet from her backpack. "You go ahead and I'll catch up with you."

"I have to buy some aspirin. I'll meet you at the register," Cindy said sunnily as she sprinted for the pain relief aisle.

The pharmacist was busy helping another customer, which gave Hatchert the opportunity to explore the pharmacy and lab. Noting the surveillance cameras in every corner and one placed above each shelf that held a row of drugs, Hatchert wandered into the lab area. She watched as the lab technician helped an elderly man into a chair and then continued a lively conversation as he cleverly distracted the man from the hypodermic needle. Before long, three full vials of blood were labeled and placed in a small, apartment-sized refrigerator. Returning his attention to the gentleman, the technician helped him up and got him on his way and was soon ushering in the next patient.

Nice job, Hatchert thought as she continued to take more mental notes. The lab technician grabbed a pair of blue latex gloves from a cardboard dispenser box and effortlessly slid his hands into them pulling them up to his wrists as he chatted with the frail, gray-haired woman whose voice quivered as she answered his questions. Hatchert watched the woman's eyes grow wide when she spotted the hypodermic needle sitting on the white paper in the stainless steel tray.

"That's a great coat you have on, Mrs. Marshall," the lab tech commented distracting her attention away from the needle. "Do you mind sharing where you bought it? My grandma's birthday is next week and that coat would be perfect for her," and while the frail woman described the purchase, the lab technician drew the blood for her tests and had her on her way home.

"Hi Kevin, that was a nice way to calm her down," Hatchert said, after she read the name on his badge.

"Thanks. It's a part of the job. Some people have a hard time with needles. May I have your lab slip?" Kevin asked as a wide smile flooded his face.

"I don't have one yet. Are you here tomorrow?"

"Yes. I'm here for at least two more weeks. The regular guy is down for the count. Apparently, he jammed his fingers playing basketball. I'm usually at Bayside up in La Mesa, but they needed somebody and I volunteered. It's nice down here and I like to fish."

"What kind of fishing?"

"I like deep sea fishing, so I jumped at the chance to work here. Maybe the guy won't come back and I can move down here," he said with a wolfish grin.

"Hi Kevin," came a voice from behind Hatchert as a thirty-something-year old man carrying a large blue ice chest with a bright red medical symbol stamped into its side rolled past her. "Got anything else to go today?"

"No. Everything's in the fridge."

"Got it," the courier said as he emptied the fridge of the vials and plastic containers filled with lab specimens into the ice chest and left.

Hatchert continued. "It's really nice in Hamilton City

with the ocean close by. I'll have to go fishing sometime. I came here last week and needed some lab work done, but I talked with another guy. Would that be the one who jammed his fingers?"

"Probably. He's about 6-foot tall, wears brown glasses, and one of those cheesy pocket protectors. He looks like a nerd and is proud of it."

"That's him. What's his last name?"

"Roberts."

"Does he go out often? He kind of hit on me," Hatchert said with a grin.

Laughing, Kevin smiled at her, "That's Mark all right. Sorry, but he flirts with anyone that has long legs and great ummm... well you know," Kevin looked kind of sheepish.

"Thanks for telling me that. I wondered about him when he said I had the greatest legs he'd ever seen since Marilyn Monroe," and they both laughed.

"Does he have a girlfriend?"

"Not that I know. His pick up lines suck and he can't seem to get a girl on a first date let alone a second date."

"Does he live local?"

"I think he lives on the west side of Hamilton."

"Do you know where I can pick up some gloves like these?" Hatchert asked nonchalantly as she pointed to the box of blue latex gloves.

"You'd have to ask supply. They bring us a box when we run low. These are hospital grade gloves so they're more expensive than the ones you get at the drugstore."

"I didn't know they had different kinds of gloves."

"Yeah. I guess they have all kinds of them. I don't pay much attention to it. I just use them. These have powder on the inside so you can get them on and off faster. I've got another patient to take care of right now. Can I help you with anything else?"

"No. Thanks. See you later."

She wandered back to the pharmacy.

"May I help you?" asked the pharmacist.

"Yes. I'm Mary Hatchert and I'm here to pick up my prescription. I was wondering if you sell those blue latex disposable gloves I saw the technician using in the lab?"

"The ones we have are white, come in boxes of 25, 50, and 100 and they aren't hospital grade quality like the ones we use in our lab. The lab gloves must comply with FDA Biocompatibility Guidance for Medical Devices and are also ISO 9001 Certified QM. Hospital supply orders them wholesale and most people don't need the level of sterility that is required in our lab. Do you need hospital grade quality or would the ones we carry in our pharmacy work for you?"

"The ones in your pharmacy would probably work. I don't need them right now, but now I know where I can buy them. I'll just pay for my prescription," Hatchert smiled.

"I can ring you up at the cash register."

After she paid for her prescription, Hatchert headed to the cafeteria. She spotted Laura and Cindy sitting at a table at the far end. Stopping at the drinking fountain, Hatchert popped two pills into her mouth and swallowed, and felt better knowing relief was on its way for the pounding in her head.

"Hi," Hatchert said as she pulled up a chair at their table.

" I remembered something," Laura said as her eyes sparkled. "When the guy was digging around inside his backpack, he accidentally sliced his glove open on some-thing. He swore, ripped off his glove, reached into the

134

backpack, and pulled out another one. He pulled it on like he'd done it a million times. Normally, when I wear those latex gloves, I kind of struggle because they're hard to get on."

"Do you remember anything about his hand?" Hatchert asked.

"Like what?"

"Were they hairy? Did he have long or short fingers? Was he wearing a ring?"

"I didn't notice. But, that's not the exciting part," Laura said as she practically bounced in her seat. "I remember he has a tattoo. He slung me over his shoulder and lost his balance. He was stumbling around and his pant leg got caught on a bush and I saw a tattoo!"

Hatchert leaned forward and stared into Laura's flushed face. "Where exactly was the tattoo?"

"It was on his left ankle."

"Cindy, do you remember seeing the tattoo?"

"No."

"Laura, you were hanging upside down, correct?"

"Yes."

"Was it on his left ankle or on the left ankle you saw as you were hanging there?"

Laura paused. "You're right. As I was hanging there, it was the ankle on my left. That would make it his right ankle."

" That's okay. It's easy to get mixed up. Was it on the inside of his ankle or the outside?"

"Inside."

"Can you describe the tattoo, Laura?"

Laura beamed. "It was an X-rated archer!" she said and almost clapped her hands.

"A female archer," Hatchert repeated as she drew in a breath. "This might be the break we needed."

"I know," Cindy said as she wiggled in delight.

"Take your time, Laura. Can you tell me more about her?"

"Yes," Laura's chest swelled as she began. "She had big boobs that had to be size 40 GG breasts. They looked like two giant inflated cantaloupes!"

"Wow! Those are seriously big," Cindy giggled.

"Yes, they were popping out of a skimpy, cut off t-shirt so you could see her belly button. Her nipples looked like two small mountain peaks sticking out of the material," Laura said sheepishly and blushed.

"You're doing great, Laura. Did she have anything else on besides the t-shirt?"

"She had on extremely short shorts and these really long boots that went almost up to her thighs."

Hatchert's brow furrowed as her mind began drawing a mental image of the tattoo. "Do you remember the color of the tattoo?"

"Her t-shirt and shorts were in bright red. The letter and her boots were black."

"What letter?"

"She had the letter 'B' on the center of her t-shirt which strikes me as being weird."

"What was the position of the archer?"

"She was holding the bow in one hand and she was loading an arrow with the other one."

"Do you remember the position of her arms? Was the bow down or up in a shooting position?"

"Oh my gosh! I knew something was different about her. She was using her left hand to load the arrow and her right hand to hold the bow. That means she's left-handed.

Most characters are right-handed," Laura face brightened like a kerosene lantern in the middle of a dark sky.

"Wow! That's awesome, Laura!" Cindy said as she high-fived Laura. "What does this mean, Hatchert?" she asked she almost somersaulted out of her seat.

Hatchert's grin stretched across her face and her eyes twinkled. "That makes his tattoo unique. It means we now have something that might help us find your attacker." Returning her attention to Laura, "Did she have long or short hair?"

"Really long hair that was almost to her waist."

"Do you remember the color?"

"Blond. Only not just any blond. It was a Marilyn Monroe blond. And her hair was in long waves."

"Was there a belt?"

"Not that I remember."

"How big was the entire tattoo?"

"About four inches tall, I think."

"Was there anything around her? Like bushes or something?"

"No."

Can you remember anything else?"

"I think that's it."

"Laura, I know you like anime art. Do you sketch?" Hatchert asked, happy to see some fighting spirit returning to Laura.

"Kind of," Laura answered blushingly.

"Do you think you can draw a sketch of her?"

"I just fool around sometimes. I'm not good, but I can give you a real rough sketch."

As Laura worked on the sketch, Cindy looked at Hatchert.

"Won't this make it easier to catch him?"

"I'm not sure about it being any easier, but it certainly helps. I don't want him to know that Laura saw his tattoo. Would you be willing to keep this between us for a while?"

"No problem," they both chimed in.

"I want to catch this weirdo!" Cindy snapped.

"He needs to be locked away for a long time!" Laura added with the first hint of fire behind her words and flushed cheeks.

"So do I. And, this gives us a much better chance of finding him. Good job!" Hatchert smiled.

"I have to go, or I'll be late for class," Laura said as she sprang out of her chair.

As Laura left, Cindy looked at Hatchert.

"She looks better. Maybe this will help her come out of her shell. She's really a nice person and she's been so down."

"It looks as though she not only helped me with our case, but with her self confidence," Hatchert agreed as she peered into Cindy's eyes. "Thanks for coming to me right away with this information. How are you doing?"

"It's hard, but I'm not going to let him ruin my life." she adamantly replied. I'll definitely feel better once he's in prison," she said as her eyes narrowed and a tiny muscle in her jaw tightened.

As Cindy walked away, Hatchert went out the side door and tapped Chief Girard's number into her cell phone.

"Hi, Hatchert. How are you doing after the party last night?" the Chief said with a smile remembering Hatchert's obvious discomfort.

"Hi, Chief Girard. It was a nice party," Hatchert said as she rolled her eyes.

"We have a great community. What can I do for you?"

"I spoke with Laura and Cindy a few minutes ago. Apparently, the perpetrator tore his glove and had to put on another one. Laura said he was fast, too fast. Her gut told her he wears them a lot. She also remembered that he has a tattoo."

"Did she get a good look at it?"

"Yes. It's on his inside right ankle and it's a sexy, female archer loading an arrow into a bow. The woman in the tattoo is wearing extremely short red shorts, a red mid-drift t-shirt with a black letter "B" on it, and long black boots. She also has long blond hair down to her waist. The kicker: she's left-handed."

"This might be his downfall. It's not something you see every day."

"He got careless. If we're lucky, we'll find someone who remembers the tattoo, and it would be even better if we can find the tattoo artist who did the tattoo. I'm going to hit all the tattoo parlors next. Any suggestions?"

"The tattoo parlors are in Hamilton City. We don't have any in Vista Point. I'll tell my guys about the tattoo and see if they've seen it."

"Thanks, Chief."

"Good luck, Hatchert."

As she hung up the phone, Hatchert stared out the window. Meade was back on the list. She headed to the elevator and punched the eighth floor button.

First things first, Hatchert thought, as she put her head down on the desk. The coolness of the metal felt good on her forehead. The jackhammer was slowing down and the nausea settling. She pulled a protein bar out of her pocket and nibbled on it as she clicked on Matthew Walton's bio. Why would a guy leave a successful therapy practice and his entire family to move halfway across the country and to start over again? He had no previous friends here and no girlfriend.

"Let's see what I can find on you, Walton," Hatchert muttered as she entered his name in a search engine.

"There you are," and clicked on the link, "Matthew Walton, Kansas City, marriage and family counselor." According to the information on his website, he established his practice twelve years ago in Kansas City at 1537 Redwing Court and was still listed on the active list at the Kansas City Chamber of Commerce.

"Looks like you weren't a good boy in high school, Matthew," as she read the list of misdemeanors for disorderly conduct, public drunkenness, and driving while under the influence in the Kansas City police database. "Your habits didn't change much either," she pondered, as she read about his probation during his college years for drunken disorderliness and inappropriate behavior at a frat party. It took him three times to pass the test for his marriage and family license.

Hatchert turned off her computer and headed to the security office.

"I have an appointment with Sergeant Jones," Hatchert said to the security officer who also acted as an administrative assistant to Jones.

"Hi, Ms. Hatchert. Come this way," Sergeant Jones motioned her to come through the door and into his office. Officer Davis was sitting in one of the two visitor chairs that faced the sergeant's desk and rose when Hatchert entered the room.

"I asked to meet with you today because I need your help. I'm Special Agent Mary Hatchert with CID and I've been assigned to investigate the recent sexual assaults on two of our soldiers. I'm working closely with Chief Girard,

140

the Vista Point police chief, since it looks like the Vista Point attacker and our perp are one in the same man."

"Girard's a good man, ma'am. I've worked with him before on some cases that involved our personnel and civilians," Sergeant Jones nodded in agreement.

Officer Davis smiled knowing she was right about Hatchert.

"We don't have much to go on. All three assaults occurred on the Vista Point trail. Apparently, our perp likes to hike or run, and he's extremely familiar with this trail. The first victim was Laura Brock. She's one of ours and lives in the same barrack as our second victim, Cindy Cunningham. I'm staying in the barrack with them until we catch him. I hope I can draw him out. The last victim is Josie Green. She's a civilian who lives in Vista Point."

"Do we need to put a special detail to monitor the barrack, ma'am?" Sergeant Jones scowled as his brows knit together like a closing drawbridge.

"The women in the barracks know about the assaults. Word got around and they've made a pact to go in pairs everywhere. I want to draw this guy out and if he's watching our barrack, it might spook him to see a security detail. We also have to consider that it might be one of ours. We do have a major concern. Dr. Calloway believes the perpetrator will hit again within the next few days. If so, he's probably already picked out his next target or he's looking for one. Either way we have to find him and we don't have much time."

"I'll do anything to find this guy, ma'am," Officer Davis's eyes hardened and her jaws clenched as she thought about her sister.

"I'm going to ask you to pull some long duty time starting tonight."

"I've got guard duty tonight, ma'am."

"I cleared it with Colonel Delaney for both of you to be assigned to me for at least the next two weeks."

"Then, I'm in," Davis said.

"Me too," Sergeant Jones agreed.

"Good. Our two military victims said he wore camouflage pants, shirt, and a ski mask. He has a medium build with brown hair."

"Eye color?" Officer Davis queried.

"He wore reflective sunglasses, so we don't have an eye color. I have reason to believe the attacker might be someone who either works here or comes to the hospital on a regular basis. He used blue latex gloves which I believe might be the same hospital-grade quality gloves they use here at Hamilton Hospital."

"That's not much to go on, ma'am. Everyone around here has access to those gloves," Officer Davis impatiently replied as she flicked at a fly.

"You're right. It isn't much to go on. Since two of the assault victims are from the base, we're going to start here at Hamilton. The victims were drugged. But, today we might have gotten lucky. Laura Brock remembered the perp has a tattoo. Here's a copy of a sketch of the tattoo," Hatchert said as she handed them a copy of Laura's sketch.

"That's a crazy-looking tattoo," Officer Davis said as she studied the sketch.

"Yes. And that's good for us. Which brings me to your assignments. She saw this tattoo on the perp's inside right ankle. I would like both of you to start going through the surveillance tapes to see if you can find anyone with this tattoo. I would also like you to go through the personnel database and see if there's any record of a tattoo that meets this description."

"We never had to record a person's tattoos until this year. If he was hired before this year, we might not have that on file," Sergeant Jones said as he rubbed the back of his neck.

"I know it's a long shot, but I'm hoping we'll get lucky. Can you sort your database by gender and date of employment?"

"Yes, ma'am," Sergeant Jones nodded.

"I suggest starting with the personnel who were hired within the last six months. How many personnel are in your database?"

"Approximately 1,871 personnel records in the active file. If he's no longer working here, I'll have to go through the archives. There are thousands in the archives."

"Do you keep a database on the volunteers that work here?"

"No. We check them in and out whenever they come."

"Could you look for Matthew Walton in the volunteer list and Mark Roberts in the active file? Walton's a volunteer here so I would like a file with the dates and times he was here."

"Sure. That's no problem, ma'am."

"If you find anything, Sergeant Jones, let me know. Here's my cell phone number. We don't have much time."

"Yes, Ma'am."

"Officer Davis. We need to look through the surveillance tapes for the past nine weeks to see if we can spot the tattoo. It's a wild shot, but we could get lucky."

"It's going to take some time to go back through the last nine weeks of video," Davis sighed as she realized it was going to be like finding the ring she lost under the bleachers at the 49er football game last season—nearly impossible.

"I know, but it's all we've got right now. If you do find him, don't try to apprehend him, or let him know in any way that we're onto him. We have to do this by the book so he goes to jail for a long time. Do you have any questions?"

"No," they both replied in unison.

"Great," Call me anytime day or night," Hatchert said and then headed outside to place a call on her cell phone to Edward Boyd, the civilian at the Department of Justice in charge of finding a DNA match from Josie Green's rape examination.

"Hi, Ed. It's Hatchert. How's your family?"

"They're fine. Jordan's a freshman at MIT and Riley's on a swim scholarship at Stanford."

"They sure grow up fast."

"Yes. We're now empty nesters. What's up?"

"Are there any matches for the Josie Green case?"

"Nothing yet. I've run it through the federal data base and now I'm running it through the states."

"Could you run Matthew Walton, Sam Meade, and Mark Roberts? Something isn't adding up about them."

"Sure. That's no problem."

"Thanks, Ed. I'll send you their personals."

Sliding into the driver's seat, she clicked on an Internet search engine on her cell phone. Let's check out the local tattoo shops, she thought, as she typed in "tattoo shop" and "Hamilton City" in the search line.

There were five tattoo shops in Hamilton City. That's a lot of tattoo parlors, Hatchert whistled as she sighed and leaned her head back for a second against the headrest noticing the jackhammer had been silent for the past ten minutes. Soldiers like tattoos of their girls, tanks, and battalion emblems she grumbled as she turned on her car and aimed it toward the highway. "Let's see what we can

144

shake loose," Hatchert smiled at her weak joke as she headed toward Shakey's Tattoo Parlor.

Who in the heck would name a tattoo parlor, Shakey, Hatchert chuckled as she merged into traffic.

Shakey's Tattoo Parlor sat on the edge of Hamilton City. As Hatchert drove by several buildings, she noticed they were covered in graffiti and gang symbols. Most had broken windows, peeling paint, and some listed so far to the side that it looked as though they would topple like dominos with one slight push.

Shakey's Tattoo Parlor sat in the middle of one of these blocks. Hatchert pulled up to the front curb and parked. Five teenagers were leaning against the charcoal-gray building smoking cigarettes. The apparent leader wore baggy blue jeans, a black t-shirt with the words, "Fuck a Bitch Today," and silver chains that hung almost to his navel. The rest of the gang looked like miniature versions of him except for the largest one, whose t-shirt was stretched to its limit across his wide expansive chest and barely skirted the top of his belly button.

She gave them a nod as the leader stepped in front of her and quite blatantly swept his gaze up and down each part of her anatomy.

"Whatcha doing in this part of town, hoe? You lost? We can help you find a home," the leader chided as he sauntered toward her.

"Thanks. What's your name?" Hatchert asked as the golden flecks in her eyes turned to steel and locked onto his dark brown ones.

"Wants a name," he snorted and gave his homies a quick glance giving them permission to surround her.

As they began to shift, Hatchert moved into position and kept her eyes fixed on the leader.

She noted that the skin below the cut-off t-shirt was painted with a field of multi-colored tattoos. Rows of silver studs pierced his eyebrow, another three on his lower lip, and the last six along his right earlobe ending with a large black plug. As he cockily leaned toward her to show her who was boss, the other young men grinned through matching studs.

"I'm looking for a dude with a hot female archer tattoo. Any of you seen him?" Hatchert asked as she focused her energy on "Pinky," a name she baptized the leader because he had a tattoo of barbed wire around his left pinky finger.

"What's in it for us? Maybe a becky?" he smiled and flicked his silver studded tongue at her.

"Not interested dude," Hatchert said as she raised herself up and tensed her muscles in an effort to make her appear taller while she flashed her military badge at the same time.

"No harm," the ringleader said as he stepped back and signaled his henchmen to back off. He gave her a nod as she kept her eyes on him while she walked toward the shop entrance.

A sickly ring sounded from a tinny, bent bell that hung on the door announcing her presence as she stepped through the splintered doorframe. A gangly, pale walking skeleton-of-a-man with tiny black pupils and smoker's breath came through the black, threadbare curtains that hung across an inner doorway. He slunk up to the long counter that ran across the width of the coal-black painted room and stared at her.

"Hi, I heard you do all kinds of tattoos," Hatchert said as she watched his blood-shot eyes sweep over her.

"Yup," he replied as he chewed the tobacco stuffed into his bottom lip and then spit out tarry stream into a plastic bucket barely missing Hatchert's blouse.

Without moving one thread of her blouse, Hatchert's dark eyes fired the first shot, "Have you done a tattoo of a female woman shooting a bow and arrow?"

"Sure. Lots of 'em. Cost you two hundred bucks," he sassed back laughing at the cop as he wiped his snotty nose on his shirt.

"When was the last time the health inspector was here?" she calmly asked.

"I'm clean," he said nervously as he bit his lip and fumbled with an unlit cigarette.

"Sure you don't remember doing a tattoo of a woman shooting a bow and arrow?" as her eyes pierced his once again.

"Nope," he said as he looked nervously around her.

"Have you been in Hamilton a long time?"

"I've been here two years," he said as his eyes narrowed into crow's slits.

"Looks like it's about time I had lunch with my buddy at the county health department," Hatchert chided knowing that she'd hit a dead end, at least for now. And she smiled as she watched him shake like an electric toothbrush before she turned and left. At least I know why they call him Shakey, she said to herself and chuckled.

She passed by the boys and nodded, did a fast sweep around her car, and then settled into the driver's seat.

"Hi, Chief Girard. It's Hatchert. I just checked out Shakey's Tattoo Parlor. Could you put someone on surveillance at the shop? I think Shakey knows something."

"Sure. I've got just the officer for the job."

"Thanks," she said and hung up.

147

After two more stops she ticked off Tattoo Mania and Ink Lives! from her list. As she pulled into the shopping mall parking lot where American Tattoo Parlor was located, she noticed the names of some of the stores: Gucci, Prada, and Armani. Nice mall, she noted as she searched for a parking space.

"Hi. I saw your shop while I was driving by. Have you been here long?" she asked a tall, medium built man with graying hair, a slight paunch belly, and dark green eyes.

"I started my tattoo business forty-five years ago and I moved to this spot nine years ago. What can I help you with?" Jarrad asked as he watched the sharp young woman move self-confidently toward him.

"I saw a tattoo of a female archer. I was wondering if you did it?" Hatchert asked as she noted he was probably in his 60s.

"Nope, and I haven't seen one around here," Jarrad answered truthfully.

"Do you know if any of the other tattoo artists might specialize in comic or anime art?"

"Rocky might have done it," he said as his brows furrowed in thought. "He does more comic characters and anime stuff than I do. I'm more into biker and military tats."

"Thanks, I'll go check him out," Hatchert said as she headed toward the door.

"It wouldn't do any good to go today. He's out-of-town this week attending his niece's wedding. Said he'd be back in the shop on Saturday."

"Thanks for the information," Hatchert smiled knowing he pegged her for a cop.

"You bet, anytime," Jarrad smiled in return. He always liked to stay on the right side of the law in this stage of his life; and his sharp eyes followed her as she walked to her Miata, and then drove away.

The sun felt good on her neck. It was time to check out the Vista Point trail and headed toward the coast. She glanced at the clock, 2:00—plenty of time to run the trail before the writing group.

The two-lane highway that was moving level with the ocean now began a slight upward ascent as it scaled the base of the first mountain range. The road that had been fairly straight became a black winding ribbon that was laid carefully in cuts that had been carved out of the steep mountains. On one side, the road's edge was only a few feet from the 100-foot cliffs that dropped into the deep blues and greens of the Pacific Ocean, and on the other side, the golden browns and muted greens of the rugged mountains shot up vertically into the sky. At one point, Hatchert could see miles down the rocky coastline offering some of the most spectacular views that she'd ever seen. She watched a flock of gulls circling over the ocean, and then one by one dive through the air headfirst into the mosaic blue waters below.

A highway sign indicated the Vista Point trail was a quarter mile farther down the highway. She turned right into a small parking lot that sat on a cliff overlooking the ocean. Pulling into an empty space, she noted there were only two other cars in the lot—a 1968 Chevy pickup and a 2010 Toyota Corolla. Not too busy on a Wednesday afternoon, she thought as she grabbed her running clothes off the passenger seat to change in the public restroom. She went through her normal warm-up routine of stretches and jumping in place while she watched an older couple hold hands as they sat on a large rock and had their picture taken against the Venetian blue sky.

The start of the trail was across the highway. Moving at a slow jog, she followed the trail across a meadow that sat at the base of the mountain. Three deer grazing in the meadow looked up briefly and then went back to grazing again. The trail started to climb as she ran past a grove of tall pine trees. She felt her heart and lungs adjusting to the steepness as she used more energy to make the ascent. The trail could easily fit two runners side-by-side she observed.

The trail wove upward around brownish-gray boulders, through 50-foot dark green pine trees, and a few California poppies that were dotted here and there between the golden native grasses that added a splash of tropical orange to the mostly brown, gold, and green palette.

She had run almost six miles upward when she reached the part of the trail that dropped suddenly downward weaving in and out among a small stand of pine trees. Hatchert stopped as her hawk-like eyes focused on the location where Cindy probably met her assailant and imagined what might have happened that day. She began to jog again spotting a few deer trails that cut across the main trail and were tucked between layers of brush. Within minutes, the trail began to climb steeply upward again.

She continued on at a fairly steady pace until she cleared the summit and dropped steeply downward where a large boulder sat in her path. Once again she slowed to a walk. Josie was right when she said you couldn't see around the boulder. Hatchert prepared herself as she cautiously rounded the massive rock. When she made the turn she saw that it was a perfect place for a rapist to taser a victim. The boulder blocked the runner's view and the large trunked pine trees that grew along the path were a perfect hiding place. *Smart man,* she whistled as she began to imagine the trail through the rapist's eyes.

Fairly soon, she reached the spot where there was no dirt trail: it was carved rock right out of the mountainside. This must be where Laura met the rapist, Hatchert thought. No wonder Laura didn't fight. There was no room to defend without a lot of risk of falling over the cliff's edge. She moved cautiously once again as she walked along the edge.

Returning to the natural dirt trail, Hatchert looked out toward the ocean and noticed the various blues and greens of the ocean currents that reminded her of the swirls of coffee foam across a coffee latte. And as the sun began to dip downward in the sky, she knew it was time to get off the mountain. Increasing her pace, she flew down the side of the mountain. As she neared the meadow, she slowed her pace to begin her cool down. Crossing the highway to the parking lot, she grabbed her clothes out of her car and changed. By the time she was done, Hatchert felt the natural buzz from the run.

As she aimed her Miata toward the church where the writer's group met, a stomachache and headache slammed into her. *Of all things, why did Josie have to be a writer?* Hatchert grimaced as she shifted into third. She hated writing as long as she could remember. Learning the alphabet was torture for her when she was in kindergarten. She got the letters mixed up as she fought to read in first grade. By second grade she was diagnosed with a learning disorder, but by then it was too late. She'd had too many embarrassing moments when the teacher asked her to read out loud and she could only stutter and stumble.

Some kids were merciless, like Bethany Roberts, Hatchert thought in disgust. She was relentless in calling Hatchert names like stupid, dumb, and retarded. Acting tough and like it didn't matter, Hatchert learned it was easier to stay alone than to risk ridicule from the other kids.

Heck, they moved so often it didn't really matter anyway. At least, that's what she told herself as a kid.

And now, look at her. She was headed to a writing group and her palms became so sweaty she had to wipe them one at a time on her jeans. They'd better not ask her to read out loud, Hatchert thought grumpily as she shrunk down in her seat. She drew a solid black line in the sand on that point, and sat bolt upright with newfound courage. *No touchy, feely poetry stuff either!* she yelled to the wind feeling more courageous. If there was any of that she was just going to sit there, she thought smugly.

As she came down a long, sloping hill covered in pine trees, she saw the road sign that pointed toward downtown Vista Point. Turning left at a signal light, Hatchert headed down a small hill that was lined with cottages. Some had steep pitched roofs and tiny windows. Others were made of rock. Still others were little wood cottages that had planter boxes filled with hanging plants and flowers draped under the windows. At the bottom, she saw the street was lined with small shops. It was a quaint town and very picturesque. The buildings were a small eclectic mix of dwarf-like dwellings, Scandinavian designed buildings, and more eclectic cottages, some with thatched roofs and others with quarried stone.

Large six-foot-wide natural rock planter boxes acted as a center divide for the main street. Each giant planter box held large, dark-green, evergreen Cypress trees that were arranged in a straight line down the middle and whose branches spread like a large canopy over the width of the main street. Beneath the old Cypress trees were rosemary bushes with short spiny leaves, lavender whose blooms were already gone, snowy white alyssum that blanketed the base of the trees, and various shades of green hanging plants spilling over the side.

It was a short main street—about five blocks in all. The shops were a mixture of boutique clothing stores, coffee shops, restaurants, jewelry stores, and real estate offices. Tourists from all over the world flocked to this tiny town to shop in the high-end stores and eat at 5-star restaurants as well as to enjoy the white sandy beach and spectacular views of the ocean that was at the end of the main street.

As she stopped at the stop sign, she smiled at a little girl who was begging her dad to buy her an ice cream cone. At Mission Street, she turned left and saw the white church steeple up ahead. Pulling into the parking lot she looked at the church. It was a classic, small, white-painted church with double doors that lead into the sanctuary. A four-foot diameter round, stained glass window of a flying dove was centered over the doors. A one-story building stretched from the main church building to the property line that held the seven Sunday school classrooms. The writing group met in Classroom 3, one of the middle classrooms.

Hatchert was headed toward an empty parking space when MISS RAV4 flew in and edged her out of it. "You've got some nerve," Hatchert almost yelled, but as she stared at the church, she swallowed back the words. She watched Josie's pair of long legs extend out of the car with a sleek trim body to follow. Josie reached in and grabbed her bulging, electric blue briefcase and her hot pink purse. Her strawberry blond hair was pulled back into a ponytail today, Hatchert noted, not in the trendy hairstyle she'd seen last night at the gala. Josie's 501 jeans hugged each curve and her long-sleeve, pale-green shirt with the tails hanging out had a navy blue, long-sleeve sweater pulled over the top. Her 3-inch tall, red heels completed the outfit.

"She obviously thinks she owns the place," Hatchert grumbled as she drove around the full parking lot and realized she would have to look for a parking space on the street. Two blocks later, she finally found a place to park. Grabbing her notebook and pen, Hatchert stomped back to the church with her nostrils flaring and her mouth clenched wanting to kick a certain someone's ass.

As she walked by each classroom, she noticed the 8" X 11" paper signs that were taped to the doors. One sign had "AA" in big bold letters along with the time and days that the Alcoholics Anonymous meetings were held. The next door had a similar sign for the Narcotics Anonymous group, or NA, and the last door had a sign that said, "Sex and Love Addicts Anonymous group," or SLAA. Apparently, this church believed in community involvement, Hatchert thought as she found the sign for the writing group.

Josie was surprised to see Hatchert walk through her classroom door. Her long, auburn, damp hair was lying in loose curls below her shoulders. But it was those icy, deepset eyes that shot her a freezing blast when their eyes met. They were intelligent eyes—eyes she could drown in when they were thawed, Josie mused.

As she assessed Hatchert, Josie noticed how her skinny blue jeans showed every muscle and curve. The long-sleeve black sweatshirt hung seductively over her hips. Her eyebrows made beautiful arches over those dangerous eyes, and those lips beckoned to be eaten. Everything about Hatchert exuded confidence, except for the twitch of a tiny muscle in her clenched jaw.

154

"Well, well," Josie thought. "Wonder why you're here Hatchert? It's going to be fun to find out what's behind all that frozen ice."

Hatchert was angry. Stealing parking spaces wasn't kosher in her book. "If that's how she wants to play the game, then game on!" Hatchert sneered as she took a seat in the back of the room. Just as she was settling in, little Miss RAV4 started to move the desks.

Apparently, Miss RAV4 wanted everyone to sit in a cozy little circle, Hatchert sneered silently. David and Matthew immediately jumped in to help. Matthew pulled his desk so close to Josie's it was almost indecent.

It didn't show in her body, but those eyes could deep-freeze an ice cube, Josie thought as she watched Hatchert out of the corner of her eye. Wait until she hears about the assignment for tonight, Josie smiled like a Cheshire cat as she pushed the last desk into position.

Walton, in his cotton khaki pants, long sleeve white shirt with the rolled up sleeves, and the green sweater that was slung across his shoulders with the sleeves tied across the front and his slip-on tan moccasins, made an obvious pass at Josie as he sidled up close to her.

Any closer and he might as well settle into her for the night, Hatchert thought as she gritted teeth so hard they made a slight scrunching sound. Maybe he already has, Hatchert speculated, and imagined a slow and merciful death by poison. "What's wrong with me," Hatchert's brain spun as she forced herself to sit at attention and take several deep breaths.

Walton leaned toward Josie putting his pec muscles in her face. He's a piece of work all right, Hatchert thought as she clenched and unclenched her right fist. Look at her. She didn't even flinch! That's not right! Hatchert's baffled mind continued as she fought to control her thoughts.

Josie smiled inwardly. Let's see how she does with the assignment tonight, as she ignored Walton's advances. Two can play the game of cat and mouse. Soon, the other students arrived and everyone was seated.

"It looks as though we might have another writer in our midst. Her name is Mary Hatchert." Turning to Mary, Josie continued. "This is a weekly writing group, Mary. Each week we have a short lesson, then a writing period, followed by a feedback session. To make Mary feel at home, let's go around the group and each of you can share your name and genre. Stacy, why don't you begin," Josie grinned.

It didn't go unnoticed by Hatchert that Walton moved his foot close to Josie's.

As Walton introduced himself, he looked like a bee that had found the sweetest nectar in the land. He was buzzing around and leaning toward Josie so close that her golden curls were gently moving in the breeze he created. Hatchert wanted to throttle him.

After the other introductions were given, it was Hatchert's turn.

"I'm Hatchert, not Mary," she snarled at Miss RAV4. "This is my first writing group. I travel a lot and thought it might be interesting to add some travel pieces on my personal blog."

"Great. It's nice to have you in our group," Josie said with a smug smile. "Tonight we're going to talk about emotions. One of the greatest gifts a writer can give to their reader is to move them emotionally through words. We can lift them up, scare them, or make them laugh. We can use words to entice, to argue, to cajole, to make believe. Our words can change a person's perceptions. I want each of you to write a short piece that will move your partner emotionally in some way. You'll have an hour. We'll break up into groups of two so grab someone and begin. I'm going to partner with Hatchert since she's new," Josie smiled so sweetly that sugar crystals formed in the air.

The shuffling of desks broke the silence and suddenly, Hatchert was facing Miss RAV4 desk-to-desk. When their eyes met, Hatchert's dark-eyes narrowed as she tensed her body like a lioness ready to strike. Slowing her breathing, Hatchert stalked her prey. She tracked every muscle and eye movement down to the number of blinks sitting perfectly still as she waited for Miss RAV4's next move.

Josie noticed Hatchert's sweaty palms and a face that looked like she was ready to take down a water buffalo rather than write.

Isn't this interesting, " Josie mused as she leaned back in her chair letting her arms fall comfortably to her sides. She would have offered to help, but in Hatchert's current mood, she didn't think Hatchert would accept it. Looks like it's going to take some time to chip the ice out of those dark eyes, Josie pondered. She liked certain types of puzzles, and Josie knew that Hatchert was going to prove to be one very interesting puzzle.

Josie picked up her pen and soon was bent over her paper lost in words and story. Hatchert sat bolt upright and didn't touch pen to paper. As the clock ticked down she watched Josie's eyebrows shift up and down as she wrote. Briefly stopping to think, Josie absentmindedly put the end of her pen in her mouth as she struggled to find the right words. Slowly, Hatchert leaned back in her chair and crossed her legs when she saw that Josie wasn't going to force her to write. Josie looked up, smiled at Hatchert, and continued to work as several minutes ticked by.

"Time's up. During the next twenty minutes, I would like you to read your piece to your partner. Then, I want each of you to write about the feelings that came up for you while your partner was reading their piece. In this way, you'll have immediate feedback on how your audience felt as they heard your work. Also, include what you would like to have heard that would enhance the piece, and what worked for you. Above all, have fun," Josie finished with a twinkle.

Josie turned to Hatchert.

"I noticed you had trouble writing tonight. I want to assure you that it's a common problem and nothing to worry about. Sometimes when we're told we have to write, our mind goes blank. That's why we have the writing group, so we can become comfortable with writing. I'll read my piece and then you can tell me what emotions were evoked. Sound fair?" Josie said too sweetly.

"That sounds good to me," Hatchert grunted as her gut warned her to watch out for the next move.

"The candles flickered softly in the rose-scented room as the logs crackled happily in the fireplace. Lilly's golden curls lightly caressed Sophia's flushed cheeks as she leaned over Sophia and looked into eyes that sparkled like a mixture of emeralds and dewy grass on a fresh spring day. As Sophia's heart melted and her dreamy dark-chocolate eyes gazed up at Lilly, Lilly took her finger that was as soft as a kitten's paw and slowly traced the curve of Sophia's dimpled cheek to Lily's lush, pink lips below. With a slight tremble, Sophia pressed her body to Lilly's sending a shower of sparks between them. Using a feather's touch, Lilly's finger lightly circled Sophia's bottom lip, and when

158

Sophia took Lilly's finger seductively into her mouth and sucked, Lilly touched her forehead to Sophia's forehead and moaned.

"I love you," Lilly murmured into Sophia's ear as she nibbled on it and cupped Sophia's breast softly, and smiled as she heard Sophia purr in delight.

"I love you, too," Sophia uttered as she stretched and basked in the river of fire that was spreading from her breasts throughout her body.

Lilly moved down Sophia's neck tasting as she went, nuzzling and kissing as she felt the beat of Sophia's heart quicken. When she reached the virgin valley between Sophia's breasts, she gently moved to circle each nipple with her tongue, and her eyes softened as she heard Sophia's breath catch, and then release. Gently now, she tasted and sucked until she felt a shudder pass through Sophia as she teased the soft peaks into hardness.

As the heat began to swirl, Lilly let her fingers search once again until they found the moist treasure that welcomed her inside. Softly, Lilly circled and stroked as the tempest began to rise. Moaning and writhing from a lover's touch, Sophia arched upward as her body screamed to be taken. Sophia gripped Lilly's hips with her hands as she felt the soft strokes of pleasure building inside of her. Each stroke brought Sophia higher as her body bucked and rose in a blinding rhythm that sought its soul mate. Lilly began to match Sophia's beat-for-beat sending them both higher and higher in a tangled mass of curls and fiery flesh. As Lilly drove her tongue into the Sophia's pool of paradise, she sucked and licked, kissed and drank sending both of them writhing and twisting toward the heavens. Exhausted, both collapsed into each other's arms and fell into a lover's sleep."

Josie had to stifle a giggle as she saw Hatchert's jaw drop open.

"Miss RAV4 is going to be a HUGE problem," Hatchert's scattered brain surmised silently as she sat there in total shock and disbelief.

"Well, Hatchert. Would you like to share the feelings you experienced while I was reading my piece?" Josie teased as she cocked her head and waited.

"No!" Hatchert snapped as she crossed her arms in front of her chest.

"Well, it's your first night and all," Josie mischievously countered.

"I think the time's up," was all Hatchert could squawk back.

"Oh my goodness. I think you're right," Josie said as she rose from her chair to address the class.

"I hope this exercise was fruitful for you. Please hand in your work. Hatchert, it's customary for me to collect the pieces so I can provide written feedback. For those who would like some extra help, I offer individual sessions at a fee where I can discuss the work in detail. Great group tonight. Next week, we'll continue to learn the various ways to express emotion through words. I hope you have a nice evening and I'll see you next week," Josie smiled and began to chat with each student.

"What was she thinking?!" Hatchert almost barked as she bolted out of the classroom door.

"Good night, Hatchert. Hope you'll be joining us again next week," Josie yelled after her as she watched Hatchert sprint to her car.

Jumping into her car, Hatchert shifted so fast she almost stripped the gears of her Miata. She aimed her car toward the beach trail that began at the foot of Main Street.

Screeching into an empty parking space, Hatchert scrambled out of her car and dove onto the trail.

As her body fell into a natural rhythm of running, Hatchert began to fume while her brain rattled off questions at the speed of an automatic rifle.

How could the Colonel even THINK about giving me this assignment? Okay, so I've never come out to him, but he should have known—RIGHT? He's head of CID in the Southwest. He's a smart man. He should have figured this out? Did he know about his niece? Holy Shit! Maybe he didn't know. Hatchert stopped dead in her tracks.

Wonder if her parents know? Does anybody know? Can you beat that? I never told my parents either, so I guess we might have something in common, Hatchert reflected as she took off running again.

She knew if she told her father, he would probably scream and yell that HIS daughter was not gay. He would order her to stand down and be a "man" and to follow his orders, she thought as she ran up a small dune and down the other side.

Her mother would cry and tell her to do what her father says so he wouldn't slam his fists through walls, smash lamps into the floor, or hit Hatchert sending her flying across the room.

She threw up quietly by the side of the trail. Her head pounded along with her heart. It always did when she let her guard down. Taking a few deep breaths and staring out across the ocean, Hatchert calmed herself. She didn't live there anymore and she would never go back. Sometimes, the only way to love someone was from a distance.

The drive back to the barracks was quiet. The stars were out and so was the full moon. This case was full of firsts and Hatchert wasn't sure she liked any of them.

CHAPTER 6

Thursday, 2 October 14
The Second Writing Group

The next morning as Hatchert was waiting in the espresso line, she noticed Dr. Calloway sitting at a table at the far end of the cafeteria.

"Double espresso, please," Hatchert said as she watched Cindy sit down next to Calloway and debated whether to join in their conversation.

"Thanks," Hatchert said as she took her cup of coffee and deposited the extra change in the tip jar. With her mind made up, Hatchert strode across the cafeteria.

"Hi Dr. Calloway. Hi Cindy. Mind if I join you?" Hatchert said as she noticed Cindy's tense smile.

"Is that okay with you Cindy," Dr. Calloway asked as she watched Cindy shift in her seat.

"Sure," Cindy replied as she continued to fidget and her face blushed pink. "I was going to call you next. You were in the shower and I wanted to pick Dr. Calloway's brain before I bothered you."

"Don't worry, Cindy. It's important for you to share at your own speed and time," Hatchert reassured her as she watched Cindy's left jaw muscle relax and her bright red cheeks slowly fade to a soft rose.

"Thanks for understanding," Cindy said gratefully.

"I was sharing with Dr. Calloway that I remembered the bottle he used to force the orange juice down me was different. The bottle had a screw cap with a plastic tube coming out the middle of the cap which is kind of weird."

162

"Do you think you could draw it for me?" Hatchert asked as she slid her notebook and pen toward Cindy.

The sketch was simple and all that Hatchert needed.

"Thanks, Cindy," Hatchert said as she took the paper and studied the picture.

"I hate to change the subject, but Laura and I were talking last night and we want to meet Josie," Cindy said as she looked at the two women who had become an important part of her life.

"What made you change your mind?" Dr. Calloway asked as she studied Cindy nervously twisting a curl of her blond hair around her finger.

"Laura and I have each other and it's really helped. Josie might not have anybody. It's kind of a sisterhood of sorts, which sounds really weird, but when you go through something like this, it's nice to have other women to talk to who understand. Especially since it's by the same creep. We both get out of class at 2:00 today. Could we do it after that?"

"I don't see any reason why not and a whole lot of reasons why this is a great idea. I'll call her and see if she has time to stop by today to visit," Dr. Calloway said enthusiastically as Cindy grabbed her pack and stood up.

"Okay. I'll see you later. Bye, Hatchert."

"Bye, Cindy. I'll see you tonight."

"That's good news, Dr. Calloway," Hatchert said as she returned her focus to the woman who was sitting opposite her.

"Yes, it is," Dr. Calloway replied as she nodded her head in agreement.

"Dr. Calloway, the attacker hasn't struck again and it's been ten days. Do you think he's stopped?"

"Sadly, no. He's attacked three women in a short amount of time. Something might have thrown him off his routine which means he might be more dangerous than before," she said calmly as she watched Hatchert's lips curl down and her forehead wrinkle in thought.

"Whatever the reason, I'm glad because it's giving me more time to find him." Hatchert said as she thought about Walton and Roberts.

"You know, the bottle Cindy drew looks like the bottles we carry in the pharmacy. We use them to hold various liquids like acetone, deionized water, and ethanol."

"He must have knowledge of pharmaceutical supplies which means we are probably on the right trail that he's connected in some way to Hamilton," Hatchert responded.

Dr. Calloway nodded in agreement. "Would you like to join me for dinner tonight?"

"Maybe another night. I've got Josie's writing group again tonight,"

"I'll hold you to it," Dr. Calloway said as she smiled at Hatchert's receding figure.

Dr. Calloway remained seated and looked out the window. Rape was ugly. The new statistics she'd read this morning on the Internet showed that approximately every 2 minutes in the United States someone is raped and the rape is typically committed by a relative, a friend, or an acquaintance of the victim. What makes it even worse is that 98% of the rapists will never spend one day in jail.

She sighed as she took another sip of coffee and wondered when the culture would change. When will fathers stop telling their sons they aren't men until they've had a woman? When will women stop glorifying those same young men as studs? Someday it has to change, she reflected as she sipped the last remnants of her lukewarm coffee from her cup.

"Are you busy, Dr. Calloway?" Laura asked pensively as she looked at Dr. Calloway's taut lips and tense jaw.

"Not at all," Dr. Calloway replied as she shuffled in her chair and focused on Laura's sagging shoulders and puffy eyes. "Pull up a chair. How are your panic attacks?" she asked compassionately.

"Lousy. I'm trying to keep them under control, but I can't. One minute I'm fine, and the next I'm breaking out into a sweat, my stomach feels like it's caught in the jaws of a bench vise, and I'm gasping for air."

"Sometimes, it's better to lose control and let the emotions come out. Would you like to come to my office tomorrow and we can work on it?"

"I guess so. They aren't getting any better," Laura said resignedly.

"Would 3:00 p.m. work for you?"

"Yes."

"Done," Dr. Calloway smiled. "I heard you wanted to meet Josie?" she asked as her brows lifted quizzically.

Laura shrugged. "We talked about it and it just feels like the right thing to do. She's all by herself and we have each other."

"It sounds like a great plan. Cindy's coming around 2:00 today. Can you come at the same time?"

"Sure."

"I think it will help all of you," Dr. Calloway smiled as she noticed that Laura was beginning to trust Cindy and her.

"Bye, Dr. Calloway," Laura said as she scooted away again.

As Dr. Calloway punched in the number for Josie Green, she marveled at the instinctual bond that women seem to have to take care of one another in a time of crisis.

"Hi. I'm Dr. Calloway. Is this Josie Green?"

"Yes."

"I work as a psychiatrist at Hamilton Hospital. I'm sorry to hear about your recent experience. I'm working with the two women soldiers who are also his victims. How are you doing?"

"I'm frustrated and angry. He shouldn't be walking the streets."

"I understand your anger, Josie," Dr. Calloway said calmly. "The women would like to meet you. Would you be open to meeting in my office?"

"That would be great! When?"

"Would today around 2:15 work for you?"

"Yes. Where?"

"My office at Hamilton Hospital. Let them know at the gate you're coming to visit me and they'll open it for you. You can park in the east parking lot in the visitor's section. Sign in at the security office and they'll call to let me know you've arrived. I'm looking forward to meeting you," Dr. Calloway said sincerely.

"Me too. See you at 2:15," Josie replied.

After Josie hung up the phone with Dr. Calloway, she sat in her car and stared at the ocean. A sea gull was chasing a fellow seagull that had a small fish in its mouth. A black cormorant with its wings spread out across the cloudless sky was gliding over the top of the water. Life seemed to go on without noticing that her life had changed so dramatically only a few days ago.

As she leaned back against the driver's seat, the attack played over in her mind. She felt totally helpless. A slow roll of terror hit as her heart raced like an Indy car and her stomach twisted itself into a square knot. Pushing on her stomach trying to work the knot free, she felt hot, angry tears roll down her cheeks. The shame sat like a bank of fog engulfing her. Her logical mind knew it wasn't her fault, but her heart only felt what it felt: shame.

"Damn you!" she yelled as she slammed her fist into the steering wheel. "You're not going to win! Do you hear me! YOU ARE NOT GOING TO WIN!" she screamed at the top of her lungs and then sat there as the next shower of tears flooded her shirt.

Through wet, glistening eyes, she looked at a little girl with long, straight black hair, blue jeans, a pink sweatshirt, and electric blue flip-flops exploring one of the tide pools that edged the surf. She watched as the girl bent down and picked up a piece of kelp that was floating nearby. The girl took the long, rope-like kelp and wiggled it along the sand forming sand waves behind her.

She felt the child's innocence and with a sacredness of kindred sprits, Josie gritted her teeth and swore the oath once again. "I'm stronger now than I've ever been. Your plan backfired. I will never rest until you're behind bars."

And she looked at the little girl and felt the unseen bond between them. "I'm going to make it safer for you little one, so you can play." With one last look at the little girl in her pink sweatshirt and electric blue flip-flops, Josie felt her resolve return. Her eyes turned to pools of blue steel as she headed her car toward home.

"Hi Chief." Hatchert said as she answered the call on her cell phone.

"I received one of the lab results from the Josie Green case. When Sheila Evans did Josie's examination, she noticed a stain on her pants. The lab analyzed it and it's from a generic brand of mouthwash called Mint and Fresh that can only be bought at Fast Mart stores."

"I'll look into it Chief and let you know what I find," Hatchert said as she headed toward the security office.

"I'll do the same," the Chief replied.

"Bye, Chief," Hatchert said as she rode the elevator. She pictured Walton bending over Josie and her tiger eyes narrowed into slits.

As the elevator doors opened, she saw Sergeant Jones talking with Officer Davis.

"Any news yet?" Hatchert almost snapped.

"I've run four weeks of tape and haven't found anything, ma'am. It could be anyone at this point," Officer Davis replied as she watched the laser sharp eyes flash.

"I've got two men who registered their tattoos, ma'am," Sergeant Jones said as he studied her.

"Is it our tattoo?" Hatchert asked tersely.

"No, ma'am. They aren't the one we've been looking for, but if a man's got one tattoo there's a higher chance he might have another one," he said calmly knowing that the woman in front of him was angry hot as a red coal in a barbecue pit.

"What have you got?" Hatchert asked as she reined in her anger.

"Jim Peterson was hired five months ago. According to his file, he has a rattlesnake tattoo winding around his right wrist. He works in janitorial service and is out on sick leave. The other man, Harry Lawrence, was hired seven and a half months ago. He served in Afghanistan and has a tattoo of a devil on his back along with his battalion

168

mascot. He works in supply, but apparently he got hurt lifting a box one and one half weeks ago and is out on workman's comp for the next two weeks. Until they return, I won't be able to check them out."

"Thanks. Do you have anything on Walton or Roberts?" she asked as her jaws clenched tight.

"Hold on, ma'am. Let me grab my notes," Sergeant Jones said as walked to his desk and back again. "Walton comes almost every Saturday to volunteer in the pediatric oncology unit. Since June, he only missed August 23rd and September 20st. Mark Roberts is out on medical leave and won't be returning to work for two more weeks. He's been out three times in the last two months on medical leave. Our files show that he doesn't have a tattoo, and when we ran a security check on him two years ago, he was clean. When he returns to work, I'll be able to check him out."

Walton was absent on the day Cindy was attacked, Hatchert noted as her eyes narrowed and the fire that had begun a slow burn within her was stoked higher. Forcing herself to focus and breathe, Hatchert replaced anger with the extreme composure and confidence of a hunter.

"Are you finished running the databases?" she asked outwardly calm as her mind continued to gather the mental notes on Walton into a subject list.

"No. I still have the civilian database to run. I should have something for you soon."

"Good. I'll check back with both of you on Saturday," Hatchert said and then headed to her car as Jones and Davis looked at her retreating figure and nodded to each other recognizing the burn that sometimes drives you on a case.

She dialed the Chief once again. "Hi Chief. It's Hatchert."

"Any new information?" the Chief asked as he sat up

in his chair.

"Yes. Matthew Walton wasn't at the hospital on the Saturday Cindy was raped. Do you happen to know anyone in Kansas City? It's a long shot, but something tells me he left Kansas City for a reason. I ran him and he's had several DUIs. Seems to be a pattern from college."

"I have an old police force buddy from my LAPD days. She moved to Kansas City to be closer to her grandchildren. I'll give her a call and see if she can find out something for us."

"Thank you, Chief. Could you put a tail on Walton?"

"Yes. I know just the officer for the job," he said as he pictured Detective Sarah Collins, one of his top officers. "How are the writing groups going?" the Chief politely teased with a huge grin on his face.

"They're fine. Gotta go," Hatchert replied as a smile slipped across her face. She knew she was now an accepted member of the "force" when the Chief teased her about Josie.

Hatchert did a quick Internet search and found three Fast Marts in Hamilton City and one in Vista Point. She punched in a request for a warrant and then headed toward the Fast Mart in Hamilton City that was closest to the base. As she entered the store she could smell the odd blending of coffee, chicken wings, pepperoni pizza, and popcorn. She spotted a woman in the candy section who was haggling with a young boy over the size and type of candy bar that would be appropriate as a reward for scooping up dog poop in her backyard. A thirty-year old something man was pulling out a case of Miller beer from the large refrigerator that spanned the length of the back of the store.

"Hi, are you the manager here?" Hatchert asked as she approached a man with "JOE" written on his nametag.

170

"Yes, I'm the manager," Joe French replied with a jovial smile. "Can I help you?"

"I'm with CID, army intelligence. I understand you can run your cash register receipts on any particular product showing the date and time of purchase along with the credit card number. Is this correct?"

"Yes. That's correct."

"I'm working on a case and I need to know who bought Fast and Mint mouthwash within the last two and a half months. How fast can you do the search?"

"It might take me the rest of the day. Do you have a warrant?" Joe asked as he began to estimate the complexity and length of the task.

"Yes, I do," Hatchert replied as she showed him the warrant on her cell phone.

"I'll have to have a copy for my files," Joe replied.

"No problem. I'll email them to you. This is top priority. Can you email the list to me?" Hatchert asked as she gave him her email address.

"I'll get started on this right away," he said as he entered the information in the office computer.

"Thanks," Hatchert said as she nodded goodbye.

It took her most of the day to drive to all four Fast Marts.

"You slipped perp and I'm going to find you," she contemplated as she settled stiffly into the driver's seat. Too much driving today and not enough coffee, she winced as her head started its daily drum practice.

As she drove along the ocean she slowed to watch a seal playing in the surf. Some gulls were dive-bombing a man who was throwing pieces of bread into the sky for them to snack on. The air was filled with the high-pitched shrill of the gulls as they made their presence and territory known to each other. An elderly couple was walking hand-in-hand along the shoreline. A little 3-year old, tow-headed blond boy was looking into a tide pool mesmerized by what he saw. His parents were watching carefully at a safe distance, giving their youngster a bit of space to explore. A few surfers were sitting on their boards waiting for that one perfect wave before they called it quits for the day.

Finding a parking space in front of a clothing boutique, she decided to walk along Vista Point's main street. She recognized the Prada, Gucci, Dior, and Gaultier clothes that were showcased in the window displays. People were scurrying across the street to greet friends or family members, while others were giggling, holding hands, and kissing. She spotted women who were dragging their husbands behind them as if they were on a mission to hit every shop in town before the end of the day. People for the most part were happy, except for those few who searched for a meandering wife, or husband, who had mindlessly wandered into one of the delightful little shops that were tucked here and there down short alleyways.

She stopped at one of the local coffee shops. Home-made pastries were displayed in a clear rounded cabinet. There was a loaf of bread shaped and decorated like a crocodile. There were cakes made with layers of white cake, red strawberry filling, and white frosting, and individual cakes intricately decorated with mini-flowers, butterflies, sea stars, or crabs. When it was her turn, she treated herself to a mocha latte with three shots of espresso.

She was hungry and spotted a quaint outdoor patio where they served fresh abalone all day. As she waited for her dinner, she thought about Matthew Walton and punched in a number on her cell phone.

"Hi, Ed. Don't mean to bug you, but have you found out anything yet?"

"I'm glad you called. Meade checked out clean. No priors. Roberts lived in South Dakota before coming here. He had two DUIs that were expunged from his record in exchange for community service. Apparently, he also roughed up his ex one time. She refused to press charges, so they let him go. Other than being late with a couple of his support checks for his daughter, he's stayed clean the last two years. Walton had a series of DUIs and has been charged three times with disorderly conduct. No jail time. He managed to convince the judges in each case to assign him to community service instead of time. So far, he's stayed clean at Vista Point."

"Thanks, Ed."

"No problem."

Something still stuck in her craw around Walton, she puzzled. She saw him in action last night and he seemed to be a player. As she savored each bite of abalone, she watched a woman in jeans and a sweatshirt and her little terrier dog walk by. The terrier had on matching blue jeans and sweatshirt and Hatchert couldn't help, but smile. What next? And just as that thought swirled away, she was dumbfounded as she watched a Russian Wolfhound on the end of a leash with a collar that was surrounded by diamonds and an owner who wore an exact replica of the diamond-studded dog collar around her neck.

Howling with delight, Hatchert paid her bill and headed toward the writing group. As she walked into the church parking lot, her abalone-filled stomach went into motion like a washing machine on the fast spin cycle. Maybe it wasn't such a good idea to fill her stomach with abalone just before class, she thought as she felt it begin to spin out of control. She took in deep gulps of fresh sea air as she fought the nausea.

Josie arrived early. She saw one of the men from the AA group placing the various 12-step brochures on the table just inside their classroom door. A large coffee pot was brewing away on a table inside the room.

"Would you like a cup of coffee to take with you?" he smiled as he offered her a cup.

"Thanks. That sounds good," she replied as she took the paper cup filled with coffee out of his hand. "How long has AA been meeting here?"

"About twenty years, give or take a year. I've been in this one for twelve years," the man with gentle blue eyes that spoke of heartache and calm.

"Thanks again. It hits the spot," Josie said as she gifted him with one of her high-wattage smiles before she headed to her classroom.

As she walked by the SLAA group meeting room, she saw more pamphlets and literature on tables along with a huge bowl of popcorn that smelled heavenly. Grabbing a handful, she leaned against the wall and nibbled between sips. Looking out across the parking lot, she watched a man with a stubble of gray whiskers, sagging shoulders, and worn blue jeans walking toward the AA door. A young woman in her twenties was busy sending a text on her cell phone as she tripped merrily toward the same door.

After she popped the last kernel of white, salty fluff into her mouth, she opened her classroom door and stood. She never thought she would be leading a writing group. She always pictured herself in far away places drinking in the culture and letting the adventure flow from her heart onto the paper.

Yet, somehow, she knew, this was where she was supposed to be right now. Call it fate or whatever, but even the rape was somehow all a part of the overall scheme of things, she reflected. Her meeting with Laura and Cindy went well. She loved Cindy's blissfully happy spirit and Laura's quiet demeanor. It's funny how people can be the exact opposite and form tight bonds, she thought. They immediately felt like sisters to her and were coming by her house next week for dinner and a chick flick.

Josie chuckled as she remembered Hatchert wiggling and twisting like a first grader on her first day in class last night. And those eyes. They were furious and intriguing, dangerous and exciting, she giggled as her stomach did a one and a half somersault.

She only knew about her feelings for women a little over a year ago. There had always been a feeling inside of her as she dated boys that something wasn't quite right. It never occurred to her she was a lesbian until she met Gina, a girl with Irish red hair and cat green eyes who stood 5'9" tall. She was wearing blue jeans and a brown plaid shirt that fateful day. Gina sat next to her in psych 102 class and had no problems with shyness.

Josie was surprised by her own over-the-top reaction to such a simple question, "Would you like to go to coffee with me?"

"Are you kidding me? You're asking me on a date with you?" Josie spat out and then stomped down the steps leaving Gina bewildered at the top of them.

But, as she walked the five blocks it took for her to reach her car, a new awakening began to rattle loose inside of her. It started as a twitch. And then it grew into an earth-shattering rumble. She slipped into a psychological cocoon where the real Josie began to form. In the beginning, there were days of terror, sadness, confusion, loneliness, and rejection. But, gradually, the pain left and curiosity took its place. Sadness turned into joy, confusion into wonder, and loneliness into expectation. Rejection became acceptance. It took her six months before the dawn broke and she came out of her cocoon. Upon emerging, she sluggishly unfolded her fresh, wet wings into a whole new world.

She began looking at women. She looked at a woman's body through new eyes. Fear, excitement, and nervousness spread as she allowed herself to imagine what it might be like to be with the exotic woman named Petra who sat two seats in front of her in Renaissance literature class. She looked at Petra's mass of black curls that went in all directions and imagined how it would feel to wrap one of those curls around her finger in seductive play. Or, how she would pull Petra's head closer to hers bringing those pert sweetheart lips closer until they touched. And imagined how those lips would feel as she nipped them, kissed them, and tasted them. And, while she was imagining, she felt her body respond in a new and exciting way that had her squirming in her seat.

And, how many times did she imagine how the athletic body of Sasha in her philosophy class would feel to her touch with all those tight muscles that rippled in every nook and cranny of Sasha's body. And, how she wanted to take the purple, V-neck sweater Sasha wore and fling it up and over those pert breasts tossing it onto the classroom floor and then put her on the large expanse of the teacher's desk.

Josie leaned against the classroom wall. Yes, Josie had imagined and dreamed, play-acted and wondered about how it would feel to make love to a woman. Would she be able to satisfy a lover? Would she have enough courage to do those things she imagined to a real woman? She wasn't brave enough to risk actually DOING IT—so she wrote. There was no heart risk or ego lost in writing. And certainly, no one knew the poems she wrote were for a woman and not a man, she sighed.

Hatchert watched her from the door. She looked at Josie and saw her changing moods from fear to dreamy contemplation.

Josie looked up and jumped when she saw Hatchert. Her cheeks felt hot as she scrambled for the front desk and began digging through her briefcase.

Hatchert turned and stomped down to the far end of the parking lot and back. Not good, Hatchert lectured to herself as she purposefully slammed her foot down on the ground. Not good to get involved with a victim or the Colonel's niece, she fumed as she abruptly turned and marched back down the parking lot in the other direction.

As if I didn't have enough things on my plate, she spat silently to the absent Colonel as she stomped from the parking lot down the street. She was supposed to figure out a way to tail Josie without Josie noticing.

"That plan was shot to Hell," her brain screamed. Josie would know when she was within a mile of her at this rate.

"Damn it all," Hatchert swore under her breath as she swatted at an overhanging tree limb. "I've had plenty of women and I don't need HER!" she blindly thought as she tripped over a six-inch succulent that had spread itself across a part of the sidewalk.

"Damn," she yelled out loud as she almost did a nosedive into the asphalt. " She's trouble!" Hatchert stomped over to a rock and kicked it. "Oh Hell!" she exclaimed and stomped back toward the room.

Meanwhile, Josie watched Hatchert's stomping and cussing as she stood in the doorway. As her eyes narrowed, she challenged, "Bring it on, Hatchert. Let's see what you're made of," and with that she turned and began to push the desks into a nice, cozy circle.

"Hi. I'm surprised to see you tonight, Hatchert," Josie smiled cattily and blinked her huge aquamarine eyes at Hatchert's stony face.

"I decided I needed the practice," Hatchert shot back glaring at her.

"Practice at what, I wonder?" Josie replied with a mischievous grin.

Slamming her notebook and pen down onto the desk, Hatchert sat and turned toward Sam. "I'm Hatchert. How are you tonight?"

"Great! I'm looking forward to tonight. Last week we did a piece on persuasion. Tonight it's on romance," he announced and then slunk down in his seat as Hatchert leveled the iciest dark cat eyes in his direction.

"Sounds just great!" Hatchert almost shouted as she glared at Miss RAV4 and wondered if she were going insane since she'd never felt this way before.

"Hi everyone. I had the pleasure of meeting Mary Hatchert at my writing group last night. It seems she can't get enough," Josie said so sweetly the sugary words hung like thick honey in the air. "Why don't we go around the room and introduce ourselves."

With the introductions over, Josie tilted her head and smiled at Hatchert.

"We'll break up into pairs. I'll be Hatchert's partner since she's new to the group. Tonight I want you to continue the scene that I will start for you. Then, share what you have written with your partner, and see if you can improve on it, based on your conversation."

178

"How much time will we have," Edna with the thick glasses and baby fingers asked as usual.

"Approximately one hour. Here's the start: Under the pale moonlight two shadows moved across the fresh-cut lawn."

"Does anyone need help before we get started?" Josie asked as she looked around her group. "Good. Let's begin."

"Well, Hatchert. Are you going to write or sit there?" Josie challenged as she sat like an arm wrestler ready to begin the fight.

"I don't know yet," Hatchert haughtily replied as she leaned back and folded her arms across her chest.

"Suit yourself. But, I don't know why you're coming to a writing group if you don't want to write?" Josie asked pointedly as her eyes narrowed.

"I didn't know it was going to be a touchy feely group. I came here to write travel features, not romance novels," Hatchert spat back.

"I guess you should have checked us out before you joined," Josie smugly replied as hot blood rather than honey began to fill the air.

With that Hatchert sat there and glared.

"All right. It's time to write," Josie said defiantly as she leaned forward revealing two plump breasts that were right in Hatchert's face.

"You've got to be kidding me!" Hatchert hissed as she picked up her notebook and slammed it down on the desk.

"Suit yourself. I'm going to write," and with that Josie picked up her pen and started writing. Lifting her head slightly, "It's going to be fun to see your reactions to this piece," she meowed like a cat that licked its first vanilla ice cream cone. And with that, Josie focused on her writing as a devilish smile spread across her face.

The minute hand of the clock sped through time.

"Time's up. Please read your piece to your partner and provide positive feedback. When you're done, you can put your papers on my desk."

"Are you ready," Josie asked as she sat back and waited for Hatchert's response.

"You bet!" Hatchert snapped.

"You first."

"Under the pale moonlight two shadows moved across the fresh-cut lawn. They walked quietly now, in unison, as two dancers who knew each other's body as well as their own. They avoided the light beam that came from the living room window and crept gracefully toward the back of the house. Keeping to the shadows, they made their way to the low bedroom window that was by the back kitchen door.

The laughter blasting from the television set in the living room could be heard as they knelt under the double hung window and the creaking of the rocking chair where one of them sat.

Peering inside, they saw a little girl sleeping on a cot placed in the corner of the room. She was clutching a worn, stuffed horse with silver-blue wings that were slightly chewed on the edges. Her breathing was shallow, but steady.

Motioning to her partner, they gently pushed up on the lower window sash. Inch-by-inch the window slowly raised. The shadowed figure slid in and moved quietly to the child in the bed. Placing a hand over the child's mouth, she watched the big brown eyes open in alarm and terror.

"Shhhh...you're safe. We're here to take you to your mommy and daddy. We have to be quiet so we don't let the other people know we're here. Your mommy and daddy send you their love, and they said to hug Beauty tight so you won't be scared. Do you believe me?" the undercover agent said with a warm, smile.

Nodding her head, the little girl clung to Beauty and let the woman with the big, dark eyes lift her and hand her to the man outside the window. Moving fast now, they kept low and ran along the hedgerow to the waiting car. Within minutes, Beauty and Kerry were hugging her mommy and daddy."

"Wow! Where did you come up with that story?" Josie asked looking at her incredulously.

"I like to read mysteries and detective novels" Hatchert mumbled as she shuffled uneasily in her chair.

Josie leaned forward forcing Hatchert to look into her eyes. As their eyes locked, Josie reached for Hatchert's hand and held it in a lover's grasp. Hatchert's mind reeled from exposing such a personal part of herself. Reflexively she dropped Josie's hand as if it were a branding iron ready to scorch and burn. Angry now, Hatchert slammed back from her desk almost sending it crashing into the classroom wall. She stomped out the classroom door leaving a puzzled Josie sitting with an open mouth frozen in her seat.

Hatchert was furious as she slammed her car door. What right did Miss RAV4 have to play with her feelings? She threw her keys into the drink cup holder and watched them slam against the sides.

Hatchert grabbed the gearshift and slammed it into reverse. And what the Hell happened in there when she wrote about a case she worked on almost three years ago, she shook her head in confusion. She never talks about a case—never! and threw her car into first and romped on the gas petal sending rocks flying as she squealed out of the parking lot.

Puzzled, Josie watched her slam her car door and speed away. Turning back to her group, she spoke with each one encouraging and supporting their writing effort, and waved them each goodbye as they headed out the classroom door. After all was quiet, she sat and thought about Hatchert. Shaking her head, she rose and gathered her briefcase and shut the door. She absent-mindedly waved to a man in a black shirt who had brown eyes the color of a June bug as he stood in the doorway of the AA room. Raising his soda can in a partial salute, he watched and catalogued every move she made.

CHAPTER 7

Friday, 3 October 14
The First Night

The reaction she observed from Hatchert last night in her writing group surprised her—which was rare. She was well schooled in how to read people and their reactions—after all, she was the "Darling of the Valley" and Josie rolled her eyes as she remembered the title the local newspaper gave to her on her 16th birthday, and the humiliation in school the next day as she walked down the main hall to catcalls and whistles.

As Josie sucked on the pen in her mouth, she wondered why Hatchert was in her writing class. She certainly didn't want to write last night, Josie fretted. The heat that was generated between them was as hot as a burning ember. As Josie remembered the aching need that raced through her last night, she set to work. The words flowed from her mind onto the page as if they had a life of their own. When the creative flow beckoned it was better than sex, she thought as she smiled and kept writing. Well, maybe not better than sex, Josie giggled, as she wondered what it would be like to sleep with a woman.

Staring at the squirrel running across the telephone wire, restlessness stirred inside of her that she'd never felt before until she met Hatchert. Her imagination had kept her satisfied until now. The overwhelming aching need to mesh flesh to flesh with Hatchert was growing stronger each time she was with her, and pulling her pen out of her mouth she was shocked when she saw that she had almost bitten it in half.

It had never been like this before. Maybe this was what the poems meant about how it felt to find your one true love? Trite, but maybe true, she pondered. Was love this wanting, this ache, this need, or was it just a sexual attraction that had her body reacting to Hatchert?

"How do I know?" she asked the squirrel who was busy running up and down the tree. Are you THE ONE, Hatchert, or will you only be my first one? And how do I stop my heart from hurting if I fall for you and you let me go, she asked her mischievous friend as she leaned back in her chair and listened to the ocean. Is the power of love like that of the ocean—surging and ebbing, creating and destroying? I know I can handle heart love, but what about its twin, heart pain, she wondered as she drank in the scent of the pine trees and sage.

Regretting that she'd accepted Matthew's invitation for lunch at the Club, Josie picked up her laptop and walked inside, putting it on the small desk tucked happily under the bedroom window. She ran downstairs, grabbed another cup of coffee, and scooted back upstairs to take a hot shower.

As the water tumbled over her, she scrubbed her white skin until it was pink. The shampoo lather slipped down the ends of her hair onto her soft, silky new layer of pink skin and made its way along the curve of her well-toned thighs and legs until they swirled in a lazy circle around the tub and down the drain. She imagined what it would feel like to have Hatchert's fingers washing her and moaned as she could almost feel her touch.

Stepping out of the shower, Josie towel-dried her long blond hair and stared at herself in the mirror. You're not the same woman you were a few days ago, Josie said to the woman whose face softened and faintly blushed like a soft summer's pink rose petal as she thought of Hatchert.

She dried and twisted her long locks into soft curls that wound their way down past her shoulders. She applied a hint of blue eye shadow to pop her aquamarine eyes and added a soft carnation pink lip-gloss to highlight her full mouth. Looking in the mirror, she liked what she saw—a girl-next-door look rather than a sexy urbanite.

She walked into her closet and slipped on her favorite blue jeans with the horizontal slits along their length and a soft blue t-shirt. She slid on a pair of white tennis shoes, a 1"-gold bangle for her right wrist and a large, round white watch on the other. She opened the sweater drawer and removed an electric green V-neck sweater and gracefully arranged it across her shoulders tying the sleeves in front of her. Grabbing her car keys off the dresser and her Gucci purse and briefcase, she grabbed her empty cup and deposited it in the dishwasher on her way out the door.

As she backed out of the driveway, she thought about Matthew. She knew he wanted her. He wasn't exactly quiet about it. This wasn't the first, nor would it be the last man, who wanted her. She'd gotten pretty good about letting them down over the years, but unfortunately, some didn't handle the rejection very well and her instincts told her that he was going to be one of them.

It was a beautiful day at the Club. The sun was out and a light fall breeze was shuffling the orange and red leaves on the ornamental pear trees that were dotted here and there. Josie walked across the white marble floor that greeted its guests at the monstrous, solid-oak double doors that were open to entice its club members inside. Her tennis shoes sunk into the rich, plush, green carpet that led its guests to the dining area.

She waved high to Dorothy, the staff manager, who nodded as she stood in her Dartmouth green uniform and starched white long sleeve shirt to welcome their guests. Other junior staff personnel looking like miniature versions of Dorothy in various sizes and shapes, stood discreetly behind potted palms as they carefully watched for any sign that one of its Club members might need assistance. Rich oak wood trophy cases were strategically placed to showcase the winners of the golf tournament and offered a subtle challenge to others to take up the gauntlet.

"Hi Josie. How are you parents?" Mr. Clifton greeted her from behind the reception desk.

"They're busy as usual and happy," Josie smiled as she continued along the wide hallway.

"Please say hello to them," he nodded.

"I will Mr. Clifton," Josie said as she shot another smile at him and continued toward the restaurant.

"Good afternoon, Ms. Green," the maître d' greeted her. "May I help you?"

"Thank you, Sara. I'm here for lunch with Matthew Walton."

"Right this way," Sara said as she escorted her to his table.

"Thank you, Sara." Josie said as she turned toward Matthew.

He was waiting for her. He knew she would come. After all, he usually got what he wanted when it came to women. It wasn't always this way he snickered silently. In high school the girls ignored him—especially Judy Angstrom. He loved her, wanted her, but she made fun of him in front of his classmates, and his eyes narrowed at the memory. He took her down a notch or two that night at a house party, he sneered as he grasped the wine glass and sipped. She was so drunk she didn't even remember what he'd done; but he remembered, and smiled as his groin began to throb. She protested, but he knew how to handle her and held his wine glass up in a victor's salute.

Majoring in psychology was brilliant if he said so himself, and he did—often. There were tricks he learned sitting in all those classes in college: subtle mind control, and then not-so-subtle control. He became an expert. They were, after all, just women. Men were superior in every way. It had been this way for centuries and he didn't see any need for that to change. Feminine rights indeed, he thought with a snicker. It's losing. They keep trying, but men will always keep women in their place. And I know how to keep women in their place, he laughed as he looked at the single red rose lying against a bed of green fern and baby's breath, wrapped in a clear plastic sleeve with a hot pink bow tied around it. He fingered the chilled bottle of champagne as it sat in its iced bucket on the table. As he looked out over the 18th hole, he smiled. His plan was working. It was only a matter of time.

Matthew sprang up and waited as Sara pulled out Josie's chair and Josie sat down.

"You look absolutely radiant," Matthew said with a cunning smile.

"Thank you, Matthew," Josie replied nonchalantly.

"Nothing, but the best for you," Matthew said reeking of charm. "Here, a rose for the rose of the Valley," he said as he presented her with the red rose that was the first step in his seduction. "May I pour you some champagne?"

"No thank you. I don't drink so early in the day, but it was sweet of you to think about it," Josie replied noting this might be harder than what she had thought.

"No problem, let's take a look at the lunch menu," Matthew hid his disgust at her denial.

"The cranberry and walnut salad looks good," Josie said while looking at Matthew's boyish face.

"Great choice," Matthew said as he snapped his fingers for the waiter. "Two cranberry and walnut salads," he ordered, dismissing the waiter without so much as a backward glance.

"Let's go over your piece," Josie said as she pulled his work from her briefcase.

"We have plenty of time for that," he said dismissing her comment as if it were a pesty gnat.

"Matthew, I agreed to lunch, but I have another appointment in one hour. We are here to discuss your writing," Josie said with more force than she was accustomed to using.

"I've planned this wonderful lunch with you. Whatever appointment you have can wait when we have such a beautiful setting to dine in," he said as he motioned to the sweeping view of the 18th hole and ocean.

"Matthew, thank you for arranging this lunch. I'm flattered with the attention, but I'm only interested in helping you with your writing."

"Ah, but that can change once you get to know me," he countered and slapped a seductive mask on his face.

"Matthew. I'm sorry, but I want to keep our relationship professional. I hope you understand."

"I understand that you're a bit nervous now, but that will settle after we get to know each other better," he replied arrogantly.

188

"No, Matthew. I don't think you're hearing me. I'm your instructor and you're my student. I think you have some writing potential and that's all I'm interested in and will ever be interested in," Josie repeated staring into his black eyes as an icy shiver ran through her.

"Relax. It's only lunch," he said changing his course of attack.

"Thank you, Matthew. Now, let's talk about your piece," she repeated as she began to point out places where the characters were well developed and showed which parts needed work.

He heard, but didn't listen. He watched her facial expressions and looked at her long, slender fingers as she pointed here and there among the pages. It would only be a matter of time. He only had a little patience, but it should be enough to change her mind. If not, well, there were other ways. It worked before and he had no concern that it wouldn't work again. All in good time, he thought, as they finished lunch and he shook her hand as they said goodbye.

She walked rapidly down the hallway and out the double doors as she gulped in huge breaths of fresh air. Shaking her hand in the air, she raced down the stairs and headed to her car.

"Hi, Mrs. Seymour. Here's a lovely rose to take home with you today," Josie said handing her the single red rose that Matthew had given her to a stooped gray haired small bit of a woman.

"Why, whatever for?" Mrs. Seymour blushed as she stared at the red rose clasped in her wrinkled hand.

"Because all beautiful women deserve a rose every once in a while," Josie smiled. "How are you doing, Mrs. Seymour?"

"I'm fine dear. It's been two months to the day that George passed away. We came to the Club on so many wonderful occasions that I wanted to come here today to celebrate all the good times we had here. Thank you for the rose, dear. I hope you have a nice day," Mrs. Seymour said as her eyes glistened because she remembered the last single red rose she received was from her husband on her eighty-first birthday.

"You're welcome. Have a good day, Mrs. Seymour."

As Josie got in her car, she thought about her next step. No one was going to stop her from living her life. No one, she stubbornly thought as her eyes narrowed and her jaw muscles tightened.

She was going to run the Vista Point trail today, just like she always did. She went home and changed into her electric blue running shorts and matching sports bra. Jumping into her RAV4 she headed toward the trail. She pulled into the parking lot and was surprised to see Hatchert running across the meadow at the start of the trail.

What a twist of luck, she thought. She was going to catch up with Hatchert and give her a run for her money and sprinted across the highway.

Hatchert glanced over her shoulder and couldn't believe what she saw. Didn't she have one ounce of sense in that blonde head of hers, Hatchert seethed. Slowing her pace, she let Josie catch up with her.

As Josie came alongside, a shockwave rolled through both of them.

"ARE YOU CRAZY?" Hatchert yelled at her. "What are you doing running this trail by yourself?"

"Look who's talking," Josie cattily replied.

"It's different. Now, go back to your car and go home," Hatchert ordered.

190

"No," Josie stubbornly replied and took off running.

"Unbelievable!" Hatchert yelled as she raced to catch her.

"No one should be running this trail alone. No one," Hatchert repeated heatedly.

"Take your own advice. It's a free country and I'm going to run it, so we can either run it together, or you can run it alone," Josie said through gritted teeth.

"OK. Let's see if you can keep up with me," Hatchert challenged as she set a faster pace.

"Game on," Josie yelled.

Hatchert wanted to throttle her where she stood. Her day had been wasted with a bunch of dead ends and she wasn't in the mood to play with this blond that sent her innards swirling. Without another word, both shifted their pace to match each other stride for stride. Within a matter of seconds, their bodies became a synchronized team, moving like a pair of angry mountain lions running side by side.

From afar, he watched them. All in good time, he thought, all in good time. He switched the radio to a talk show. He loved to hear the announcer screaming and yelling. That's man-talk. No pussy footing around, just telling it like it is about keeping a woman in her place and he settled in to wait for their return.

At the three mile point Josie felt the invisible bond that had formed between them. Few things scared Josie: she was a "take the horns by the bull" type of gal, but this sensation was so new she wasn't sure what to do with it. She could feel Hatchert's anger as she ran beside her: and her stubbornness, determination, and fear.

Hatchert looked at Miss RAV4 and didn't like the feelings she was having at the moment. She should be home doing what writers do, Hatchert thought angrily. Not running this trail by herself!

The bursts of heat kept rolling through her as she maintained the pace they'd silently set. This was the commander's niece, she chastised herself as she ran up and then down the rolling land. Damn it! I need to run this off and charged ahead of Josie.

Oh no you don't, Josie grinned as she shifted her pace and stayed right by Hatchert's side. Catch me if you can, Josie thought as she took off down a small incline.

Breasts heaving and sweat streaking down their backs, both were pushing the other's limits. No greater contest could have taken place on that mountain as the heated battle waged on; up and down through the pine trees, around boulders, and over small patches of level ground; one parried, the other countered. Heart and lungs were pushed to the max as they rounded the final curve before the rugged descent.

Looking at his watch he knew it was just about time they should be showing up at the meadow. Time to move my car where they're less likely to see it, he muttered to the radio announcer as he turned on the key and headed back towards the highway. Turning right, he drove to the next turnout and parked his car. He walked back to the parking lot and hid himself in the tall bushes that bordered the west side of the parking lot and waited.

Small rocks flew and limbs bent as they streaked down the mountain. Lungs fought for oxygen as the war played out on the descent. They fought gravity and each other.

Their senses sharpened as they drove their bodies to their maximum. Running neck and neck, they ran across the meadow and at the end of the trail they looked like two thoroughbreds racing for an invisible finish line. Only the deer and he were witnesses to the war that was being waged. Smiling, he sat and watched through the bushes as the blond and brunette fought for the lead. He liked fighters.

And when it was over, they jogged in circles with chests heaving and blood flowing, tossing their manes into the wind and looking at each other--neither a victor. And as they stood within inches of each other, Josie made the first move.

"Here," Josie yelled as she ripped the chain off her neck that had her house key dangling on it. "I live at 419 Ocean View Drive. If there's something between us, we need to find out what it is. I'm not afraid. Are you? I'll see you at 9:00 tonight unless you're too scared!" And with that, Josie climbed into her RAV4 and drove away.

"What the Hell," Hatchert yelled to the wind as she stared at the pink house key and chain dangling in the palm of her hand. Pink! Didn't she have any common sense? Hatchert fumed as she stomped over to a rock and kicked it.

She climbed into her car and threw the pink key and chain into the passenger seat and watched it bounced around until it settled to the bottom. She threw her car into gear and skittered out of the parking lot.

And he watched it all. Laughing out loud, he headed back to his car. This was going to be better than killing ground squirrels, he chuckled as he aimed his car toward Hamilton City. Soon, a new plan began to form in his mind as he took another swig of mouthwash.

It was 8:58 p.m. when Hatchert looked up and saw Josie's silhouette in her upstairs bedroom window.

You're lucky it's me, and not some thief, Hatchert thought as she paced around in circles in Miss RAV4's driveway. Someone's got to teach you a lesson and it looks like I'm elected. I didn't ask for this, Hatchert wanted to scream as she kicked a rock with her toe and heard it clank off the house wall.

She took the pink key on the end of a silver chain out of her pocket, put it in the lock, and turned. With one light push, the door swung open. The chandelier that hung in the entryway was of 17th-century cut glass with swan necked branches and crystal beads that spilled down from the branches looking like a jeweled waterfall. It was a showstopper, Hatchert thought as her sharp eyes quickly darted back and forth logging the details of her surroundings into her mind.

She recognized the painting on the left wall from an art catalogue she'd studied during one of her cases. It was Monet's "Woman in the Garden." The burst of cream and red-orange flowers in the painting worked well against the soft sage green wall color. The oak hardwood floors had wear patterns from years of foot traffic and a hint of lemon polish lingered in the air. An 18-inch bronze sculpture of a nude woman sat on a nearby Chippendale table, whose image was reflected in an oval antique mirror that hung strategically behind it.

As Hatchert walked across the large entryway, she glanced to her right through a door into the library. Each book was sitting neatly in its spot on the shelves of a dark oak bookcase that ran from floor to ceiling and circled the entire room. A matching brass and oak ladder that could be

194

moved along its rail allowed someone to reach the top bookshelf that stood about fifteen feet high.

The chairs were upholstered in different shades of blues and greens with a pop of orange that matched the flowers in the Monet painting in the entryway. Botanicals in frames were placed cleverly here and there on various shelves providing a nice break among the hundreds of books that were archived there. Most looked like they had been read, not once, but several times throughout their life, Hatchert thought as she noted many of the bindings had folds in them that could only have occurred through repeat use and wear.

Glancing to her left into the formal living room, she saw a massive marble fireplace that was the focal point of the room. It had flecks of greens and blues in the marble that tied into the color motif of the home. French wingback chairs were upholstered with rich materials of various patterns in the same hue of greens and blues as the fireplace marble. Each chair was carefully placed to beckon someone in to sit.

The grand staircase curved upward toward the second floor. As Hatchert slid her fingers along the worn handrail her body began to tighten.

She was here on business, not pleasure, she chastised herself as she kept climbing the stairs. The nerve of that woman to hand just anyone her house key! For all she knew, Hatchert could be an art thief out to steal her Monet or jewels. Or maybe, Hatchert only wanted a quick night of sex while her partner was home waiting for her. And if her partner found out about Josie's little tryst, it could land her in the morgue—just like the innocent lover Hatchert had the unfortunate job to identify on one of her last duty assignments in Chicago.

As Hatchert ascended the staircase, she began to realize how lucky it was that Miss RAV4 gave her the key rather than someone else who would take advantage of her. The Colonel told her to keep an eye on her and he was right! She needed someone to look out for her, Hatchert growled as she thought of how risky it was for Miss RAV4 to be running the trail by herself. Hatchert had seen too much in her career. As Hatchert brought her full weight onto the third step from the top, it responded with a loud "CREAK."

Josie looked nervously around her room. She loved her four-poster bed with the tall spires of dark oak. She'd walked over to the bed and fussed with the pale tea green comforter until each edge hung artistically down the side of the king-size bed. She shifted and shuffled the decorator pillows of varying sizes and shades of green and robin-egg blue until they were formed a soft mound at the head of the bed.

Two dark oak nightstands, one on each side of the bed, held candles of varying heights that were lit and flickering softly. A white desk painted with tiny flowers of various shades of pink was standing under one of two, large double-hung windows that were on the wall facing the ocean. A vase filled with fresh blush roses was sitting on one corner of the desk, adding a sweet fragrance to the air. A small fireplace stood against the wall opposite the bed, and a wood fire was snapping and popping happily as it cast off a soft glow around the room.

Josie heard the creak from the staircase and felt her heart beat faster. She turned to face toward the door and waited. "What am I doing?" she thought as she nervously fidgeted with the black silk bathrobe ties. And just as she was about to bolt, Hatchert opened the door.

Hatchert stared at Miss RAV4 standing before her in a short black negligee with a matching black silk robe spread open in the front. The long, black ties fell gracefully along Josie's thighs. Hatchert swallowed hard as she followed the deep "V" of the negligee's neckline to Miss RAV4's cleavage. As the heat of desire swept through her, so did her anger.

"You're playing with fire!" Hatchert spat out as her nostrils flared.

"I'm a big girl. I've been playing with fire for a long time," Josie volleyed back with blue sparks flying from her aquamarine eyes.

Hatchert's eyes narrowed and her teeth clenched as she moved boldly and steadily toward Josie.

"You shouldn't give your key to just anyone. It could be dangerous," Hatchert snarled as she slowly continued to walk forward.

"You aren't just anyone," Josie simmered as she stared into Hatchert's fiery cognac flecked eyes.

As Hatchert's nose came within six inches of Josie's, she stopped. Josie's heart beat wildly and her chest heaved as she fought the fire that was slowly being kindled inside of her. Retreating, Josie took one step backward and found she was pressed into the bedroom wall.

"What now?" Hatchert challenged as she put one hand on each side of Josie's body trapping her against the wall while she stared into the most gorgeous pair of crystal blue eyes she'd ever seen.

And without thinking Josie plunged her tongue into Hatchert's stunned mouth.

Fire flared as match struck tinder. The heat of the kiss scorched and burned as a firestorm was born. Buttons flew as Josie ripped Hatchert's shirt open revealing two perfectly round breasts sitting seductively in an athletic bra.

Hatchert's eyes flashed sending golden sparks flying. "You don't understand the size of the fire you've set little girl!" she sneered as she stepped back and placed both hands on her hips where they were safe.

"I think I do," Josie haughtily replied as she nipped Hatchert's lip.

With two swift flips, Hatchert had Josie's black silk robe and negligee lying in a pool on the floor. Josie shivered in surrender while Hatchert's breath caught in her throat at the sight of Miss RAV4, and her own heart beat out a warning signal.

Josie was mesmerized by the twin peaks that were straining against the gray cotton material of Hatchert's sport bra and shocked by the unleashed blinding hunger that would take an unlimited feast to fulfill.

Hatchert cupped Josie's breast in her hand and took her nipple between her thumb and forefinger and pulled. Josie's eyes went wide as a sumptuous jolt sent her reeling.

Josie stripped Hatchert's bra from her and trembled at the sight of the two olive-colored breasts standing before her.

Hatchert bent and drew one nipple inward and gently sucked, and then using the tip of her tongue lightly teased the top of Josie's nipple sending the blue-white flames skyward.

She never dreamed that a tongue could elicit the blazing heat that rose as she felt the scorching flames lick and whip inside of her and threw her head back and moaned.

Josie's creamy white neck begged to be tasted. Hatchert groaned as she felt the soft, pink roughness of Josie's nipple against her tongue and forced herself to move slower. She rained fire around Josie's breast, and with each sumptuous taste, Josie's eyes widened as she felt the scorching heat reach an almost unbearable temperature.

Fumbling, Josie fought to release the zipper that held Hatchert and yanked as she forced Hatchert's jeans down to join the silky black pool that lie at their feet. She grabbed Hatchert's white jockey underwear and swept them down over Hatchert's thighs gasping when she saw the dark curly hair that was revealed.

"Oh my," Josie moaned as her body shuddered and a flash of burning ache streaked like lightning through her.

Blind now from the burning flames, Hatchert flung Josie into the mountain of pillows on the bed. For one brief moment, Josie wondered if she would be any good, but another wave of white hot sparks flew as Hatchert nipped and suckled Josie's other nipple driving the fire out of control throwing them both into the depths of a rising inferno.

Hatchert lost all sense of time as the out-of-control firestorm commanded. She fed on milk-white virgin breasts until the flames engulfed the innocent peaks driving them into hardness. The tempest ruled as she plundered and tasted. Relentlessly lost in the inferno, Hatchert could only ride out the firestorm.

Their bodies soon glistened as the raging inferno could not be tamed. Hatchert's tongue burned a trail of searing kisses down Josie's stomach until she found the only place where moisture grew.

Josie groaned as Hatchert's tongue drove them both into the heart of the blazing firestorm. She arched and

199

bucked as she felt the scorching flames sweep over her body. Believing she couldn't reach any higher, Josie screamed to be taken, and her eyes widened in disbelief as her body twisted and strained to meet an even greater tempest that Hatchert created with her tongue.

White-hot flames spiraled higher and higher as the raging inferno filled the room. Licking and sucking, sipping, then tasting, Josie screamed and jerked as both she and Hatchert rode the winds of the firestorm, whipping and dragging both of them into the inferno's belly.

Exhausted and spent, Hatchert swept Josie into her arms and held her. Josie nuzzled in and lay there quietly, taking in the aftermath of the storm. As Josie looked into Hatchert's eyes, she saw flecks in each that looked like golden bits of fire radiating out from the center. Hatchert fell into the blue pools of Josie's eyes and lightly circled a strand of Josie's blond hair around her finger. Both slipped into exhausted sleep entwined around each other until deep into the night.

Josie stirred. She explored Hatchert's nipples with a feather's touch of her finger. Gently she circled one and then the other watching Hatchert's nipples respond to her touch. Empowered by her success, Josie became bold and slid her body over Hatchert's as she let her tongue follow where her fingers had been. She took a nipple in her mouth and gently caressed it with her tongue intrigued by the feeling of warm molasses that spread through her own body and the soft, slightly rough texture of Hatchert's nipple. Experimenting, she placed her breasts against Hatchert's and gently rocked back and forth allowing the slow simmer to boil.

Hatchert silently allowed Josie to explore and taste, feeling the heat rising between them again, only this time, it was like the gentle flame of a candle's light. Josie nipped and teased and began kissing her way downward.

She was nervous wondering how it would feel, wondering if she would be any good. She tasted with each kiss letting the heat and her own desire guide her. When she reached Hatchert's downy softness, she swept her lips back and forth, tickling her nose, and then buried herself in the dark curls. And with an angel's touch, she found the moist garden of desire and knew what it felt like to fly through the clouds on the wings of paradise. And when she was done, Hatchert softly embraced her once again and both fell into a deep lover's sleep.

CHAPTER 8

Saturday, 4 October 14
The Longest Day

Hatchert woke first and found her arm resting on Josie's thigh as she lay with her full nakedness against Josie's soft creamy skin. She watched the soft upward and downward motion of Josie's chest and looked at the one errant blond curl that was lying gently across her cheek. Quietly, she slipped out of bed, gathered her clothes, and crept downstairs. She dressed under the chandelier in the entryway, turned the front doorknob, and soundlessly shut the door behind her. Just before she climbed into her car, she paused, and looked up at Josie's bedroom window. Her stomach twisted so tight she thought it would twist in half.

"Fuck! She's the Colonel's niece," she thought and had just enough control remaining to gently close her car door and creep toward the highway.

Turning south onto Highway 1, she slammed down the clutch pedal, yanked the stick shift as she shoved it through its gears, and smashed down on the accelerator petal. "How could I have done this?" she yelled as her car slunk down the highway.

"I knew better, damn it! This is why I never, I mean never, get involved!" she screamed to the wind.

But, she had, and she couldn't take it back.

"She was a fucking virgin!" she yelled at the top of her lungs, feeling like the used bubble gum stuck under the playground bench because even after she knew she didn't stop.

202

And as she struggled for air, she stomped on the accelerator pedal sending the back tires into a spin leaving one year's worth of rubber on the pavement.

The threat of the steep 100-foot bluffs only inches away from the highway edge was what she needed right now as she flew around the first curve sending pea gravel flying.

The adrenaline pulsed through her. She rammed the accelerator pedal down forcing her car to heel over as she went around a turn. She could feel the tires slide as she stretched them to their maximum. The wind whipped at her face. She could feel the car buck and holler as it fought to stay on the road.

"This job sucks!" she shrieked as she let three years of emotions of the grueling and sickening work blast out of her.

Fury took over. Her tires squealed as she took the next curve. Through her narrowed eyes she focused on the road crushing the brakes one minute and slamming down the accelerator pedal the next. Rocks were flung against the cliff side as squirrels and birds scattered away as her Miata fought to stay on the road. One curve and then another disappeared into a thundercloud of dust.

She only saw the black asphalt and blurred white lines streak by her as she slammed and swore, swerved and yelled, until finally the only voice that could be heard was that of the screeching tires. Mile after mile Hatchert drove sending her anger spinning over the cliffs until she felt nothing at all. The crashing waves against the rocks below echoed her anger. Miles later, fuzzy eyed and numb, Hatchert pulled over into a turnout that sat on a cliff's edge facing the sea.

For a long while, she just sat, gripping the steering wheel as if it were her only friend. When she removed her hand, her fingers were cramped into the steering wheel's shape and tiny ridges from the stitched seams were imprinted into the palm of her hand. She slowly moved each finger until the tingling of a thousand steel needlepoints, overtook the numbness. As she got out of the car and started to take a step, she grabbed the door as her legs nearly buckled under her. She aimed her body toward a large, flat rock that acted as a natural barrier to the 100-foot drop to the rocks and ocean below. On wobbly legs she flopped onto the rock. Bending over, she threw up the bile that was the only thing left in her empty stomach.

Bleary-eyed she pictured Josie's beautiful, naked body beside her, and for the first time since she was a two-year old child she cried from her heart. She began to shake violently as the cold swept over her and the hot tears of pain spilled down her cheeks. It had been so long her body didn't know how to react to the rolling waves of sobbing that racked her body. But, once the flood began, there was no stopping it. The tears came from a hidden pool that grew larger over time, with all the tears that her child and adult had dared not cry until now. It was a deep, and seemingly, unending pool.

A sea gull flapped its wings and settled on an old wood post that was jammed into the ground a few feet away. The gull sat there quietly staring at her. When their eyes locked, Hatchert felt her wisdom; that of one who had learned to accept the perils and mystery of life. When Hatchert's heart calmed, the gull stretched her wings and silently floated away on the updraft of air that lived by the cliff. Hatchert watched her as she dipped and turned, dove and fished, ate and soared. With one final pass, the sea gull flew over

Hatchert and then headed south as Hatchert watched her until she became a pin dot in the sky and then disappeared.

"What am I going to do now?" she wondered and was surprised when more tears fell. They rained down softly on Hatchert's cheek as her heart slowly opened and the ache of love slowly spilled outward from its center. Sweet, almost painfully sweet, the foreign warmth spread in a sultry wave of grace throughout her body. It was beautiful, yet frightening, knowing that her heart was now unfettered and vulnerable to pain.

Hatchert was a lot of things, but she was never a coward. She stood up and leaned over the cliff's edge letting the updraft dry her tears. As she watched and listened to the surf pound below, she knew what she had to do. Resolutely now, Hatchert climbed in her car and headed back to Josie's.

As Josie slowly awakened, she basked dreamily in the afterglow her body felt after a night of wild hunger and passion. It was magic, and for the first time she knew what it felt like to love.

It was never this way with Jimmie, the boy she took to the prom and then to bed.

"Let me touch you," Jimmie said with calculated eagerness as he moved toward her breasts.

"Sure, Jimmie," she replied as she prayed she would feel something.

He stroked her nipple through the shiny blue satin of her prom dress and she waited—waited to feel anything. And as she let him unzip her dress and slide it to the floor, she waited once again. And when her bra followed, she fervently hoped her feelings would change. And when he kissed and caressed, pinched and pulled with his thick thumb and forefinger, she felt nothing.

"It's okay. Don't be nervous, "Jimmie said gently as he tucked his hand under her panty band and slid his hand down to the fuzzy softness below. And she stared into his light brown eyes and wondered—when? When would she feel that something that all the girls so candidly talked about at school. And she waited once again and watched as Jimmie became hard.

Soon her panty joined her prom dress. She watched him stand and pull off his bowtie and unbutton the tuxedo buttons one by one exposing a few strands of dark curly chest hairs. She didn't want to touch them or twirl them around her fingers. She felt panic as he unzipped his pants and slid them off letting them join the growing pile of clothes on the dingy motel floor. His white jockey underwear with the faint gray letters along the waistband soon joined the pile. And she stared at his maleness, waiting to feel anything except the gnawing dread that was sweeping over her.

"You're beautiful, Josie," Jimmie said with passion in his voice as he caressed and kissed her curly mass of blond in her magic triangle of softness. And as much as Jimmie tried, she didn't respond. Not a twitch, not a tweak, not a speck, not a spark: nothing. Except dread, to get it over with so she could get dressed and leave.

And the next day she joined in her girlfriends' chatter about how great prom night was for each of them. Those who already tasted the sweet weren't as giggly as the rest. For those who dined for the first time, the giggles and awe, and the feelings of adulthood that swept in, passed Josie by. She only felt emptiness and confusion, isolation and desolation. She pretended she loved it, she giggled and laughed, but deep inside she wondered what was wrong with her.

After last night, she knew and purred. She knew what her high school girlfriends were talking about when they said how wonderful it was to shoot into the heavens riding the waves of passion and desire. A woman's warmth flooded over her as she smiled sleepily to herself. She'd come home.

She stretched and rolled over, her body seeking her lover's, and recoiled from the icy cold sheets that only hours before had burned blistering hot from the firestorm that branded love into her heart. Her mind couldn't take it in. Hatchert was gone. The ice sword pierced her heart, and for a moment, there was no feeling, only numbness, and then the searing pain tore through her sending shattered rivers of ice everywhere. She couldn't stop the shards of pain as they ripped through her.

She was a fool, she sobbed as tears spilled over and flooded her pillow. She knew it was a risk. She thought she could handle it; after all, it worked well in her dreams. But, this was no dream.

She tried to get up, only to slide in a heap on the floor. Leaning against the bed, she dragged a pillow down with her and rocked back and forth. It was so ironic, she maddeningly laughed. She remembered all those times she wondered if those feelings of desire and passion were there at all? She hoped they would be there and prayed they would be there. She was overwhelmed at first, when those feelings burst through the unknown into the known last night. The feelings of heat, desire, and passion filled her with such jubilation that while Hatchert slept beside her, she found herself marveling at how she'd ever believed that these feelings never existed.

And now those feelings of love, jubilation, and desire were gone into an abyss, and what was left in its place was a searing pain and ache that engulfed her and sent her reeling. She never imagined anything like this before. She never knew her heart could feel like a shredded napkin left tossed upon a chair after a feast of plenty.

She forced herself to stand and look at the empty bed so her mind could absorb the reality. She fought to keep the love she felt only moments before to remain. But, the emptiness of the bed moved into her heart leaving a chasm so deep she couldn't feel the bottom. What was she going to do now? Now that she knows what it feels like to love a woman. How could she survive the emptiness without her?

She wrapped the sheets around her and walked across the room in an effort to warm her heart. But, the crushing heart wound could not be bandaged. Instead of love, there was pain. Instead of warmth, there was ice. Instead of joy, there was shadow. Instead of hope, there was despair. The sobs that shook her body brought her to her knees once again. The river of ice felt endless. After a while, she slid down the bed to the floor.

And the seed of anger was planted and fed by the feelings of betrayal.

"How dare she treat me like a piece of meat!" Josie screamed as she flew off the floor and threw the double-doors open to her bedroom balcony.

"Coward! Pig!" Josie screamed to the wind again and again.

"I hate you!" she shouted and stomped back into the room and slammed the double French doors behind her.

She grabbed a pillow and slammed it again and again into the white, wrought iron headboard until she sat on the bed with her chest heaving. The fire was back only this was a different fire than the one that burned so brightly the night before. This fire coiled and whipped, snapped and cracked, hissed and spit, wanting to destroy everything in its path.

"Is this how women treat their lovers?" she screamed.

"Does it feel so incredibly blissful and luscious one minute and so destructively gut-wrenching the next?

She collapsed onto the bed, sobbing and crying into the sheets, the sheets that still had Hatchert's scent on them. And as she buried her face in them to drink in the scent, she burst into tears all over again.

Her heart was racked with pain and then anger. Waves pulsed through her at unexpected speeds as she battled to overcome the shards of emotional ice that were piercing her heart.

Spent and exhausted, she sat in a pile with the sheets pulled around her. Numbly, Josie wondered how she could have been so wrong about Hatchert. She was always a good judge of character—until now. It was no use sitting here any longer. Nothing was going to change.

"You can't come back, do you hear me?" Josie screamed at the top of her lungs as she stomped into the shower, turned on the water full blast, and stepped into the icy blast of the spray. It pounded her head. It pounded her back. It pounded her breasts. It pounded her heart and Josie burst into tears once again. It was so beautiful, and you left, she wailed as she leaned against the soft-blue tiled shower wall. And as the water droplets began to warm, she softened the spray, and let the soothing warm water cocoon her.

As she dried her long hair, she looked into the mirror and saw heartbreak staring back at her. Her eyes were drawn and tired, and the twinkle that normally lived there was replaced with despair. Her long, damp, tangled hair looked lost as it searched for a place to land.

She took the soft, green terry bathrobe and wrapped it around her. Barefoot, she walked down the stairs to the kitchen and poured a cup of coffee. She stared at the refrigerator. Even the sunlight streaming in through the large window looked lost as it bounced from place to place.

She stared at the blooming azalea tree outside the kitchen window. Funny, but until now, she never saw the spent, sickly-pale, orange blooms that were hanging by a thread, struggling to hang on. Or, the dead tree branch that moved in a ragged spear across the horizon from the old pine tree across the large expanse of yard.

She walked back upstairs. As she came into her bedroom, she looked at the candles that had burned brightly during the night were now a mass of hardened distorted blobs of wax. The fireplace that produced delicious warmth was now cold and filled with ashes.

Another searing wave of pain shot through her heart as she walked across the thick white carpet to the French doors. Opening them, she let the fresh salty scent of raging ocean waters flood into her room. The sound of the crashing waves on the rocks matched her mood. She slid her coffee and journal onto the bistro table, and sat, then looked across the landscape toward the ocean.

It didn't take long before she was bent over her journal as the pain flowed from her heart onto the blank pages. She looked up every once in a while at the gray squirrel performing gymnastic feats in the tree beside her balcony. Normally the little squirrel made her laugh, but now, her heart couldn't even muster up a sliver of a smile.

The heart pain overtook her and swept her under again and again. When she thought she had no tears left, more flowed. When she thought her heart couldn't hurt anymore, the pain exploded sending her reeling once again. Now she knew what the poets were saying when they wrote about the depths of despair and emptiness, she thought as she sniffled and watched a blue jay soar overhead.

"How could you?" Josie screamed, where only the blue jay and gray squirrel could hear her mournful cry.

"How could you make love to me and then leave me?" she wept in anguish as her heart screamed in agony.

Once again, she bent over and did the only thing that could save her heart now: like a lover, she gently fingered her pen and placed its tip to the face of the soft paper that waited patiently for her. And soon, her heart spilled onto the blank pages in front of her and she got lost in them.

As Hatchert drove back to Josie's house, she began to practice what she would say to Josie.

"I want to apologize to you, Josie. What happened last night was wrong."

Crap, that's perfect, Hatchert! Just tell her it was wrong and really make her miserable.

"This is why I don't get involved. This is exactly what I've been trained not to do!" she screamed to the wind as she cut the corner barely missing the face of the rock cliff that was only inches from the highway edge.

As her car came around another curve she pulled to the side. Barely making it out of the car in time, Hatchert threw up beside the road. Taking her water bottle out of the drink cup holder, she swirled it around in her mouth and spit.

"Stop this!" Hatchert chided herself as she climbed back into her car again.

Her palms were sweaty. It felt like a thousand jack-hammers were at work inside her head. Her eyes squinted against the sunlight as she turned her car into Josie's driveway. She looked like she'd driven through Hell. A spray of dirt coated the sides of her car from where the ocean mists and road dust met in flight. Her face matched her car. The sweat and road dust formed a thin, brownish paste that was splayed across her face except for where her sunglasses sat. There were tiny rivers of caked mud from falling tears and road dust that lay in streaks down her cheeks.

When she saw Josie on the balcony with the light shining on her blond hair, her heart shattered as she saw what she had done.

"Get it over with," Hatchert muttered to herself, trying to muster up the courage it would take to confess to Josie about what she'd done. She put her car into first and slowly crept to Josie's front door.

Josie heard her car and didn't look up. She couldn't. Anger, heart pain, and confusion ruled her now. Her spirit was ripped and torn lying in a heap on the bed along with the tangled sheets she'd thrown there earlier. But, as Josie heard Hatchert's car moving up the driveway, pride took over. She stopped her tears and took several deep breaths. She would treat Hatchert with dignity and grace because she was a Green. But, she was not allowed in her bedroom ever again.

With a plan in her mind, Josie moved rapidly. She threw on her jeans and a t-shirt and slipped through her bedroom door shutting it behind her.

Once again, Hatchert opened Josie's front door. She saw the pink key and chain lying on the table where she'd left it the night before. It seemed like a long time ago. As she tried to climb the first step, her nerves got the best of her. She had to stand for a bit to get herself under control again.

When Hatchert looked up she saw Josie coming down the stairs and almost lost her nerve. "Remember your training, damn it!" Hatchert stammered as she willed herself to stay calm.

Josie came to the bottom of the stairs and stood facing Hatchert. Steel replaced love.

"Hi Josie. I came to apologize. What happened last night shouldn't have happened. It was wrong for me to come to you. It won't happen again," Hatchert mumbled.

"So last night was a huge mistake?" Josie coldly replied as her heart shattered like a broken mirror. She'd expected an apology, or an explanation, but never, did she imagine that Hatchert would say it was all a mistake.

"Look, it won't happen again."

"You bet it won't happen again! Josie icily replied.

"You're the Colonel's niece. This shouldn't have happened. I'm trained to handle these kinds of situations and I blew it."

"What are you talking about?" Josie replied with a stone-face that hid the unbearable grief locked inside.

"I'm here on assignment. Your uncle is my boss. He sent me here to find the attacker. I work with intelligence. I'm not supposed to get involved with anyone who is involved with the case. I blew it. I'm sorry," Hatchert croaked out looking absolutely miserable.

"See that chair in there," Josie said as she pointed to one of the wing back chairs in the living room. Sit down," Josie commanded. "And, start from the beginning."

Hatchert walked like a petulant child who was getting punished for stealing from the cookie jar, Josie thought as her writer's eye observed her lover. "But, she wasn't a child and it wasn't a cookie she stole," Josie fumed to herself.

"I've been an intelligence operative for the past three years. I'm Special Agent Mary Hatchert and my missions involve catching perpetrators of sexual assaults of military personnel. Your uncle is my boss and has been since I joined the army. He assigned me to this case. Then, you end up being beautiful and I blew it!" Hatchert blurted out and ran for the front door to throw up outside.

As Josie watched Hatchert throwing up in the bed of orange poppies, the steel that protected her heart melted away.

As Hatchert returned and sat in her assigned chair, Josie folded her long legs under her as she sat on the small, cushy sofa opposite Hatchert.

"I saw you at the gas station," Josie began.

"Yes. I saw you too. That was the day I arrived. I didn't know who you were because the person who made the files for this case forgot to include a picture of you in the file."

"Go on."

"There are two other victims who are soldiers that live in the same barrack at Fort Oaks," Hatchert continued.

"The Chief told me about Cindy and Laura. At first, he didn't want me to talk with them since they're military, and he felt if the attacker was following any of us, it might tip him off that the local police and military were working together. But, I finally met them the other day. They're wonderful."

"Yes, they're great women. Chief Girard and I are working together to find this guy."

"What have you found out?" Josie's eyes narrowed.

"Look, I'm not supposed to share my information. It's against my orders," Hatchert defended as she squirmed in her seat.

You're going to tell me everything. Those are my orders! We're going to work together to find that jerk starting right now!" Josie demanded as her eyes flashed fire.

"The Colonel will kill me," Hatchert wearily replied.

"I'll shoot you now if you don't!" Josie countered as her steel blue eyes locked onto Hatchert's somber ones.

Hatchert stared at Josie, then sighed. "We know that he wore blue latex gloves and that he has a tattoo of a female archer on the inside of his right ankle. I've talked to every tattoo parlor owner in the area except for Rocky. He was on vacation and he should be in his shop today. You were the only one brave enough to go to S.A.R.T. and have a rape exam performed. Which, by the way, I think is pretty awesome," Hatchert smiled for the first time since she arrived.

"Thank you," Josie replied hesitantly as she was caught off guard. "Keep going."

"Sheila Evans, the program director of S.A.R.T. noticed a stain on your pants during the exam. The police ran it through their lab. It's Mint and Fresh, a mouthwash sold at the local Fast Marts. I have the store managers tracking down the sales of that brand of mouthwash sold in the last three months. If we're lucky, he used a credit card to buy the mouthwash. If he used cash, then we have the dates that the mouthwash was purchased. It could tie into something else later."

"Go on."

"He knows the Vista Point trail by heart and the surrounding area. He has to be in good shape and we guess he has a medium size build. Do you have any idea about his size?" Hatchert asked as she started to regain her composure.

"Sounds about right. He had trouble with me because I'm tall, and come to think of it, my body didn't fit on his shoulder."

"We also know the type of plastic bottle and tubing he used to force the orange juice down your throat. It's used in hospital lab settings. I've got a strong feeling that he has access to Hamilton Hospital. The security chief and police officer Davis are looking through the video of the surveillance cameras in case one of them accidentally filmed his tattoo. It's a long shot, but it might pay off. I really should go over there to see how they're doing," Hatchert almost pleaded as she squirmed in her chair.

Josie's heart skipped a beat as she watched Hatchert. "It's almost twelve thirty. We need to eat something. I don't know about you, but I'm starved."

"I'm pretty well empty," Hatchert replied as she thought about the number of times she'd thrown up today.

"How are you in the kitchen?" Josie's eyes twinkled as she saw Hatchert's face scrunch up.

"I'm not a cook. I do mostly take out," Hatchert sheepishly replied.

"Well, I'm a great cook. How are you with a knife?" she teased.

"That's one thing I'm good at—handling knives," Hatchert beamed.

"Okay. You chop and I'll cook. Deal?" Josie laughed.

"Deal," Hatchert happily replied.

As they ate the mushroom and spinach omelet, both looked into each other's eyes.

"I'm sorry I left you this morning," Hatchert said softly.

"Thank you."

"I needed to figure this all out. I've never had a reaction like this before."

"What type of reaction?" Josie prodded as she leaned forward in her chair and waited.

"This feeling."

"Explain it to me," Josie pushed.

"I...I mean...I feel...this is too hard to explain."

"Does it feel warm?" Josie nudged.

"Yes. But, it also feels swirly."

Josie laughed lovingly at Hatchert's attempt to explain how love felt and leaned over and kissed her lightly on the lips.

"Right now, I want to take you to bed."

"I'm not sure that's a good idea," Hatchert replied as her breakfast began to spin.

"You don't have a choice. Either you sleep with me or I'm calling my uncle to tell him you blew the case!" Josie said, not afraid to use a little emotional blackmail to get what she wanted.

Hatchert knew she was no longer in control—and for once—she was happy to follow instead of to lead.

As Josie stepped on the third stair from the top it creaked.

"Why don't you get that creak fixed?" Hatchert asked.

"It's the creaks and moans that makes this house a home," Josie lovingly replied.

As they stood in front of the bed, Josie slid off her jeans, pulled off her t-shirt, and dropped them to the floor revealing her soft naked body.

Hatchert's body shuddered as she looked at Josie's body. Glints of gold in Hatchert's eyes met Josie's twinkling aquamarine ones. Slowly, Josie slid Hatchert's shirt to the floor revealing the soft sport bra underneath. Noting Hatchert's nipples already at attention, Josie gently skimmed her finger around one nipple, and then the other, as Hatchert groaned in response. Sliding Hatchert's bra off, she let her tongue roam and glide over each peak softly, gently, circling, tasting, feasting.

Hatchert moaned as her body felt warmth spread through her. She let Josie's tongue feast. The warm molasses began to bubble and boil.

Josie slid Hatchert's jeans and black panty to the floor. Josie looked like a golden goddess as the light from the window shimmered across her naked body. Gently, Hatchert lifted her and carried her to the bed.

Hatchert fondled the blond strands of hair, twisting them around her fingers, feeling their softness. She let the curl float away and watched the wisps of blond drift through the air. She nipped Josie's ear and let her tongue play along its edges while her hand moved gently to Josie's magic triangle of softness below. Her fingers played with the blond tufts of curly hair. And then she slid her fingers into Josie's moistness, and with a feather-light touch Hatchert circled and teased as Josie moaned while the warm molasses began to turn into a molten river of burning sugar.

Hatchert licked Josie's nipple as her fingers explored and commanded. Josie arched upward and as she threw her head back she begged for Hatchert to take her. And the molten river of molasses bubbled to a boil and exploded like shooting stars across the sky while Hatchert took them both into the heavens.

As Josie purred softly, she was content to settle her head on the pillow next to Hatchert's.

As they lay in bed snuggling, Josie felt Hatchert's antsy body. She knew it was time for Hatchert to go.

"What's next?" Josie asked.

"I'm going to stop by Rocky's Tattoo Parlor on the way to Hamilton Hospital and see what he says. If we're lucky, he did the tattoo and remembers the guy. The perp's made a mistake that's going to cost him."

"What time do you think you'll be home?"

"Give me a couple of hours—probably around 8:00."

"I'll miss you," Josie said as she planted a deep kiss on Hatchert's mouth.

"Me too. But, right now I have to go," she said as she scooted off the bed.

"I'll cook dinner."

"Great!" Hatchert said as she grabbed her cell phone out of her pants that were on the floor and checked her messages. Nothing.

"If Rocky doesn't have anything, then I hope Sergeant Jones and Officer Davis have found something on the surveillance tapes. Do you know anyone that works at the hospital?"

"I know some people who work there, but only through the charity work I do. I don't go there too often at this point. But, after the S.A.R.T. unit is there, I plan to become a patient advocate."

"If you remember anything, call me. Stay off the Vista Point trail. I mean it," Hatchert commanded as she looked into Josie's contented blue eyes and Josie nodded in return. "We feel he'll attack any time and he's probably selected his next victim. I'm going to run the lab and pharmacy personnel through some of our databases and see what I find. One of the lab techs named Mark Roberts has been off work a lot lately. Josie, I didn't want to tell you earlier, but I think Matthew Walton might be involved."

Josie sat up and stared at Hatchert.

"I had lunch with him yesterday," she said angrily. "What happened?"

"Matthew made an appointment with me for extra help on his writing. We met at the Club for lunch to review his work. When I got there, he had a single red rose and champagne waiting. He didn't take the subtle hints so I had to tell him I wasn't interested. He was mad, but he covered it well. "

"Do me a favor? Stay away from him until I know more about him, okay?" Hatchert said with raised brows.

"Do you really think it's Matthew," Josie asked as she looked at Hatchert's stern face.

"I don't know," Hatchert said shaking her head as she looked into Josie's eyes. "I'm going to find out. In the meantime, what are you going to do this afternoon while I'm at work?"

"I want to help," Josie shook her head angrily dislodging a curl that fell across her cheek. "I'm tired of sitting here and waiting."

"Look, I know you're angry, but I'll do a better job if I know you're safe. Could you just stay put today until I come back?" Hatchert pleaded.

"Only if you promise to call me if I can help," Josie huffed.

"Deal. If I need your help I'll call. What are you going to do this afternoon?"

"Write. I've got some great material to work with," Josie giggled as she looked at Hatchert and planted another kiss on Hatchert's lips.

"That was nice," Hatchert replied as she placed her hand around Josie's head and gently brought her toward her as her tongue played gently in Josie's mouth.

"Whew!" Josie said as she leaned back a little and lovingly ran a finger down Hatchert's cheek.

"I don't want to leave you, Josie, but I have to find him before he hurts others," Hatchert said softly as she put her forehead to Josie's.

"I know that now," Josie said as she leaned back so her soft blue eyes could gaze into Hatchert's dark ones.

"Josie, keep the doors locked. If he's ready to rape again, he could break his pattern and go back to his previous victims."

"Don't worry. I already thought about that last night. That creep needs to be in jail where he belongs and if it's Matthew I want to look him in the eye and tell him a thing or two," Josie said angrily as her eyes flashed blue sparks.

"That tattoo's going to sink him," Hatchert said resolutely as she kissed Josie goodbye.

Josie watched Hatchert from her balcony as Hatchert looked up and waved goodbye. She watched the black Miata until it disappeared around the corner. Soon, she was writing at the little table on her balcony, and the world disappeared.

Hatchert headed to Rocky's Tattoo Parlor along the ocean boulevard. The sun was out and the air had a crispness to it that signaled fall was descending on the valley. Sea lions barked and the surf pounded as clouds marched by on their way east. Pelicans and cormorants floated on the wind currents above the jade-green and blue ocean that was dotted with white caps. People walking on the beach wore jeans and down jackets instead of t-shirts and shorts. A black retriever was busy frolicking in the surf and a young girl was holding onto the string of an orange and red box kite as it skittered and dived in an indigo blue sky.

Taking the Poppy Street exit, Hatchert drove into a large suburban community of Hamilton City known as Farmer's Park. As she drove down the tree-line streets, she saw that the homes had a coat of fresh paint, the lawns were meticulously mowed, colorful flowerbeds welcomed visitors as they lined the walkway to the front door, and waxed cars sparkled in the driveway.

She smiled as she slowed to watch a boy and a girl involved in a basketball shooting match. From the looks of it, the girl was winning and the boy wasn't too happy, she thought. She saw an elderly woman sitting in a rocker on a front porch holding a baby while a young woman was sipping tea as she rocked in a chair close by. Hanging plants bursting with oranges and reds were displayed on many of the porches. Pride showed in the community as she drove by the local playground and saw freshly painted slides, jungle gyms, and swings. The grass on the baseball field was still green, even though it was fall. Hatchert wondered how her life might have been if she had grown up in a community like this one.

Rocky's Tattoo Parlor was located in Farmer's Park Shopping Center. The store buildings were artfully constructed composed of exposed beams and natural structural supports that were cut from logs of rough pine. Each was carefully varnished to bring out the grain and knots that made each log unique. The storefronts were covered in river stone. Large planter boxes held trees and greenery. A fountain stood in the middle of the main square. Restaurants, boutiques, small stores, and four huge department stores made up the shopping center. It also boasted a movie theater. This might be a nice place to bring Josie after the case was over, Hatchert thought as she felt warmth spread through her.

But, now it was time to work, she sighed as she parked her car and searched for the mall directory. Finding Rocky's on the map, she began walking toward the shop. She smiled when she saw a young girl eating an ice cream cone with a huge chocolate moustache. Pushing open the door to Rocky's she was greeted by a small black poodle.

"Her name is Daisy," said the gray haired man from behind the counter.

"How are you, Daisy?" Hatchert asked as she petted her curly black head. "How old is she?"

"Almost ten years old. She's a store fixture. People come in to pet her and she loves it. What can I do for you?" asked Rocky as his sharp blue eyes assessed her dark intelligent ones.

"Do you do tattoos of archers?"

"I've done one or two in my day."

"Have you done any recently?"

"The last one I did was in 1996 when Justin Huish won a gold medal at the Atlanta Olympics. The girls came in and wanted him on their arm," he said as he studied the cop standing in front of him.

"Thanks. But, I'm looking for a female archer done more like anime art."

"Nope. Haven't seen that one," Rocky shook his head.

"Any ideas who might do something like that?"

"Not around here. Up in the city maybe," he guessed.

"Thanks. And Daisy, you're just about as sweet as they come, " Hatchert said as Daisy batted her eyes while Hatchert scratched under her chin.

223

Back in her car, Hatchert checked Rocky's off her list. She read a message from one of the Fast Marts. The list was done, but their computer was down. Lucky I'm close by, Hatchert thought as she headed toward the Fast Mart off Lavender Lane.

"Hi, Mr. Allen. I understand you have a list of numbers for me," Hatchert said as she shook his hand.

"Yes, it's in my office. I'm sorry I couldn't email it to you. Our computer is down."

"That's okay. I was in the neighborhood, so don't worry about it."

"There are one hundred and thirty charges, and fifty cash sales in the last three months. This mouthwash is really cheap and believe it or not, it's one of our top sellers. We can't seem to keep enough of it in stock."

"That's a lot of sales," Hatchert said as she walked into Mr. Allen's office.

"Here it is," Mr. Allen said as he handed her the list.

Hatchert looked at the rows of numbers and noted the dates and amounts were listed, but only the last four digits of the credit card numbers were shown.

"Is there a quick way to find out the names of the people who made the charges?"

"Joe, I'm sorry to interrupt, but the computer system is up and running again."

"Thanks, Kathy," Joe answered as he turned back to Hatchert. "Now that our computer system is running, I can get that for you if you like. It won't take too long, maybe thirty or forty minutes tops."

"Okay. I'll wait for it. Thanks," Hatchert replied and then stepped outside to dial the Chief.

"Hi Chief. It's Hatchert. Any news on Walton?"

"No. He's out playing golf today with three of the local

big shots, so he should be there for about another hour."

"I'm at the Lavender Lane Fast Mart waiting for the list of buyers."

"I'll let you know if my officer finds out anything about Walton."

"Thanks," Hatchert said and hung up the phone.

"Here it is," Mr. Allen said as he handed her the list.

"Thank you, Mr. Allen," Hatchert replied and headed to her car.

Quickly scanning the last names, Hatchert's shoulders dropped when neither Walton nor Roberts was listed. Aiming her car toward Hamilton, she thought about Shakey. So far, they didn't see anything out of the ordinary at his tattoo parlor. Apparently, the same gang of kids stood in the same place in the late afternoon and evening. There were one or two regulars, but none fit the description of their assailant. Her gut told her that he was involved somehow, but it looked like the connection was going to be more challenging than what she thought.

She pulled into a parking space and headed to Davis and Jones.

"Hi Officer Davis. Any luck with the surveillance tapes?"

"Nothing yet, ma'am," Officer Davis said as she sat back in her chair. "Anything else on the tattoo?"

"No. I was hoping you or Sergeant Jones got lucky," Hatchert replied as she cocked her head and glanced at the monitors.

"I spoke with Sergeant Jones a few minutes ago before he went for a quick round of the building. He's come up empty like me."

"How much footage do you have left?"

"I've got last week's footage and this week's left to do. I might have something by late tonight."

"Let's hope something's there. I'll check back with you later."

"Yes, ma'am. I'll let Sergeant Jones know you were here."

"Thanks. I'm headed up to my office for a while in case you find something."

"Yes, ma'am," Officer Davis replied as she returned to her monitor.

Hatchert leaned back in her office chair and rubbed her eyes. Picking up her cell phone she dialed Josie.

"Hi, Josie. I'm not going to make it back by 8:00. I've got a hunch I want to check out. Can I borrow your car?"

"Sure, but why do you want my car?"

"There's a fire road on the mountain by the Vista Point trail and I want to check it out. I'll swing by in a little while to pick it up."

"I'll be waiting," Josie said, delighted at the prospect of seeing Hatchert again so soon.

Hatchert paused in the driveway and looked at Josie's house. The sun was kissing the rooftop where shadows played. Hatchert watched a gray squirrel running across a telephone wire that connected the house to the pole and a blue jay darting and diving at the squirrel letting it know it wasn't happy with her being so close to her nest. The squirrel stopped and chattered angrily at the blue jay as it swooped overhead once again making Hatchert smile.

"I've got steaks and potatoes ready to go when you come home tonight," Josie almost purred as she gave

226

Hatchert a big hug at the kitchen door. "Did Rocky know anything?" Josie asked as she tilted her head and waited.

"No. He didn't do the tattoo and he doesn't remember seeing it on anyone. The first list I picked up from the Fast Mart doesn't have Robert's or Walton's names on it. I'm waiting for two other lists. Hopefully, we'll have some luck on one of those. What have you been up to since I left," Hatchert asked as she kissed Josie's neck.

"Ummm...that's sweet," Josie muttered as she melted into the kiss. "I'm working on a great piece," she smiled as she turned and gave Hatchert a long, deep kiss on the lips.

"You can read it to me when I get home," Hatchert smiled as she grabbed Josie's car key off the black marble counter.

"Bye," Josie said and smiled as she gave her one last kiss and then watched Hatchert drive away in her RAV4. She said "home," Josie murmured as she went upstairs to her balcony and sat in her chair. And with a warm, soft heart, Josie began to write.

Hatchert thought about Walton. Arrogant asshole came to mind, she growled as she thought of Josie and him together and romped on the gas. He wanted to be seen with Josie. He sure painted a romantic picture with the red rose and champagne, Hatchert scowled. But, that didn't explain Laura and Cindy, she thought as she gripped the steering wheel.

She looked at the clock and saw it was close 4:30. It didn't take long to reach the fire road that was close to the Vista Point trail parking lot. She rattled over the cattle guard and past an old wood picket fence. Dust swirled in clouds so thick that even the car felt parched and begged for water. Plants clinging to the side of the road were covered with inch thick sheets of gray particles. Hatchert's butt came off the seat and slammed down again as she popped into-and out-of a deep hole cut from rains long forgotten. Brush drier than a matchstick stuck awkwardly into the sky. A gray squirrel scrambled over the road scampering over the rocks and jumping the ruts as if it were an obstacle course. Slowly, the RAV4 climbed the mountain. As she rounded a sharp turn near the summit, she almost ran smack into the back of a black Chevy Blazer.

She looked inside the windows and saw empty gum wrappers and old towels wadded up and thrown in the corner. A dirty Raiders hat was tossed on the seat. As she turned to look in the back window, she caught a glint of something shiny under the car. Getting down on her knees, she looked at the bottle of Mint and Fresh that was lying on its side.

As she reached to slide the bottle toward her, an electric shockwave froze her in pain. A rookie mistake she acknowledged to herself as he drug her backward. He slapped a pair of handcuffs on her. Just as she felt her muscles relax, he tasered her again.

"Look at you," he grinned as she winced in pain. "I got me the Hellcat that was running with that blond the other day. I must have been good this year since Santa brought me my Christmas present early," he roared with laughter. I need to think about what I'm going to do with my present," he chuckled as he quickly tied her ankles together with a short piece of rope.

Hatchert's eyes formed dangerous dark slits as she studied her opponent: 6'1" tall, medium body frame, definitely in good shape, she thought, as she focused on his weathered face that looked like the skin of a carcass that had been dried out by the sun. His dirty brown hair hung in thick, waxy strands around his head like a mop that had been used to clean a filthy bathroom. His thick, dark eyebrows were low on his forehead, almost blending in with his burnt-toast colored skin. Hatchert knew his nose had been broken at some point in his life since it sat crooked on his face. His mouth was narrow and thin, but it was his eyes that seemed to define his character. His deep-set, almost coal black eyes, were more distant than the eyes of a robot she saw at a technological show in Denver last year. I wonder who you are, she thought as she was thrown into the back of the Blazer and a heavy gray moving blanket was slung on top of her. Her visual world went black.

Soon, fresh cigarette smoke blended with the stale along with the smell of rotten meat and sweaty shoes. The car radio blasted out Brad Paisley's *I'm Still a Guy* as she twisted and turned her feet testing the rope that was twisted around her ankles. It gave a little, but not enough to free her. She felt with her feet and hit a box in one direction and the interior wheel well in the other. Her hands found an old paper wrapper along with some dried up meat that was covered with a soft, fuzzy texture. Great, she thought, a rotten hamburger as she wiped her hands on the dirty carpet and felt around to see what else she could find.

Sweat began to form on her face and body as the air became stuffy and hot under the heavy gray moving blanket. She shuffled around to move the blanket enough to get more air. A small bend in the blanket brought in some cooler air and she drank it in. She found the perp all right, although not in the way she had anticipated, she thought and chuckled at the irony. There was nothing she could do to escape right now. She made a mental note to look at his ankle for the tattoo, then settled back and forced herself to breathe deeply and slowly.

He looked at the sun that was descending in the horizon. Wouldn't take him long to get her up the mountain. He had plenty of daylight left. He would make another woman pay for taking his Barbara away from him and he became hard just thinking about it.

He was lucky all right, he thought, as he blew a smoke ring. Lucky that he met Bobby Jo in prison two years ago. He remembered counting out the dollars and quarters into Bobby Jo's hand in exchange for the fake papers behind the Fast Mart on Eleventh. Damn cops. They needed to mind their own business, he snorted as he took a long drag on his cigarette.

Monica was his wife and it was his right to take her whenever he wanted. Damn bitch called the police after he taught her a lesson when she told him no. One missing tooth and a black eye wasn't much to ask when your woman denies you what's rightfully yours to take, he snarled as he took another drag on his cigarette. And those shit-assed cops believed her two-bit story that she didn't do nothing wrong. She should have been the fuckin' one in jail for not taking care of her man. Now, he had a record. No one was going to hire an ex-con. But, Bobby Jo took care of all that, he grinned.

Bobby Jo was good, really good, and he chuckled when he thought about the day he handed that woman cop the fake papers he paid Bobby Jo to make. Women: they were stupid, even women cops, he laughed uproariously. She looked at the fake papers and handed him his new identity card for Hamilton Hospital. Look at me now, he thought as he smiled and took a swig of Mint and Fresh. Jesus, this stuff tasted like shit he muttered as he choked and coughed. "That's enough of that crap," he yelled as he slung the bottle out of the passenger window.

He thought about the tenement building he was raised in that was held together with paper clips and glue. He knew each stair by its creak. He got pretty good at guessing who was coming up the stairs by the sound of their footstep. It was a game he played to keep himself company as he waited for his momma to return. She taught him about patience when she left him alone in the corner most of the day in their studio apartment with the leaky shit pipe and paper-thin walls. Don't move, she said when she left to go to work. He didn't always stay there, he chuckled.

Momma didn't know he left many days to go play outside. No one cared if he went to school or sat at home by himself. Only Mrs. Farley cared, he thought as he smiled when he pictured Mrs. Farley in her fire-engine red nightie and her dyed red hair to match. She was missing a front tooth because one of her johns threw her against the wall one night when he wasn't satisfied with her performance.

Mrs. Farley knew how to keep him company. When his momma was gone she would come and get him and teach him all sorts of things. She knew how to treat a man, he grinned when he thought about all those days in her bed. Yup, good ole Mrs. Farley was a wise woman teaching him so young about women.

Mrs. Farley shoved him in the closet more than once when Big Papa, her pimp, walked in the door. Big Papa was 6'5" tall and weighed around 300 pounds. No one messed with Big Papa. He had a big ass ring with points and if anyone got out of line he used those points to cut them. He wore a fancy green shirt and black suit and wore several heavy gold chains around his neck.

He wanted to be just like Big Papa when he grew up, but he never got that big. Big Papa came by every day like clockwork to collect his payment. Sometimes, he collected more than money, he thought with a smile remembering what he saw through the slats in the closet door.

Nobody thought Ray Wilson would amount to anything. Look at me now, he chortled as his chest swelled. He had a job and a place to live that was nicer than what he grew up in.

The motel was decent enough, even though the red vacancy sign still wasn't fixed. He doubted if they would ever fix it. The "vacancy" sign only spelled out "can" at night since the other letters burned out. He smiled. Shakey said it was called the "can" because the place was worse than a stinkin' toilet.

It wasn't no fancy hotel, he snickered. The dull, pink paint looked like the remnants of a dead pink flamingo. The shingles on the roof were curled upward, the broken downspouts were being held in place by the rust leaving red water stains striped down the side of the building. The planter boxes were leaning over so far the plants that were hardy enough to survive were poking up between the boards of what should have been the base.

He had to admit the mattress on the full-size bed sagged so much his butt almost touched the floor. But, he had a tiny refrigerator that doubled as his night table and that was better than anything he ever had at home. And he even fixed it up with a lamp he found on the curb one day. It had a wrinkled and torn lampshade and its frame tilted dangerously toward the bed, but it gave him enough light to make the hookers comfortable and that's all that mattered. That... and Barbara, he thought as he pictured the wall back in his hotel room.

232

The eight-foot by twelve-foot wall was filled with photos that had been arranged in a collage. He had pictures of Barbara bending over to get a diet soft drink from the vending machine, Barbara smiling at the delivery man when she signed for a package, Barbara going into the grocery store, and Barbara reading a book while lying on her couch at home. Over one hundred pictures of her on the wall: He counted them one day when he had nothing better to do. And now, she was gone, he growled.

She'd be back they said. And he was patient, he thought as he held up a dog-eared corner picture of Barbara smiling at the camera. Like a cat watching a gopher hole he waited for them. His momma didn't raise no fool.

It was Shakey who first pointed out that he should make Barbara his own. They were talking and razzing each other and he accidentally slipped about Barbara. Good ole Shakey, he laughed. Charles Phillip Gathus, or Shakey, as he was called in prison. Shakey could sure tell a joke! It was fate that Shakey was in the cell next to his. Shakey's jokes kept his cellmate Bobby Jo and him from going crazy when things got boring. Most everyone liked Shakey's jokes. But, the person who laughed so hard his whole body shook like a runaway vibrator was Shakey himself, so it didn't take long before Charles became Shakey to the regulars. Shakey got out two years before him, but he stayed in touch all these years.

He thought about the conversation he had with Shakey yesterday as he blew another smoke ring and watched it drift around the cab.

"Hi," Shakey said as he came out from behind the curtain.

"What's hanging?"

"Not much. Had a cop in here earlier asking about archer tattoos," Shakey said as he looked at a smoke ring he'd just made.

"When was the cop here?" he nervously asked as he chewed on a wad of tobacco wedged in between his teeth and lip.

"Couple days ago."

"Did you tell him anything?"

"Didn't tell HIM a thing. Could have told HER something," Shakey teased as he puffed out another smoke ring.

"A woman?"

"Yup, about 5'8 or 5'9" worth of woman. A real looker too. Long legs, long dark hair. Great body. I'd like to get my hands on some of that if I could get away with it. But, I don't want no cop. They're trouble," Shakey spoke as he watched his friend squirm.

"A cop, huh? Did you say anything?"

"Sure. I gave her your address and told her about all those fake papers of yours," Shakey burst out laughing.

"Okay, I had that coming to me. What are you doing tonight?"

"I got me a new woman and I'm taking her to that new chick movie that's playing at the Reel."

"Hope you score!"

"I plan on it. Just don't you come by tonight and spoil my fun!" Shakey said half jokingly, half seriously.

"Don't worry. I got my own woman to keep me warm."

Ray's lips curled up and his body went hard as he thought about the brown haired woman in the back and decided it was time to play.

"This is lady luck," he said as he laughed out loud and pulled the heavy, gray moving blanket off Hatchert.

Hatchert blinked her eyes as the late afternoon sun hit them.

"What's the matter? Didn't I tell you we were going to a party? And he snorted as he shoved the medical ice chest against the back of the rear seat.

"No one's going to hear us up here. Go ahead, yell! You ready to have a good time?" he snickered as he brought his face within inches of her nose.

"I'm ready to have a great time," Hatchert replied calmly as she stared into his crazy eyes.

He stared at her. "What, you giving up so soon? Where's that fire I saw when you were running with that blond bitch yesterday?"

No one would have noticed the tiny jaw muscles that tightened as Hatchert fought to contain her anger.

"That wasn't fire. If you want fire, we need to start the party," Hatchert replied without a break in voice.

It unnerved him that she was so calm. He tossed her onto his shoulder face down and held her legs as he began walking. She felt the brush scrape her thighs as he pushed through the thick bushes that hugged the narrow trail. A long branch stung as it whipped against her cheek. They were climbing steadily upward. The sun was low now. She shivered as a light, cold breeze swept over her. Her face slammed into the backpack when he nearly dropped her as they went around a boulder.

"How're you doing? Wouldn't want any damaged goods," he chortled as he stopped and slung her down onto the ground. Grabbing her by both arms, he pulled her into a sitting position and leaned her against a tree.

He studied her. She was a looker all right. He did pretty well for himself this time, he thought as he reached into her pant's pocket and moved his fingers through the material and stroked her upper thigh. "That's just a sample of what's to come," he sneered as he stared into her dark she-cat eyes.

"I got me a wildcat," he snorted again as he played with her pant's zipper. And he laughed hard once again when he saw that her eyes almost glowed so bright from the anger they could melt steel. "You won't be needing these," he said as he took her car key and put it in his pocket. "You're not so calm after all," he heehawed as he took off his backpack and reached for a bottle of 90-proof whiskey that was carefully nestled into the pack.

"Now's the time to start the party," he said as he smiled and twisted the top off the bottle. He took a long, deep slug. He swirled it around in his mouth, savoring it as a vulture would their first taste of red, juicy, fresh-killed meat. He swallowed, and savored the burn as it made its way down his throat.

"Now that's whiskey! We got us a party going on and you're the guest of honor," he cackled as he took another drink. Screwing the lid back on, he carefully returned it to the backpack and then strapped it on again. "Time to go before the sun goes down. We're going to party all night."

He grabbed Hatchert and slung her over his shoulder. Steady now, he said to himself as he almost stumbled over a rock. He followed the trail as it wove its way up the mountain. Another forty minutes and they would be at camp. It was worth all this trouble, he thought as his foot slipped a little on some loose dirt and rocks.

Hatchert watched him as he took his first drink. The way he swallowed the whiskey showed her that it was his first drink in a long time: he cherished it as a child would a toy. The mouthwash made sense now. He chose Mint and Fresh because it had a high alcohol content. She wondered

236

what type of drunk he was. Some get friendly, some get mean, some fall asleep, and some get angry. It looked like she would be finding out real soon.

She looked at his camouflaged pants and the dirt trail. She wondered if he would untie the rope around her ankles and take off the cuffs before he raped her. If he did, that would be a fatal mistake. She knew she could take him. Even if he only took off the ropes, she knew she could get in at least one kick that might knock him out. She would have to time it right and aim well but, that's all she needed: one chance. The only thing she could do now, was wait as her nose hit the backpack again.

He was getting excited as he passed the tall, skeleton of a dead pine tree that stood watch over this part of the mountain. Another ten minutes and he could settle in for a long sex-filled night. He continued upward, sliding a little where the rocks and dirt were loose, and slowly weaved his way through a maze of boulders. His heart beat faster and he began to sweat, not from exhaustion, but from excitement.

Camp was his and his alone. His eyes teared up as he crested the final rise and looked down at what he'd built. The 15-to-20 foot boulders formed a natural fortress around the small open space. His tent blended in with the muted green brush and brownish-gray boulders. It squatted under a large pine tree whose canopy acted as a natural camouflage cover for his tent. He looked at the board across the two rocks that formed an outdoor table. It was home.

He flipped Hatchert off his back and onto the semi-level ground covered in pine needles. He removed his backpack and set it down by the tent opening.

"This is you new home," he told Hatchert as he sat her up and looked into her Hellcat eyes. "We're going to have fun on the mountain tonight," he laughed as he stood up and looked around.

He hiked up the small trail that wound around a 20-foot boulder. He found the small "tunnel" that had naturally formed between a swarm of boulders. Bending over he walked in a stoop until he reached the far end. Standing now, he looked down the mountain to the small valley below where a creek ran between the two mountains. Farley Mountain—that's what he named *his* mountain—was set back behind the other and few ventured here. He could see off to the north the parking lot for the Vista Point trail that looked like a miniature postage stamp from his vantage point. His eyes swept the clear blue sky and then looked at the sliver of black, curling ribbon that was the coast highway. No cop cars anywhere. He would have seen the red lights from here and turned back toward camp.

"You don't give me any trouble and I'll treat you to a night you won't forget," he laughed as he was coming down the incline toward camp sending rocks skittering.

"I'm ready to party whenever you are," Hatchert replied as she forced a seductive smile across her face.

He studied her once again. Maybe she liked the kinky stuff and he got hard just imaging what those long legs and dangerous breasts could do together.

He unzipped the tent and went inside to make sure there weren't any critters who took up residence in his absence. He flipped the sleeping bag that was on the cot into the air and unzipped it to look inside. He squashed one spider and tossed it onto the ground. A flat board sat across two rocks and had a kerosene lamp on top of it. He would use the lamp to keep the party rolling, he chortled. Too bad they couldn't have a fire, but the cops were just too damn nosey and might check it out.

He went back outside and gently pulled the whiskey bottle out of his backpack. He sat on a rock that made a perfect seat for his butt. He held the bottle up and looked at the pure, amber color against the sunlit sky and swirled it around watching the liquid dance. "Your eyes have flecks that look like whiskey," he said as he watched Hatchert. "I'm going to drink you!" he said as he leaned over so far he almost touched her nose and bit her lip.

Hatchert froze as he leaned toward her. His breath smelled of Old Kentucky bourbon as he bit her lip. Forcing herself to calm, she waited for her chance.

Returning to the bottle, he ran his finger gently around the label feeling the paper edge against the cold smooth glass. Slowly, he twisted off the cap, and took a swig letting it roll around in his mouth. As the liquor burned down his throat, he gasped. "It's been a long time friend," he smiled. That shitty Mint and Fresh they told him to use to wean him off the real stuff was a bunch of horseshit, he snickered. Now, this was a man's drink, he thought as he took another swig and as if a lover's kiss he moved the cool liquor around in his mouth once again.

He looked at his Hellcat watching him and savored the moment. He had planned this for a long time; bringing a woman to camp. He always thought it would be Barbara, he thought with deep regret. But, this one would have to do as he looked at Hatchert once again.

Hatchert saw him go after the bottle like it was a gift from heaven. One slip and you're going down, Hatchert hissed silently as he rooted around in her pockets and tried to shove his finger where no man had ever gone before while she fought her need to turn him into a pulpy mass of blood and tissue.

"You're not going anywhere, so it's no use trying if you're thinking about getting out of here," he chuckled as he kissed her on the lips.

She smelled his breath and was glad he used alcohol before he kissed her to kill all the rotten germs that he probably carried, she sneered.

As he adjusted his butt on the rock, his pant's legs slid up. Hatchert saw the archer tattoo and knew she'd found her perp.

"Tonight you're going to know what it's like to be with a REAL man, he roared as he took another swig of golden liquid. "Mrs. Farley taught me well. She sure did," he snorted as he drank again. "You can scream and holler for help. There's no one to hear you except me, and I like it when a woman gets all fired up! Some spit and fire makes me hornier than hell!" he laughed at his own joke.

"What's your name big guy?" Hatchert spoke for the first time noting that as the alcohol began to take affect, he also started to talk more.

"Ray Wilson—and don't you forget it!"

"Who's Mrs. Farley?" Hatchert asked as she studied him.

"She taught me everything I know about women. To Mrs. Farley," he toasted as he raised the bottle into the air and then sipped.

"Is that Mrs. Farley in your tattoo?"

"Hell, NO! That's Barbara!"

"Barbara is your girlfriend?"

"Damn straight. And she and I were going to be together until that damn Josie Green got in the way," and tilted the bottle up once again and drank.

"You mean Barbara left you?"

"She left because of that damn Josie Green!"

"Why would she leave such a great guy like you?"

"Hell, I don't know. You women think you know it all. Well, you don't. I did everything for her and I got nothing," he spat out a wad of spittle that landed at Hatchert's foot.

"Was she living with you?"

"Hell no."

"Was she your girlfriend?"

"Didn't I just tell you that?" he said angrily as he almost reached over and whacked her.

"Does she like to use a bow and arrow to hunt?"

"I don't fuckin know!"

"Well, that's one hot looking babe on your leg and she's holding a bow and arrow. Don't get burned, baby 'cause we're going to ride the stars into the heavens tonight," Hatchert crooned as her stomach turned over.

"Her name's Barbara Archer. Get it! Shakey thought it was real clever to draw an archer instead of writing out her full name," he laughed uproariously and took another swig.

Hatchert watched his face twist as the burn ran down his throat. "I have to say, that's pretty smart," Hatchert nodded her head and shifted a little to get into a better position. "Where'd you meet Barbara?"

"Work."

"Where do you work?"

"You ask a Hell of a lot of questions!" he leaned forward and glared at her with slightly glassy eyes that were starting to lose their focus.

"Look, I like you. I think you're hot. If we're going to party, I want to know who you had before me and what you did so I can be better than them, OK?" Hatchert lied.

"Want some whiskey? Here take a slug," and he shoved the bottle into her mouth and poured.

The whiskey burned as she held it in her mouth. When he turned, she spit it into the pine needles and dirt.

"What happened to her?" Hatchert asked as she rolled what was left of the bourbon around in her mouth to get the taste of him out of her.

"She left. She just left" he said as he drank once again.

"Why did she leave when she had such an obviously great guy like yourself?"

"That damn Josie Green scholarship, that's why."

"What did the scholarship have to do with her leaving?"

"She got the scholarship money and left. Those damn rich folks. They think they know it all, but they don't. They took Barbara away from me."

"I heard Josie Green was taken down a peg or two by a man. That man wouldn't have been you would it, sugar pie?" Hatchert forced another wide smile onto her face as she coated the words with thick honey.

"Sure did. That uppity bitch had it coming to her. She was a fighter. I like it when they fight. Are you a fighter?" he laughed as he leaned toward her again.

"No. I'm just someone who can appreciate a good man," Hatchert sweetly replied as she batted her eyes and controlled her stomach from upending right then and there.

That stopped him. Maybe this one liked him. He began to imagine her as his woman and the idea began to grow on him.

"Damn, we ARE going to have a good time tonight," he hollered as he took another drink and laughed uproariously.

"Where did you see this bitch? I'll take care of her for you."

242

"Her fucking pictures are everywhere. She strutted by me so many times with her nose in the air. Before I knew who she was, I tried to get friendly with her, but she blew me off. She's one cold bitch and I ought to know," he hee-hawed at his own joke.

"Where did you see her? After we're done up here, I want to tell her you're my man and to keep her grubby hands off of you."

"Church. She comes to church and runs that stupid-ass writing group every Wednesday night. And you don't need to worry, she won't be coming after me soon. I took care of it."

"You go to church every Wednesday night? I didn't figure you for a preacher man."

"I go to meetings. Have been since March 3rd," he snickered as he took another long drink and held up the bottle in the fading light to see how much was left. "One day I heard Barbara say that she doesn't like men who drink, so I quit. And what the Hell did I get in return? She left. She left without telling me. That ain't right," he snorted as he finished the bottle.

He walked to the tent and gently removed two more bottles of whiskey. He cracked open another bottle and took a long drink as he stood in front of the tent flap. He walked back to his rock and almost rolled off the side when he tried to sit down. Hatchert watched as he finally got his balance and settled on the rock.

"I'm the jealous type. If you've been with other women, I want to know. Have you ever been with any other women?"

He laughed so hard he almost fell off the rock.

"What the Hell do you think? I've been with women since I was seven or eight years old. I'm the best fucker in the country. No, the world," he laughed.

"Have you brought any other women up the mountain?"

"Not here."

"Should I be jealous?"

"Hell no."

"I want to know who they are so I can tell them to leave my man alone."

"Shit, they don't mean nothing to me. They were only to get me some fucking time."

"I like to fight for my man. What are their names?"

"Hell, one was a blond and the other gal, shit, I can't remember. She was the beefy one. I almost brought her here, but I couldn't carry her up the hill," and he bellowed until he choked on his saliva at his apparent joke.

"I heard about a heavy-ass mechanic that works on the base. Know her by chance?"

"That's her."

"How did you know she was a mechanic?"

"I hauled their bad ass lab crap to the central lab and then I watched them. Shit, they run like princesses up this damn mountain. Didn't take much to have some fun. Like shooting hens in a hen house. Git it!" he laughed and almost lost his balance again.

"I like that I've got a working man for my man," Hatchert said as she forced a smile.

"That's right. I work hard and don't get shit!"

"What do you do, big guy?"

"I told you. I take the lab speci… speci…oh shit, I take lab crap, pee, and blood from the hospital to the main lab."

"Wow, that's a mighty important job," Hatchert said as

she studied him and suddenly remembered where she'd seen him before. He was the courier who came in to collect the specimens when she was talking with Kevin, the lab technician at Hamilton.

"Damn right it is. That's why I'm pissed at that stuck up bitch for taking Barbara away from me as if I were a gnat or a nobody. I got her. I got her good. She's colder than a God damn ice cube in Alaska."

"I don't think you're a gnat. I think you're a big hunk of a man," Hatchert said as she fought to control her facial expression and the extreme urge to rip him apart. "Did you bring them to our special place up here?"

"No. But, I sure got them bitches all right. Three times each," he said laughed victoriously.

" Weren't they any good? Why'd it take three times?"

"Cause I stopped drinking on March 3rd. Get it, 3 and 3. And they were piss poor women in bed, that's for sure," he drunkenly laughed as he took another giant gulp.

"Why didn't you pick me?" Hatchert asked as she batted her eyes.

"I saw you running with that bitch the other day. She never moved like that with me. Why the Hell were you with her and not me?" he asked angrily.

"I didn't ask her to run with me. That bitch ran up behind me and was trying to beat me around the trail. I showed her. I beat her."

"Here, that deserves a drink," and he shoved the bottle and tilted another shot into Hatchert's mouth.

She waited until he turned to go back again and then spit out the whiskey into the pine needles and dirt where it joined the other small puddle of whiskey.

"That's damn good whiskey. You sure know how to pick out the good stuff."

"Damn right."

"Let's toast to your manhood," Hatchert said hoping she could keep him drinking.

"One for my manhood," he shouted and took another long pull.

"You know sugar, I play a lot better when my feet and hands are free. How am I going to please you all tied up like a freakin' pig?"

He tried to focus on her, but she was a big blur.

"I don't know about that," he slobbered.

"What's the matter? You're such a big man. You couldn't be scared of a little woman like myself? Or, could you?" she baited him and waited to see if he bit.

"I ain't scared of no bitch!" he shouted.

"If you really want to play, wouldn't it be better if I could touch you in all the right places?"

"I don't know," he shrugged.

"Look, where would I go? You're so big and strong you could stop me, right?"

"Yeah. You're not going anywhere. Besides, a woman's got to mind her man."

"Don't you deserve to have some real fun?"

"Damn right I do."

"Well, why don't you untie me and uncuff me. We could really play if I'm free, sugar?"

She made sense to him. After all, he was a big man and no woman was ever going to get the best of him. He could take her down in a second if he had to. And he went hard thinking of where her fingers and mouth could go. He walked over to her and fingered the knot.

"God damn knot. I tie 'em good when I tie them," and started cursing as he struggled to untie the knot.

"It's okay, sugar, you're doing fine. We have all night."

"It's coming," he said. "I should be on TV, get it? Coming!" he laughed as the rope came free and he let it drop to the ground.

He reached into his pocket and almost fell over. He tried again and took out the key and waved it in front of Hatchert's face.

"I think I should handcuff you to that tree? We could play cops and robbers! What do you think?"

"Sure, sugar. How about you uncuff me. I'll pretend like I'm running. You can catch me and handcuff me to the tree and do what cops do to the bad guys. Doesn't that sound like fun," Hatchert said as she forced a giggle.

"Play acting. I like that. And I'm the cop! Holy shit!" and he fumbled as he dropped the key on the ground.

Finding it, he held it up and smiled at her.

"Here you go sugar," and taking the key, he unlocked the handcuffs.

The kick sent him flying and the wind blew out of his lungs as his back slammed into the ground. He shoved himself upright and she kicked him in the stomach sending part of the whiskey he'd drunk flying out of his mouth. As her foot caught the side of his head, he spun around and fell face first into the dirt. Fury rose inside of him as he swung and got lucky sending her flying backwards. He grabbed the cuffs and used them as a weapon lashing out at her face. She ducked and fell backwards over a rock. He lunged again and missed.

She delivered another kick to his head that sent him flying down a bed of graveled rocks. As he turned over, he grabbed the pistol he kept in his leg band and fired. The pain was like a bee sting as the bullet skirted the top of her left shoulder. He fired again and another sharp sting hit her left upper arm. She ran behind a tree and started to climb.

Another bullet hit wildly to the right of her. Upward she climbed, zigzagging and ducking. Bullets flew past her as she scrambled. Another bullet ripped the bark off a tree and a large piece slammed her in the face leaving a nasty gash.

"God damn it bitch! You said you wanted to please me!" and she felt the wind of a bullet slip by her ear.

The moon provided some light as she scrambled over low bushes and rocks. Rocks and dirt slid as she hit loose dirt and scrambled to get some footing.

"God damn it! I knew I shouldn't trust no bitch! I'm going to find you and then I'm going to do things to you that you never thought could happen! You hear me, bitch!" he yelled as he lumbered up the mountain. "Shit!" he yelled as he slid down to his butt on some loose rocks.

Her shoulder and arm started to ache and pound. Keep going Hatchert, she said to herself. You can do this. Slow and steady. One step at a time, she made her way around a tree and a large rock. One branch slapped her in the face and another tore at her pants. She stumbled over a rock and fell. Blood began to trickle off her chin.

"I'm going to find you bitch! Do you hear me?" he yelled as he started to climb again. "And when I find you, I'm going to beat the shit out of you for disobeying your man! Do you hear me? Jesus Christ," he screamed when he fell down the mountain again.

"Keep right on falling you dickhead. You're going behind bars forever, " she thought angrily. She was gaining ground as she noticed his curses were becoming more distant. Her heart pounded, and her lungs screamed. She touched her shoulder and felt the warm slick blood between her fingers. She had to get off this mountain before light. He knew it too well and could track her faster in the daytime.

248

She fell over a plant runner and landed flat on her face.

"I hear you! I'm coming!" he screamed. Breaking branches and sliding rocks gave away his position letting her know he wasn't gaining much ground. The moonlight was a steady beacon as she continued her climb along the mountain.

"God damn it!" she heard along with the cracking sound as a large tree limb snapped off and rocks slid once again.

You keep right on swearing and breaking branches so I know where you are, Hatchert sneered as she heard some rocks fall down below her.

She kept going as the pain settled in her left shoulder like a cauldron of fire. She moved parallel to the mountain headed north putting distance between her and camp. Pausing mid-stride, she listened. She heard breaking glass against rock in the distance. She sat on the ground and took some deep breaths. As she focused on her breath, she forced her body and mind to settle.

She felt the hot moisture of the fresh blood with her hand as she found the entry point for the bullet that was still in her upper arm. She hadn't figured on the gun, but from the feel of it, she would be all right. The bullet seemed to be lodged in the flesh and missed her major arteries or veins.

"Crap. I love this blouse," Hatchert thought, as she took out her small pocketknife and cut off her left sleeve. Tying the cut shirtsleeve around her arm, she tied it snugly over the wound to slow the bleeding. There was a short, but deep rip along the top of her right shoulder where the other bullet had lodged. She winced again as she gently probed to see where the bullet entered. Pushing gently, pain exploded once again as the bullet slightly moved against a nerve.

Breathing deeply again, the pain began to subside as she slowed her pulse. She felt her cheek. Slippery fingers told her it was still bleeding, but it was superficial and she would be okay.

She knew she couldn't sit here long. She was on the east side of the mountain and at some point would have to climb the summit and head west to find the coast highway. For now, she needed to put some distance between herself and him.

Wincing, she got up and began walking north, parallel to the mountain range. She slowly wove her way around the large rocks and trees that clung to the steep slope. Keep going, Hatchert. You can do this, she said to herself as her teeth began to chatter from shock as much as from the cold. A piece of brush grabbed her left pant leg and brought her down and pain rocketed down her arm as it hit the ground.

She rolled over and listened. Silence. Make a sound you asshole so I know where you are, Hatchert wanted to scream. Silence.

She pulled her cell phone out of her shirt pocket. No reception. Punching the text button, she typed, "Meet at VP fire road, med courier is our man, send help," and hit "send" hoping that Chief Girard checks his text messages often and the signal got through. The leaves rustled behind her. Instantly Hatchert's body moved into a fighting position. A branch bent and whipped as Hatchert listened to an animal slipping away into the night. Using a nearby rock, she hoisted herself up again.

Hatchert inched her way along the mountain. She looked up at the stars and hoped Josie was not worrying about her. Her arm throbbed as she crept her way around a large rock. She looked down at the small valley below. Sliding her feet sideways, she carefully moved across the

250

open cliff face of loose rocks and dirt. It was so steep, if she spit it would land three-quarters of the way down the mountain.

There was a large grouping of boulders in front of her. She scooted sideways as she moved slowly along the rock face. At one point, she found a large, 6-inch high deep crack where she slipped her fingers inside to help her maintain a grip. She slid her hands along the crack inch by inch. Her fingers bumped into something leaving only her fingertips clinging to the small rock edge. Slowly she felt her way down the crack and then the crack moved. The skin was soft and the body long. Slowly, she pulled her hand out of the crack as sweat broke out across her forehead. The snake stopped moving as she crept along until she reached the other side of the boulder into an open space with enough room to sit down.

Shaking, she looked across the valley at another sister mountain to the east. Brush broke and sweat poured down Hatchert's face as she strained to hear any noise that might give away his location.

Her arm ached and pain stabbed through her as her salty sweat flowed into the open wounds. She heard a man's howl from far below and the sound of glass breaking against rock and leaned her head back and rested.

He cussed at women and threw the bottle sending it crashing into a rock. The shards of glass sprayed the area. Damn it! She was a liar and he fell for it. Letting out a long howl he stumbled over the board that acted as a table. His world spun and the ground rose up to meet him.

He picked himself up and screamed like a madman as he stood there in the middle of the opening, "This is my mountain. I own it. I'll find you and when I do you're gonna pay!" and as he kicked at his rock stool he yelled and plummeted head first into the dirt tearing the skin off the bridge of his nose. "Shit!" he yelled as the blood poured down the side of his nose.

"Now you've gone and done it, Bitch! I'm mad. I was going to do you all nice and romantic, but now, I'm going to take you and make you beg! You hear me, Bitch?" he shouted to the dirt as he tried to get up and promptly fell over. Dragging himself over to the rock she'd just left, he pulled himself up onto it and sat. "Bitch!" he repeated again.

"I hope the mountain lions get you!" he yelled into the sky. "Naw, I want you. I'm going to find you and dissect you. Yea. I'm going be just like that ole mountain lion I saw up here a few days ago and I'm going to tear your legs off you. That's what I'm going to do. I'm going to fuck you first, second, and third, then I'm going to cut your arms and legs off you. And I'm going to feed the pieces to that lion myself," he said as he drank some more whiskey. "It won't take me that long to find you. You can't get away, girly! No one gets away from me on my mountain, do you hear me?" he shouted and as he took another drink.

He staggered up the mountainside. It was slow going with the bottle in his hand, but the whiskey gave him courage now. He was the master of his kingdom and she was his woman. She needed a man and by damn he was the best fucker in the whole world. Just ask the girls he's taken and the women too for that matter, he chuckled as he remembered Ms. Farley and how good she said he was at fucking her.

He slid down some rocks and cussed again. Damn women, he thought as he tried to step around a bush and managed to get all tangled up in it. "Shit!" he screamed as he slammed his leg back and forth ripping the tiny bush into pieces.

"You were right, Big Papa! I should never trust a damn woman!" The only thing they were good for was one thing—and he was going to get it, he snorted as he looked around him. He sat down on the ground and drank some more. The liquor convinced him that she was too stupid to make it off the mountain by herself.

"You'll die out here if you don't let me find you," he screamed. "If the mountain lions don't get you, then the rattlesnakes will, and if they don't get you, I will," and he laughed at his own private joke.

Dragging himself up, he headed back to camp. I'll find you, but I have to get another bottle, he said as he tossed the empty bottle down the cliff. I'm going to hunt you down and then I'm going to have fun with you. You'll thank me when I'm done, he said with the arrogance of a man who'd grown up on the streets.

Hatchert could hear him once again as he cursed and screamed. Thank you, you drunken perp." Now I know where you are, she thought as she scanned the mountain. It was time to cross the summit. She began looking for an easy place to begin her ascent. She found a trail that had a gradual slope upward. Step by step she climbed. Her arm and shoulder sent another river of pain through her as she grabbed a branch to pull herself up a small, sharp incline. The bullet in her shoulder moved yet again.

Under the last group of trees before the barren summit, she sat and rested. The throbbing in her shoulder beat unrelentingly now as she felt warm drops of blood slide down her breast. She leaned against the tree and shifted around until she could find a position where the throbbing began to lessen.

She planned her route in her head. The summit was above the tree line and she would be exposed. She had to cross it fast and go down the other side to where there was more cover.

Hatchert heard the distant thump of a helicopter. As she waited and listened, the thump, thump, thump became louder. She watched for it. Soon, a small black shape floated in the sky. It swept across the summit of the Vista Point trail mountain first and then swept directly overhead. Hatchert looked skyward and smiled as she watched the helicopter until it was a tiny spot in the distance. The Colonel was looking for her. He would only take one sweep to make it appear as a routine flight that just happened to cross over the trail. She looked at the moon and knew it was around midnight.

She couldn't sit and wait for the Colonel to find her. The perp knew this mountain too well. The Colonel wouldn't use the helicopter. It was too noisy. They would set up a base camp somewhere near the entrance to the fire road. She thought about the perp. He heard the helicopter too, so he knew they were looking for them. He would follow her; she was certain of that. She had to head to where the fire road met the coast highway and hope she gets there before he finds her.

Brush broke and rocks slid just below her. Her pulse rose and every muscle tensed as she waited and winced as the bullet let her know it didn't like all the jostling. A deer shot across a small opening thirty feet away and brush broke as it raced down the other side. It's only a deer, Hatchert told herself as she forced her breathing and heart to slow. She waited and listened. Only silence greeted her.

Time to move again, she said to herself as she stood up and waited until the pulse beat of the pain went from a boil to a simmer.

Moving painfully slow, Hatchert kept moving. The moonlight reflecting off the rocks acted as a lantern as she wove her way upward. Just before the summit she sat and leaned against a large tree. She felt her left arm under the shirtsleeve and found some dried, caked blood and a few drops of fresh blood. She adjusted the makeshift shirtsleeve bandage over the wound clenching her teeth as a lightning bolt of pain shot through her as the knot pushed gently on the hole.

Gingerly, she touched her shoulder wound. A few parts of the wound had clotted, other places were still moist and wet. She felt the dried waterfall of blood that spread down her shoulder and was caked on her blouse. Looking up at the stars, she saw that she was still heading north. Once she reached the top, she would have to move rapidly across the rocky, almost barren surface. The moonlight was her enemy now.

He shook the backpack and then slammed it against a rock. Empty. Party was over. And he froze as he heard the distant thump of a helicopter. He strained his eyes looking for the black dot that would give away its location, but they were too blurry to focus on much of anything. Sweat poured off his brow and swept in a flash flood alongside his pockmarked, blood-caked nose and onto his shirt. The helicopter flew across his mountain and he cursed quietly as he watched it disappear into the dark autumn sky.

He grabbed a bottle of water and dumped instant coffee into it. Swirling it around, he drank. Sitting on a rock, his eyes narrowed and looked blacker than a starless night, and madder than a madman's. After he taught her a lesson, she would get her final lesson all right, he snickered as he patted his gun in his ankle holder and checked the extra ammo in his right front shirt pocket. He filled two other bottles with water and instant coffee and started up the mountain. I'll find you bitch, and when I do you'll regret the day you lied to me.

He moved from tree to tree and kept in the shadows. His footsteps became steadier as the caffeine started to kick in. Slipping on some loose rocks, he slid down into a tree. Not a word did he utter as he pursed his lips and listened.

She leaned against the rock's surface and stood up. Weaving and ducking she made her way across the top as her shadow danced on the ground. She could see the stars all around her. As she reached the edge of the westward side she contemplated for a split second, then lunged forward sliding down the rocky embankment sending dirt and rocks flying. The gamble paid off as she dug her heels into the loose patch of dirt bringing her to a stop. Wincing, the pounding beat in her shoulder forced her to her knees. As time passed, the pounding lessened allowing her to scramble between two large boulders where she rested once again.

Suddenly, the crickets stopped singing. Shivers ran down her spine. She strained to hear any noise. A twig snapped down below. She moved slowly into the shadow of the boulder. A branch whipped in the distance. Her heartbeat pounded in her ears. Her eyes could only see rock and dirt. She pushed herself further into the rock's shadow, waiting. Her lungs struggled as she fought the fear that was trying to explode to the surface.

The pot roast was cooking in the oven and Melissa was reading a book on the couch. She handled being a police chief's wife with apparent ease. She still looked as beautiful to him as the day he met her when he was a rookie cop. They were twenty-four then. She was giggling with some friends in a local store when she accidentally caught his eye and he was hooked. Her hair was the color of caramel and honey and her eyes were a mixture of a dark Hershey's kiss and red pepper. When she laughed her dimples showed and her eyes sparkled like a thousand points of starlight. He smiled warmly now as he studied her lying on the couch across from him engrossed in one of her romance novels. She was never boring, he chuckled to himself as he thought about last night when they were together in the tub.

He took in the scent of fall as he settled back in his recliner for a quiet evening of football. The smell of baby red potatoes, chunks of farm-fresh carrots, and rings of red onion with a dash of salt and pepper drifted through the air. He'd made the pumpkin pie earlier that morning compliments of his mother's family recipe. He was looking forward to Thanksgiving in a few weeks when both their families would come together in a cacophony of scents, sounds, and laughter.

His cell phone wiggled in his pocket. When he read the message, he pushed out of his chair and went over to Melissa and knelt by her side.

"What is it?" Melissa asked as she studied her husband's troubled eyes.

"I've got to go, Sweetheart," he said gently as he kissed her lips. "It's going to be a long night and day tomorrow."

She never questioned him about his work. It was one of the things she learned to accept as a cop's wife. "Be careful, Darling," was all she said as she kissed him goodbye.

Josie knew something was wrong. Chief Girard sent her a text to meet him at the hospital. The lights from the harbor went by in a striped blur of pale yellows and bright white. She paid little attention to the flashing red light on the other side of the highway where a police officer was issuing a speeding ticket. Her jaw clenched as the adrenaline flowed and her stomach formed a square knot.

The Miata bounced over the iron drainage grate at the garage door entrance. Her car screeched as she slammed on the brakes and squealed into an empty space.

"What's wrong?" Josie asked anxiously as she stepped out of the elevator and almost directly into the Chief.

"Hatchert found your assailant."

"That's great! Where is she?" Josie asked as she scanned the lobby for Hatchert.

"Josie, I think he has Hatchert," the Chief replied quietly as he watched Josie's reaction.

"He can't have her, Chief!" Josie screamed.

"I'm sorry, Josie. When did you last see Hatchert?"

"About 4:30. She wanted my RAV4 to check out the fire road near the Vista Point trail. Is that where he's got her?" Josie panicked as a wave of terror shot through her. "I love her, Chief!" Josie sobbed as she fought to pull herself together.

He looked into Josie's eyes and saw confirmation of what he'd suspected long ago. "We're going to find her, Josie," he said as he placed a loving hand on her shoulder.

Sergeant Jones and Officer Davis bolted out of the stairwell door.

"What's up Chief?"

"We think the assailant has Hatchert. Have either of you seen her this afternoon?"

"She stopped by the office around 3:00. I've been looking at surveillance tapes and I haven't had any luck yet," Officer Davis replied as she whistled under her breath.

"She asked me about the personnel records for the man with the archer tattoo. She was going up to her office and that's the last time I saw her," Jones said.

"We need to look at the surveillance footage from this afternoon," the Chief commanded.

"They're down. The surveillance cameras were pulled off-line today for a software upgrade," Sergeant Jones said quietly as he shook his head.

The Chief inhaled and looked at Jones and Davis.

"I want everything you have on the medical courier for the lab," he said just before he stepped away to take a cell phone call.

As the Chief was busy talking on the phone, Officer Davis and Sergeant Jones looked at Josie.

"We'll get him," they reassured her, as Josie swayed back and forth.

"I want him. I want him now," Josie said angrily. "He can't get away with this! Not again!" Josie yelled as she fought back the tears.

"Hi Dr. Calloway," the Chief said as he hung up the phone and smiled with relief as Dr. Calloway joined the small group. "Dr. Calloway. It looks like the perpetrator might have Hatchert."

Dr. Calloway looked back into his eyes and knew she had to stay calm.

"Josie could use some help right now," the Chief said as his eyes motioned toward Josie who was pacing to keep calm.

"I'll take care of her. For what it's worth, he's changed his routine. It could mean nothing or it could mean something. Would you like my opinion?"

"Yes," the Chief said as he looked at Dr. Calloway.

"He could be getting bolder because he's done three rapes and hasn't been caught. He's also getting careless. He's not thinking things through. He might not only want to rape. He might want to keep her for himself, or when he gets done with her, he might kill her," Dr. Calloway said as she looked for the Chief's reaction.

"I agree with you," the Chief said quietly as his eyes hardened.

"Josie, we're here," Cindy yelled as she and Laura burst through the front doors.

"Looks like you can add two more women to that list," the Chief said as he watched the two other women running toward Josie.

"I'd be happy to stay. This is one of their own, and they need to feel they're helping Hatchert. I'll try to keep them out of your way, but the best thing you can do right now is be honest with them about everything and to keep them informed. It will not only lessen their stress, it might help your stress as well," she said with calm demeanor as she glanced at the Chief.

"I hear you, Dr. Calloway. I'll do the best I can. I've got to call the Colonel."

"I'll do my best to help the women," Dr. Calloway said as she turned and headed toward the three angry women.

"What's going on? Cindy said as she looked at Josie's red flushed face and razor-sharp eyes.

260

"He's got Hatchert," Josie said angrily.

"Holy Shit!" Cindy screamed.

"When?" Laura asked as she bent over to stop the dizziness.

"I talked with her at 4:30 and it's close to 8:30 now. We've got to find her. We've got to stop him," Josie said as she clenched her fists.

"We'll find her," Cindy said resolutely.

"How are you doing, Josie?" Dr. Calloway asked as she approached the small group.

"He's got her. We've got to find him. We know where he's got her. We're wasting our time here. We've got to go to the trail," Josie said vehemently as her eyes flashed and her lips pursed shut.

"You're right. We've got to go to the trail right now," Cindy said fiercely. "We can't just stand around while he's doing…while he's…" Cindy said as she struggled to come to terms with what was happening.

"We know what he does and we have to get there," Laura said angrily as her face paled, her stomach recoiled, and her chest heaved in and out.

"Take some deep breaths, Laura. She's a professional and can take care of herself. You're safe right now. Breathe. Breathe. That's right. You're safe." Dr. Calloway said softly as she watched Laura's fight against terror.

"Thanks, Dr. Calloway. But, it's not me I'm worried about. I'm okay. We have to help Hatchert," Laura responded as she stoically fought off the panic attack while Cindy put her arm around her.

"The Chief knows what he's doing. Why don't we go up to my office so the Chief and his team can do their job," she suggested knowing already that her plan wouldn't work.

"I'm not going anywhere unless it's to the trail. She needs help and I plan on finding him, and when I do, he's going to pay!" Josie fumed.

"Josie. I know this is hard right now, but the Chief has experience with this sort of thing. It might be better if we wait in my office."

"No. I'm not going anywhere unless it's up to the trail," Josie said stubbornly as she gritted her teeth.

"Okay. Let's go over here so we can talk and give them some space," Dr. Calloway said as she motioned for them to move across the lobby to the far side.

"Dr. Calloway, he's gotten away with this before. We've got to stop him," Josie said angrily while standing her ground.

"Hatchert would want you to stay calm. She would want you to take care of yourself. Hatchert's smart and strong. This is her job. From what I understand, she's been in similar situations and managed to come through them with little less than a bruise. She's a professional and I think we need to give her some credit that she's handling whatever is happening right now."

Josie looked at Dr. Calloway and knew that what she was saying was true. Hatchert was a professional and Josie thought about how strong she was when she had to be.

"The text from Hatchert says that it's the medical courier for the lab. Do either of you know him?" Chief Girard asked Sergeant Jones and Officer Davis.

"Sure. That's Ray Wilson. I check him in and out each day," Officer Davis responded as she thought "scumbag" in her head. "Wait, he's on one of the surveillance tapes yesterday," and she sprinted to the security office. As Davis entered some codes in the computer, everyone gathered around the monitor.

262

"There he is," Officer Davis said as she pointed to a medium built man with dark stringy hair who was carrying an ice chest with a medical sign on its side.

"That's the rapist!" Josie's stomach lurched. "I recognize his boots!"

"Officer Davis, can you give me a printout of that picture?"

"Yes, sir." And as she hit "print" she thought of the dozens of time she smiled and said "Hi" to him as he walked back and forth past her desk. "You dirtbag," she said under her breath. "We're going to bring you down!"

The Chief stepped away and began making some calls.

"Do you remember him looking like that?" Cindy asked Laura.

"No. The body shape's right. I'd remember his snort anywhere," she thought disgustedly.

"I've got officers going to his residence," the Chief said as he approached the group. He drives a black 1975 Chevy blazer license number EQU163. He's been working as a courier for the last two years. My guys are running him through our database right now. Sergeant Jones..."

"I'm already on it, "Sergeant Jones responded as he began typing in codes into their computer system.

"His papers check out clean," Sergeant Jones said as he leaned back in his chair so the Chief could look at the monitor.

It was getting close to ten o'clock and it seemed as though nothing had been done. Josie paced the same strip of marble in the front lobby over and over again. "I'm tired of waiting. We need to do something!" Josie said in total frustration to Cindy and Laura who were seated on a leather couch in a quiet discussion with Dr. Calloway.

"Hatchert's smart. She knows all sorts of things," Cindy said trying to convince herself as much as Josie.

"She knows what she's doing, Josie. It's hard, but we have to believe that Hatchert can handle herself," Laura said trying to console her.

Dr. Calloway stood up and went over to the Chief.

"Any news yet, Chief? The girls aren't going to budge until they know about Hatchert," Dr. Calloway asked.

"Nothing yet. Thanks for staying."

"No problem. I like Hatchert too. After all, she is my assistant," Dr. Calloway smiled slightly as she looked at the Chief's furrowed brow.

Just as Dr. Calloway sat down in the lobby, Rachel came bursting through the hospital front doors.

"Josie, how are you?" Rachel said as she threw her arms open wide and Josie fell into them.

"Oh Rach," Josie said tearfully, "He's got Hatchert."

"Let's sit over here and you can tell me all about it."

"She spent the night, Rach. It was so wonderful. Candlelight, a fire in the fireplace, and then she left. I woke up and she was gone. I was so angry with her and hurt. I yelled that I never wanted to see her again. Oh, Rach, what if I don't get to tell her I love her?" and Josie wept into Rachel's arms.

After a while, Josie sat upright, dried her tears, and blew her nose with a tissue as she looked at Rachel.

"She came back, Rach. A couple hours later she came back looking like she'd been drug through the dirt. She was so cute with the white circles around her eyes from where her sunglasses had been. She'd been crying. Hatchert crying! Can you imagine," Josie laughed and then cried softly. "We talked. She told me about the case and how she's an undercover operative for the Army. He's got her,

264

Rach. We've got to do something!" Josie pleaded as she gripped Rachel's hand.

"Dad's the best. He'll find her."

"Yes, but will he find her in time?" Josie sobbed. "I love her, Rach."

"I see that," Rachel said as she held Josie's hand tighter and looked at her friend's glistening eyes. "We have to believe she'll be okay. If she's an undercover operative, she's been trained to handle this kind of situation."

"She works for my uncle, Rach. I've got to call Uncle Steve," and Josie punched in his number as she stopped sniffling. "Hi, Uncle Steve. It's Josie."

"Hi, Josie."

"Uncle Steve, Mary Hatchert told me she works for you."

Colonel Highland sighed. The Chief filled him in earlier on Josie and Hatchert. "Yes, Josie, she works for me."

"She's in trouble, Uncle Steve."

"I know Josie. My crew and I are in route now and should be there within thirty minutes. I'll let you know when we arrive."

"I'm with the Chief, Uncle Steve, and I'm not leaving until we have Hatchert back," Josie said adamantly.

"All right, Josie. I'll see you soon," the Colonel replied. After he hung up his cell phone he thought about the sweet little dark-haired girl who mustered up the courage to sit on his lap sometimes, and the little honey-blond girl he used to swing around in the air. He should have retired last year, he thought, as he looked at the serious faces of the ten of his best undercover ops in their camouflage gear who sat quietly in their seats as their Black Hawk helicopter lifted off the ground and aimed toward Fort Oaks.

265

Nothing. Not a twig snap, not a rustle of a bush, not a mouse step. Make a noise! She wanted to scream. He was too quiet. She'd heard his cussing even from here as it echoed off the rocks and it calmed her to know where he was. Now, she felt like a grasshopper sitting in the open on a foggy day with a blackbird circling overhead. Where the Hell are you? She strained her ear to pick up even the slightest rustle of a branch or the slip of a lone rock. Nothing.

She leaned against a tree trunk and waited. Something small crawled over her left shoe and scurried away. She looked up at the moon that was making its night's journey across the sky. Judging by its location, it was around 2:00 a.m., and she wondered how Josie was doing. She shivered as the cold night air touched her moist, bloody skin. As she shifted her weight, a small tree branch whipped against the shirtsleeve that was wrapped around the bullet wound. Wincing, her body shook from the sharp, stabbing pain that ensued. Her stomach growled. She listened carefully once again. Nothing.

He was moving like a mountain lion after a rabbit. It was only a matter of time, he smirked and he would find her. This was his mountain and no one comes or goes from it unless he allowed it. He snaked around a large boulder carefully placing one foot down and then another. He slid on loose rocks and froze at the end of his descent. Moving his head around, he listened for the slightest hint of her. A branch snapped and bushes rustled to his left. Sniffing the air, he smelled deer—a frightened deer. Prison time gave him time to learn. The Internet was a treasure chest full of ways to survive in the wilderness. It fascinated him and he became a student. He snickered as he remembered his teacher-parent conference when he was in the first grade and where he sat on at his desk while his momma and the teacher talked.

"I'm afraid your son has a learning problem. He's behind the other students and it wouldn't be fair to promote him," Ms. White said.

"Are you telling me my child is stupid?" his momma snapped back.

"No. I'm saying that he's behind everyone and we need to retain him in first grade," Ms. White smiled hoping her friendly manner would calm his mother.

"My son is just as smart as any other kid in his class. It's the teacher who's stupid," momma's eyes flashed back at the silly smile.

"I'm not saying that your son is not intelligent. I'm saying he doesn't know the things he needs to know to go to second grade. I'm sorry, but the second grade teachers and I looked at his records and achievements from this year. He will be retained."

Momma slammed out of her chair sending it flying across the first grade classroom floor and into the wall.

"Come! We're leaving!" momma said as she took my hand and with her head held high she stormed out of that school forever. That's when she left him at home with books and television.

"You're smart baby. You can teach yourself better than that stupid woman. I'll be home tonight to hear what you learned," and with that momma went to work as he sat in the middle of a pile of worn-out books in the room.

Look at me now, momma. You'd be proud of me, he thought as he stepped over a rock and continued the hunt.

Sunday, 5 October 14
The early morning hours

She must have fallen asleep. The moon was lower in the sky. She almost moaned out loud as the wave of pain hit her. Her shoulder wound cracked open and pain shot through her as droplets of blood trickled down her chest. Her arm was cold and stiff as she moved it gingerly in a small circle. Her shirtsleeve bandage was now frozen to her bullet wound. She rubbed her legs with her right hand trying to warm herself. She slowly lifted one leg and it was numb. Rubbing it, she soon felt the pins and needles as her leg awakened. Stretching it in and out, the pins and needles slowly subsided. She listened. Nothing. Pushing herself off the ground, she leaned against the tree and listened once again. Silence. Damn you. Make a noise so I know where you are, she sent out to the winds hoping he would hear and slip.

He kept moving steadily toward the summit. She'll try to get to the highway, he figured as he methodically put one foot quietly in front of the other. Pausing, he drank more coffee water. She'll try to get there the shortest way possible. I know just where she's headed, he smiled as he thought about how he was going to surprise her. He knew a shortcut once he cleared the summit. It was an easy deer trail to follow if you knew it was there. Otherwise, it takes a long time to weave around rocks and trees going down the front side of the mountain. Yes, he smiled, I'm going to have a little surprise waiting for you when I find you, and he laughed uproariously not worried she would hear.

She thought she heard someone laughing behind her and kept moving. Sticking to the shadows, she stepped over rocks and around trees. Inching her way down, she kept a steady pace. Carefully, she wove her way around some huge boulders that were blocking her path. She felt something was watching her as she walked under two twenty-foot tall boulders that were leaning against each other. Stopping, she listened again as she leaned into the shadows.

The feeling that something was there was stronger now. Looking up she saw a shadow move across the side of the west-facing boulder. She looked for a place to defend herself and found it as she slipped between the boulders and into an opening. She needed room to fight him as she thought about his weight and her right arm. Adrenaline poured into her as she planned her moves and how she would bring him down. She knew his gun was strapped to his right ankle. If she could, she was going to knock him down and get his gun. It was a long shot, but at the moment it seemed to be the only one she had. Looking back at the boulders, she waited. What she saw shocked her.

He was crossing the barren summit when he heard a branch snap far below him. Well, she's made better time than I thought, he grinned. She's tough. I like them tough, he smiled as he kept moving with purpose. We're going to have a good time. Well, I'm going to have a good time. I don't think you will, he laughed again. It will make catching you all the more fun, he snickered as he watched his shadow move with him.

Crossing the flat, slick rock that sat on the summit, he headed for the deer trail that was just north of the rock. There it is, he laughed again when he thought about all the work she was doing and how tired she would become making it easier for him to catch up with her. It's only a matter of time, bitch, only a matter of time, and he laughed out loud once again and got hard thinking about what he was going to do to her when he caught her.

She froze. The mountain lion stared at her from its perch on top of the boulder. This is not good, Hatchert thought to herself. Of all the rotten luck, she would have to find a mountain lion, she grimaced, as they both stared at each other. "Make yourself big" was all she could remember from the material she'd read about mountain lions never believing she would ever need it. She raised her arm high over her head to look big.

The cat continued to stare at her. Hatchert slowly started to back down the mountain. Steady, Hatchert said as she moved backwards. When she was free of the clearing, Hatchert stood beside a tree. The cat seemed to be content up on the rock ledge. Moving slowly, Hatchert walked carefully stepping over rocks and small plants. As she put more distance between herself and the cat, she felt her body start to shake. The adrenaline rush that she'd kept at bay now flooded through her.

Hatchert increased her pace weaving down the mountain. She could hear the sound of water splashing over rocks below and knew that she was coming close to the bottom. She had to work her way through taller brush as she neared the bottom. She heard the bubbling and bustling of the busy stream as it made its way to the ocean. Reaching the stream bank, she stayed in the bushes for cover. At last she was to the crisp, cold water and kneeling on the bank she cupped her hands and took her first sip. The water coursed down her parched throat and as she felt the cold water making its way down into her stomach, she sat in the sand to let her body rest.

He waited for her where the stream formed a series of small rapids. He could have taken his car, but after hearing the helicopter he knew they were looking for them. He had to change his plans a little, but that's okay, he thought as he cunningly smiled. His momma didn't raise no fool. They might know where his camp and car were located, but he knew where he could take her and have some fun before he dumped her.

He'd hidden his motorcycle just for a special occasion like this and he laughed as he thought of all the cops who were probably looking for them in his Blazer. He'd be long gone before they would find him. Kneeling down he splashed the cold water on his face. When he sat back on his knees he looked up the stream and sniffed the air. She wasn't here yet. I told you bitch I had a big surprise for you, he snickered as he stood up and saw the perfect waiting spot: out of the wind and her direct line of sight. Patience his momma taught him as he walked across the patch of high marsh grass and down into a small trough behind some young willows. He settled back against the back of the sandy walls of the trough and waited. Patience, he thought as he smiled and closed his eyes.

Hatchert sat back and listened to the night. Crickets were chirping in the tiny scrub brush that ran here and there in patches. A cold breeze wove through the willows that bordered the stream sending shivers up and down Hatchert's body. A doe broke through a clump of young willow saplings on her way to get a drink from the stream.

Hatchert sat quietly as she watched the doe straddle the bank and bend her long sleek neck to sip the cool water. Her ears moved backward without fear as more rustling of the saplings revealed her two fawns. She barely flinched as they butted against her in their competition to drink by their mother's side. Patiently, the doe waited for her fawns to drink and to splash in the shallow pool. Suddenly, the doe stood tall and her ears swiveled. Her eyes followed the sound of breaking brush. She sprang back toward the saplings and her children bounded after her.

Hatchert scrambled back toward the thick stand of willows and hid in their midst. Patience, Hatchert told herself as she waited to see what or who emerged. Within minutes, a mountain lion wandered to the stream's edge. It drank its fill and looked around. Hatchert stood quietly and watched as the big cat licked its paws. Picking up on the doe's scent, the cat moved through the saplings and disappeared.

Hatchert let out the breath she had carefully held. She breathed the night air deep into her lungs as she turned her attention to the moon. It was low in the sky—it would be daybreak soon. She needed to keep going before he found her. Quietly, she stepped out of the willows and began to follow the stream to its mouth.

Josie paced around the same set of white marble floor tiles in the Hamilton Hospital lobby.

"Uncle Steve," she yelled in relief as she saw him scanning his security ID in the door scanner.

"Hi, Sweetie," the Colonel said as he kissed her on the cheek. "It's been pretty rough for you, I hear."

"Yes. Hatchert's been kidnapped by the guy who raped me. We've got to find her, Uncle Steve," Josie demanded with her hot blue eyes.

"We'll find her. I've brought my best team with me, and they know Hatchert," the Colonel said as he signaled to his team toward the security office.

With a wave of hands, Bill and Samantha Green stood at the front doors waiting for someone to buzz them in.

"Samantha, Bill, I'm glad you're here," The Colonel said as he hugged his sister and shook hands with his brother-in-law. "Josie's had a rough night and I'm not sure it's going to get any better soon."

"Thanks for calling us, Steve," Samantha replied. "She's so strong headed. She rarely accepts help from us."

"Yes, thanks, Steve," Bill said as he looked at his daughter. "We'll take care of Josie."

"I'll keep you informed as best as I can," the Colonel said as he walked over to Chief Girard.

"Hi, Chief Girard. I've brought ten of my best soldiers with me. What have we got so far," and as the Chief and the Colonel were deep in conversation, Bill and Samantha went to Josie.

"Josie, dear, we're sorry that your friend is in trouble. Perhaps it would be best to let Uncle Steve and the police handle this situation while we go home," Bill said looking into his daughter's troubled eyes.

Standing straight as a lightning rod, Josie looked at both her parents and crossed her arms.

"I'm not budging unless it's to go to the trail to find Hatchert," she said with blazing blue eyes.

"Sweetie, you'll only get in the way. You barely know this woman," her mother said off-handedly.

"You're wrong, mother. I know her very well. I know her so well I slept with her last night," Josie retorted through clenched teeth.

"Oh," her mother replied as confusion swept over her face and then reality settled in. "OH MY!"

"Why don't we go over here so we can talk," her father said as he tried to steer her toward an alcove off the lobby.

"There's nothing to talk about. I love Hatchert. The rapist has her and I'm not leaving unless it's to go with Uncle Steve to find her."

"Let's be sensible about this, shall we," her mother tried once again.

"No, mother. You can be sensible. I'm furious and worried and terrified for Hatchert. That creep has her! Don't you understand?"

"No, I can't say I do at the moment, Josie," her mother looked at her as if for the very first time.

"We can discuss all of this later. Right now, all I care about is Hatchert," Josie said as she turned and walked over to the Chief and her uncle.

"What are we going to do?" Josie demanded.

"Colonel," the Chief said.

"Yes, Chief Girard?" the Colonel replied.

"We ran him through our system. He was sentenced to six years for assault on a woman beginning in 2008 and served time at the federal penitentiary at Lompoc. He was released on good behavior in 2012. I also received a call from one of my officers. The hotel manager where he rents a room hasn't seen him since approximately 7:35 p.m. Saturday night. She noticed the time because his black 1975 Chevy Blazer backfired and she missed one of the answers to a Jeopardy question and thought about yelling at him to fix his car."

274

"Thank you, Chief Girard," the Colonel said as he turned to Sergeant Jones desk and spread out a map of Vista Point Mountain across the surface.

"As you can see by the map, there are two rows of mountains that make up the El Diablo mountain range. My guess is that he took her to the backside of this range. It's not on the Vista Point trail, but if you look here, there's the old fire road that leads up the backside of this mountain where Hatchert said she was located. It's far enough away from the trail that no one would hear them, but it's still on his turf. I'm going to send our chopper over that region and see if they can spot his car."

"Isn't that dangerous, Uncle Steve? What if he sees them?"

"We've got to know where he is. It's a chance we have to take," he replied as he turned toward his helicopter pilot and relayed his orders. With the ops team in the air, the Colonel looked at his watch: 11:45 p.m. She'd been missing since 7:30. He didn't want to think too deeply about what had happened during that time frame. She was good, but he wondered, "how good?"

As he bent over the map, he looked at the wide expanse of mountain where he could have taken her. If they were lucky, he didn't go too far from the fire road. His crew had night vision goggles, and with luck, they might see him, although he could only admit to himself, it's like looking for a tagged fish in a river.

The helicopter crew stared through the darkness as they flew over the Vista Point mountain trail and along the fire road.

"There! At ten o'clock!" one of the team members yelled as they looked at the image of a Chevy blazer parked near the summit where the fire trail snaked along the ridge and the RAV4 sat beside it.

"This is Red dog, over," the team lead said into her headset.

"Red dog, we read you, over," a member of the Colonel's team replied as the Colonel and Chief listened.

"We've found the target parked on the fire road near the ridge and the victim's car parked beside it, over."

"Continue on your flight path. Wait for my orders."

"Officer Davis. Would you please let the other women know we've found the cars on the ridge."

"Yes, sir."

"Chief. Now, we've got our work cut out for us," as they both bent over the map and began to form a plan.

"They found the RAV4 on the ridge of Hawk Mountain," Officer Davis said as she scanned the tired and frustrated group of women. "They're working on a plan right now. All we can do is wait."

Hatchert was tired. The sunlight was starting to melt the night. She hadn't heard the perp in a long time. He sobered up faster than she thought and he knew the mountains. She found a loose willow branch and walked back up the muddy incline and then walked south again making sure her footprints showed clearly in the muddy soil. As the bank sloped to the stream, she stepped into the creek and walked north once again. The water swirled around her legs as she slid over the moss-covered and slippery river rocks that lined the bottom. It was slow going, but it would cover her trail for a while. She found the same spot where she had come down to the stream the first time. Using the willow branch, she carefully swept her footprints away leaving only those that headed south. He

276

would guess she was headed to the highway. But, maybe, he would follow the footprints south long enough for her to cover some distance. Turning north, she began her walk in the icy cold water.

The profiles of the Humvees against the dawn were surrounded by other profiles of men and women who quietly moved back and forth between them as they set up base camp. The air was chilly as it absorbed each morsel of heat from the rising sun.

"Uncle Steve. Do you think Hatchert knows we're looking for her?" Josie asked as she swatted her arms to stay warm.

"Yes, Josie. She heard the helicopter. She knows."

"Thanks, Uncle Steve," Josie said as she scanned the top of the ridge across from her.

"I know it's hard, but Hatchert's a pro. She's been in tough spots before and has always come out okay. Look, I've got to focus now. Trust me," he said as he looked into his niece's tired eyes.

"Are you ready to go, Red Dog?" the Colonel asked one of his team leads.

"Yes, sir."

"Are you ready to go, Yellow Dog?"

"Yes, sir."

"All right. Move out."

As Hatchert's teeth chattered in a new rhythm she thought once again of Josie. When this was all over, she had some decisions to make. Not now. She had to focus now. Looking down the stream, she noticed a place where there was a bank of rocks. Working her way toward them the water swirled around her. She grabbed onto an overhanging limb to steady her as she climbed over the rocks and up the bank. She hadn't covered much distance in the water, but hopefully it was enough. Her stomach growled loudly as she sat and rested. She looked at the shadows of the willows against the far rock wall. They formed a beautiful geometric pattern that at any other time she would have enjoyed to sit and watch as it changed with the rising sun that was making its way into the sky.

He heard her coming and pressed himself against the mud. It wouldn't be long now and his fun would begin as the soft movement of the willows gave away her position. The thought of catching her made him hard once again. Her dark hair caught the light as he watched her stepping carefully around a large rock. He'd wait until she passed him before he made his move.

The wet clothes clinging to her body almost had him come as he looked at her nipples showing through her blouse. Like a pigeon to breadcrumbs, he thought as he congratulated himself on knowing HIS woman. And she was HIS woman now, he chuckled. No one else would feed on her after him. She was moving away from him as he stood up and began to walk quietly toward her. It was only a matter of minutes now, he grinned. Only a matter of minutes, as he licked his mouth and thought about the sweet taste he would have soon.

"Look who I found?" he chortled as his eyes hardened and he raised his pistol.

She turned slowly to face him and stared.

"You thought you could outsmart me. Didn't I tell you men are smarter than any stupid woman," he spat as he advanced toward her with the barrel of his pistol aimed at her chest. "You thought you'd fool me," he hissed. "No one fools me. You and I are gonna have that party I planned last night. And then, you're going to have your own one-woman party," he snickered. "Now move that way," he said as he waved his pistol toward the right stream bank.

Hatchert took several deep breaths and began to plan. His eyes were bloodshot and were squinting against the morning sun. Chances are you have one whale of a headache, she thought as she began to slowly move toward the bank and faked a fall going down onto the ground.

"Stand up you bitch!" he screamed as he stomped toward her. "I said get up!" and he grabbed her arm and yanked her to her feet.

The pain rocketed through her arm as she gasped for air to bring her reaction under control.

"Now move!" he said as he shoved her sending her flying.

She looked for anything to use as a weapon as she climbed up the stream bank and saw nothing.

"Head on over to those two big rocks that are leaning against each other," he gestured with his gun.

Hatchert thought of Josie with him and her eyes turned to black ice. She would find a way, she thought as she forced herself to focus.

"Walk through them," he pointed as Hatchert nodded and ducked into the opening that was formed by the rocks. As she reached the other side, she walked into a small secluded clearing of sand surrounded by rocks and the hillside. There was no way out.

"Now's the time to have our little party," he laughed as he held out a small white pill in his hand. "Take it!" he demanded as he kept his gun aimed at her.

Hatchert took the pill out of his hand and dropped it in the sand.

"Now why'd you go and do that, bitch!" he swore and slapped her across the cheek sending her reeling backwards. Reaching into his shirt pocket, he pulled out another pill. "Think you're so goddamn smart, bitch! Here's another one. I'm gonna shove it down your throat and when I'm done with you I'm gonna dump you in that creek," he sneered as he leaned over to shove the pill in her mouth.

He never saw what hit him. The tranquilizer dart hit dead center in his jugular. He fell face forward into the sand. A soldier in camouflage scrambled over the rock while others appeared in the opening. Within minutes, Ray Wilson was handcuffed and flipped.

"Hi Hatchert. Out for a nature walk today?" Special Agent Lawson beamed as she saw Hatchert's face return a wide smile.

"Yeah. I thought I'd take a stroll through the mountains. Get some air," Hatchert teased right back.

"Well, if you're done with your walk, we've got a Humvee on its way to pick us up," Lawson smiled.

"Yes!" Hatchert yelled and high-fived Lawson.

ABOUT THE AUTHOR

Sherlyn Stahr lives in California on the Monterey Peninsula among the sand dunes and scrub oaks where turkeys strut in the spring, coyotes sing odes to the moon, and rabbits sunbathe on the walking trails. After a successful teaching career, followed by working for the military as a writer and editor, she finds herself in creative writing. This is her first novel.

Made in the USA
San Bernardino, CA
05 April 2016